The Structure of Delight

By

Nelson Zink

The Structure of Delight

Copyright © 1991 by Nelson Zink

All rights reserved.

Printed in the United States of America

For information address:

Mind Matters, Drawer SS, Taos, NM 87571

Cover layout by Willi Wood

Cover photograph by Stephen Bradley

Published by Mind Matters, Drawer SS, Taos, NM 87571

ISBN 0-9629621-0-4

because of Melissa

Chapter One

≈≈≈≈≈

The old man quietly selected smooth, fist-sized stones and tossed them into the river. Some of the rocks splashed loudly and sank from sight. Others floated serenely on the water's surface. Following the current they danced on ripples as the river carried them away in the afternoon light. Dressed in the faded khaki shirt and pants of a practical desert prophet, he gazed after a floating stone. When it reached a certain spot, he directed a very slight nod across the water and sent the rock slipping under the surface to sink soundlessly. The old man watched. Close cropped white hair framed his broad tanned face, a face on which lines of the Vedas would be at ease. He waited, alert and listening. When the stone reached the bottom it discharged a flash like a crystalline rainbow that sprang across the river and lapped up onto the bank. A pulse to be remembered.

With economy of motion the old man walked along the gravel bar, studying the rocks. Selecting another, he threw it far out over the water. The man's movements were steady and sure, like a bear's, shambling but purposeful. When he bent to gather a stone his body was limber and each toss smooth and strong. Workmanlike he proceeded, steadily performing his task. Stroking his short grizzled whiskers he inspected the stones. The man was deliberate in his choice of stones and after picking one never exchanged it for another. Each choice was final and absolute. The selected stone, lifted with a wide strong hand, flew high over the water and sank with a splash, or it would ride the current until a small nod sent it cutting through the surface.

The river's surface tension split, then flashed another rare keen slice of the waterknife.

ΩΩΩΩ

The river created itself. Its history was its present. It did not flow through time; it flowed with time. Old now, it had become sedentary, a permanent fixture of the land. But this was not always so.

Long, long ago a young river wandered into this part of the country and decided this would be a good place to go into business. To become a working river. In the transportation trade. The child river knew two things: How to cut and how to haul. And these it would do forever, sculpting a whole region. With the power of flood and friction it would slowly grind its way down into the earth, cutting a deep channel as it went. The river ground and abraded huge boulders until they cracked or crumbled. Then the debris was hauled away. The river could collapse mountains and set entirely new courses. Endurance was its power, long periods of contented grinding, chewing at the rock. Then a sudden lurch, a new channel or an interesting bend added. The river was playful while it worked.

As it honed its skills, the young river was curious and seeped in new directions. Watery fingers were always exploring and testing, searching in yet uncovered bedrock. It tickled the earth and scratched her back. The young river had found a land to explore and in the process slowly became time itself.

With no schedules or expectations, it is now a worryless river that surprises itself at each turn and is curious before every bend. It may dally or rush but never hurries. Strong and sure, it renews itself each day and so is tireless.

Some say this river has moods and it may. News travels slowly over busy water. Undistracted the river sings while it works.

¥¥¥¥¥

Jay Thomas didn't know why he kept returning to his secret camping spot in northern New Mexico. In fact, Jay Thomas didn't really know why he had done most of the things in his life. Now at twenty-eight, hiking toward the river, he impatiently brushed his black hair away from his sharp angular face while avoiding cholla stickers before they tore at his pants.

Every year or so Jay imagined that the river was calling him, calling him to return at a time that always coincided with an intense period of introspection. Lonely periods that dulled the light in his blue eyes and drew the corners of his mouth tight. Picking his way through sagebrush and cactus, metal clips on his pack clicked out a steady cadence. This time would be different he hoped, this time .... Always this time.

Jay had been an engaging young man with a quick tongue, but the normal adjustment period after college lingered into years. Part time jobs allowed him to delay as his bloom of promise withered. At first it didn't bother him, but then he began to perceive a dismal future stretching far out in front of him. A small cramped line pushing into increasing darkness, a darkness that felt like misery. As he thought about his difficulties the pack frame rode heavily on slim shoulders and his favorite plaid camping shirt stuck to his back. Leaning forward under the load he craned his neck, squinting to catch a glimpse of the river's foliage.

In the past, empty arrogance kept Jay shielded from his future. But now his pride was wearing thin and the fear wolves were beginning to circle, attracted by the scent of uncertainty. Plainly it was time to return again to the solace of his secret retreat.

There the river ran flat. Upstream were small rapids that giggled at night when the air was cool and still. Along the banks large green cottonwood trees loomed over thin stemmed willows. A clearing kept smooth and sandy by the river's yearly floods lay between the slow green water and dense willow stands. Two heavy columns of undergrowth protected the river, one on either side, marching along its course, savoring water that seeped to their roots. Lush vegetation attracted raccoons and porcupines, muskrats and coyotes. Finches and sparrows, tanagers and grosbeaks nested in its midst. Less than a hundred feet from the river moisture stopped and a dry thorny landscape began. It in turn was replaced as the land rose into low hills covered with the stubborn southwestern evergreens, piñon and juniper. It was a place where Jay could be alone, watch and listen to the river until it ran through his dreams as he slept. This time of year the water level was low and he could safely wade across, wandering far back into the hills. He would sit for hours watching calm

3

water as it passed effortlessly on its way to the sea. In the past, when his mind was washed clean of self-doubt Jay would return to his world with renewed confidence, but without any change in competence.

Approaching the river, Jay heard splashing sounds as he picked his way quietly through the underbrush. Using sounds to guide him, he wondered what was creating those disturbing noises in his special place. Creeping forward slowly he peeked through the willows and saw an old man throwing rocks into the river. Jay brushed his hair back again and knelt down to watch the man throw stone after stone into the water. Finally the man stopped and sat, calmly watching clear green water flowing in front of him. Jay Thomas summoned his courage, pushed through the last of the willows to advance cautiously. "So what were you doing?" he called out.

The man turned slowly and looked at Jay. The gaze was long and certain, his face solid and sure, like his movements.

"I was sorting those stones," the old man answered, gesturing toward the gravel bar over his shoulder. "All rocks have a desire to float at least once and with some rocks that desire is strong." He gazed down the river toward the spot where the floaters had gone. "Given a chance they float, but the rest don't."

Watching the reflection of the opposite bank on the water's surface, Jay wondered about the rocks he had watched serenely floating downstream. Looking at the spot where the stones had sunk, he asked. "So what will happen to them?"

The old man shrugged. "After they've been sorted they continue with their own business."

§§§§

Jay had never thought about a rock's business before; in fact he realized he had never thought much about rocks at all. The idea that stones could have individual lives, let alone desires, puzzled him. Camping here before, he was aware of the gravel bar, but had never thought about individual stones. The rocks were there, had always been there and always would be there. As he thought about it now, he contemplated how each stone had its own history, its own origin and journey to this place. Nestled with others, each would in time continue its journey, continue with the affairs of its own business. Continue on to find new lodgings along the river's course. As Jay looked at rocks on the gravel bar he dimly began to realize that each stone's shape and texture could be determined by just two things: The internal properties of each rock and the circumstances of its journey. Each stone's character was its history. The ground where he stood had witnessed the passing of untold legions of stones, silently noting their histories as they continued on. During spring floods the river rumbled with these migrations.

"There's just one thing I want to know," Jay said as he turned back to face the old man. "I want to know," but he was stopped by the man's upraised hand. The hand was strong and callused and each finger looked as if it could live alone without the others.

The old man slowly blinked. "Just one thing? Come, sit down. If there were a question, a single question, which directly guided your life; if there were a question that you'd always asked yourself deep in your mind," he paused and then continued in a whisper, "what would that question be?"

ΩΩΩΩ

On the river long ago a slim brown hand plucked a single blue pebble from the water at the edge where small ripples play. Deposited in a soft leather bag hanging from a waist string the stone began its journey. Over many years it made its way steadily westward. It was traded, given as a gift, passed from hand to hand. This stone was highly valued, for it never dried out, always keeping a direct link to the river of its birth. The pebble was a water stone and prized because of its color, texture and ability to summon and retain water. Many rains were called forth using the stone. During winter the pebble was hidden deep among corn kernels in a clay seed jar. Its presence insured the seeds would remain alive and healthy and that a fruitful harvest would follow their planting. Deep in the seed jar the stone was contented. It was a stone of fog, of mist and its soft lustrous surface always sparkled with a liquid sheen.

The Structure of Delight

One spring the owner of the water stone failed to retrieve his seed jar. The stone waited for a warm hand but it never came. As it waited, the water stone kept its faith alive by reliving events of its origin. It waited for several hundred years until the jar was found again and moved to a museum.

At the museum bones and skulls, arrowheads and stone scrapers are old now in their waiting. Most wait with their eyes closed, drifting in lightless depths of memory. Some are blind, milky white scales of time gluing their eyes closed forever. They exist beyond sleep, beyond dreaming, waiting with dust-laden backs. The museum staff occasionally lifts them from their cases and dusts them off, setting each upright again. The world passes in front of them, pointing and staring, but they will outlast us and our children's children. For them there is nowhere to go. They have been left behind to wait and remember.

In one of the cases flint corn spills from a huge pottery jar. Black lines, painstakingly painted, embellish its smooth gray surface. At the edge of the kernels sleeps a small blue pebble. The stone has dried after centuries of neglect, but beneath its surface just enough moisture remains to create a cornucopia. The water stone is content, still waiting for a spring in which to plant.

≈≈≈≈≈

The old man had waited for Jay and now he had come. In his dreams Jay was slightly different, taller and a little thinner; but he was sure that this was the young man for whom he had waited. The quickness was there and nervousness, a head full of false certainty and confusion. An intense intelligence slumbered, waiting for a circumstance in which to flourish. Yes, this was the one. The old man noted worn running shoes, a tense mind with tense feet. The young man's nervousness came out in his feet and hands. He ran his thumb across the tips of each finger, starting with the little finger and ending with the index finger. Repeatedly. Silent finger drumming was an attempt to ease endless ragged mind rhythms. Sometimes one hand drummed, sometimes both. Yes, this was the one.

As the old man watched Jay searching for the one question, his eyes slowly defocused and he seemed to be looking through Jay's head and far beyond toward the horizon. He remembered a time some fifty years ago and a place far distant. He remembered himself as he struggled for that very same question, how important and vital it seemed at the time. He had carried youthful bitterness in his mouth and the question forced him to taste it fully. A simple but relevant question marked the beginning of a new life; one he was still completing. He spent fifty years learning all ramifications of the question and so was in no hurry for this young man to formulate his own.

Looking back on it now he knew the question itself was unimportant. The knowledge that an acrid strain existed in his life, that he would have to swallow or spit it out was what set him on a new road. The knowledge that he would need to act every day, perhaps every minute for the rest of his life was what was important. At first, the thought had disturbed him. It appeared to be a life dedicated to endless struggle, but with the bitterness gone his thoughts began to have clear meaning. His life became more fluid and effortless. He now knew that to hesitate was to live with a mouth full of fear.

Before the question, his life had been one of endless hesitation. Hesitations leading to more hesitations. Fine silken threads of hesitation that seemed secure and comforting. He had wrapped those threads around and around himself to form a barrier, to create a protection against the uncertainties of life. A protection made of hesitation, a tangle that clogged his throat and his mind. The question began the realization that his safe cocoon was actually a prison. The question of what was really important, what was the one thing that mattered above all else, became his knife. Became the sharp edge of intent which allowed him to cut through the web of his indecision, to clear the way and point his direction. Anxiety ceased to be his currency; the fear wolves became loyal guard dogs.

ΔΔΔΔΔ

A past must be repeated to be retained. Past memories are winnowed by grinding on the broad stone of experience. A gentle breath will separate the husks from strengthening events that grow into our bones and carry us on. The constant grinding of life separates surface from substance, leaving sweet roughage for us to devour. Living without a past is constantly to create one.

≈≈≈≈≈

This young man sitting by him, came to the river seeking a sign, an indication from the cosmos, something that would give him direction in his confusion. He came to camp by the river, hoping to be redirected, to be told what he should do. To be found special by it and receive secret instructions meant only for him. But the river flowed on, unmindful of his presence. And now Jay sat straining and uncomfortable, unaware that when he took the arrow of certainty firmly in his hand it would deeply mark his palm. A mark truer than any compass, a mark that would always calculate his bearings instantly. A mark that would allow him at last to draw a map for his life and find a way home.

ΩΩΩΩ

As Jay began to sit up straight the old man's attention returned. He knew the question was near.

"Let me stop you again," he said lifting his hand. "My name's Noom."

Jay's brow furrowed. "That's not what I was going to ask."

"Good, then you wouldn't have wasted your question."

"My question is this. What's the capital of North Dakota?" Jay fell to his side laughing.

Noom was pleased and smiled broadly. At least the boy had a sense of humor. "As a matter of fact I once lived in North Dakota," he said leaning back to begin a story. "I worked on a ranch far back in the Dakota hills. One morning I set out to find a herd of horses that I'd been hunting for a week or so. Just around noon I was riding by a stream at the bottom of a little canyon. It ran along the north side of the ranch right where the big timber grew. That summer was extremely hot but it was cool down there in the canyon by the water. So I was riding along not paying much attention when I realized something was flying straight at me. I noticed it five or six feet in front of me and just had time to duck out of the way. When I jerked to the side my horse spooked. I reined him in and looked over my shoulder to see a large pale owl still gliding right down the trail. I don't know why the horse didn't see the owl first but he hadn't, maybe he wasn't paying attention either. After I got myself settled back down I started to get curious, because the owl was out in daytime and because it passed over me with absolutely no noise. For a minute I wasn't sure but that I'd made the whole thing up. Anyway, the owl landed and perched in a tree so I rode back to get a better look at him, and when I got close he flew away. I'd find him and then he'd fly and I'd lose him again. I spent maybe half an hour following that owl and then lost him entirely. I never did get a good look at him, so I rode on to find the horses. At the head of the canyon I climbed a ridge and rode along the fence line but the missing horses weren't to be found. No tracks or anything. I was starting to get discouraged. I didn't know if I'd ever find those horses." Noom glanced across the river as if he were still hunting them.

"Anyway it was getting late so I turned back, and coming down the trail, I saw that old owl again. It flew by another time and vanished again in the trees. So I decided that I'd just wait and see what happened. I dismounted and sat on an old log there by the trail and waited. It would fly by and disappear, so I just sat. After about the third pass the owl landed across the trail some thirty feet away in a little grassy clearing. It would blink at me and I'd blink at it, and finally I got up and went over closer. The owl hopped around some but it didn't leave, and so we just sort of studied each other. After a while I cut a big bushy branch about six or seven feet long and when I got close enough pinned him down with it. I got him up in my arms and folded his wings and smoothed his feathers, and all the time he didn't struggle. He just looked at me with those big yellow eyes, blinking occasionally. He was large, maybe a couple feet long and his wings were about as wide as my arms." Noom stretched out his arms to demonstrate the bird's wing span. "And he was extremely light, didn't weigh a thing. I'd expected a bird that size to have some heft but he didn't, and he had these pale, pale feathers. Up close you could see little brown spots, like he'd been dusted with ochre. I'd never heard of an owl like that. We looked at each other for awhile and I finally decided to wrap my jacket around him so I

9

could carry him under my arm. When I had him all bundled up with his head sticking out I mounted up and started to ride back to the barn. I don't think my horse ever was aware of the owl or at least he never seemed to see or smell him. I rode along with the owl tucked under my right arm. He kept his head cocked, just staring at me. I talked to him, trying to find out who he was or what was going on. I didn't have any clear idea what I was going to do with that owl, I just knew that somehow he was a very peculiar bird. I tried to figure why he scared the wits out of me and then why he stuck around. It seemed that he came to me for some reason. When I asked him he just blinked and then his eyes began to dilate. The pupils grew to the size of dimes and slowly his lids closed. With each step the horse took the owl's head began to lower, bit by bit, then he was dead. During that whole time he never made a sound, not during flight or when I picked him up, nothing." Noom slowly shook his head in amazement.

"The next day I wrapped him up in some burlap and put him high up in an old pine tree. I kept one of those pale feathers to remind myself that he wasn't a spirit owl after all. Sometimes at night I'd get the feather out just to make sure. Anyway, right after that I found the horses. They'd been around the whole time."

§§§§§

Jay had watched the river all during the story. "What about those rocks?" he asked.

"What about them?"

"How did you make some of them float?"

Noom had thrown with a smooth sidearm motion. Jay remembered his limping slightly as he walked back to select another rock. He walked with a stride that was long and slow and whenever he changed direction the old man's hips seemed to turn just before his shoulders. Watching the old man made Jay think of soft angles.

"I didn't make them float I told you, I was just sorting them."

"Okay, why were you sorting them?"

"It was something to do while I waited for you to come."

"You knew I was coming? You knew I was coming to this very place?"

The young man's face began to redden and one hand silently drummed.

"Jay, I knew sooner or later you'd come here. You've come here before haven't you?"

"Yes, and how do you know my name, anyway?"

Noom looked into the hills far across the river, his brown eyes slowly scanning the terrain. At last his gaze returned. "I know your name the same way I know that you come here from time to time. It seemed like a good place to wait for you."

≈≈≈≈≈

In his youth Noom struggled to understand life. He felt the world directly interfered with him and that his well being was dependent on controlling his surroundings, an enormous undertaking well beyond his knowledge and ability. Noom's frustration with this impossible task was immense until the moment he realized that the universe didn't need to be managed; he needed to be managed. He discovered that it wasn't the world's turbulence which frightened him, it was his own.

That was when he began to search for a way to order events that seemed to arise and then disappear spontaneously. Events within himself, external events, unrooted happenings. Natural phenomena of this type began to fascinate him. He watched the formation and disappearance of clouds, the beginnings and ends of storms. He listened to the delicate music of lapping water in small streams. He noticed his own moods as they came and went. These events weren't the culmination of circumstances, they were the creation of circumstances. He suspected that contained within this chaos was great beauty and power, and he wanted to experience it directly.

When Noom was older, an idea came to him during a raging sand storm in the middle of Australia. Caught alone in a featureless wasteland, a violent wind sprang up suddenly, whipping sand and small pebbles all around him. At the moment when his fear was greatest the winds created an eye of calm into which he stepped. From the safety of one event he could witness the wildness of the other. While the bubble of calm existed the storm was incapable of reaching him and he was safe within an eventless vacuum. Out of chaos came order. Noom called his idea hycation. And though he never felt he could adequately describe it to anyone, it became an important part of his life. For him, hycation was the process by which chaos revealed its beautiful patterns. From that day on confusion became a cherished state of mind, because he anticipated the natural process of hycation would soon deliver him a splendid gift. He learned to employ confusion creatively, for at the very center of this process is the source of imagination. He never figured out how it worked, but instead found out how to allow it to happen. The most precious use of hycation, he found, was the generation of thoughts themselves, those wonderful moments when his mind delivered enormous strokes of clear lightning. To Noom hycation was the origin of surprise.

§§§§§

"It's just that I wasn't expecting you," Jay stammered.

"People rarely do."

Noom's eyes, soft and relaxed, gazed at Jay, never wavering. Set wide apart they seemed to focus not on the young man's face but somewhere at the back of his skull. Jay's uneasiness grew as he realized that the man wasn't paying attention to him but to the back of his head. Every time Jay glanced at the river Noom's gaze probed the hair just behind his ear. Jay struggled to leave, but part of his mind kept seeing rocks as they floated calmly downstream. He was used to meeting people head on, feeling a slight pressure of other people's nearness, but with this old man there was none. He had an odd sensation that he was trying to keep himself from falling forward.

"Okay, so what happens now?" Jay said aggressively. It was a question he asked whenever he was confused, when he was unsure of how to proceed.

Noom pondered the question. "You've got me there. I suppose we could watch the river while we wait."

Both men watched green ripples while Jay nervously chewed at his lower lip.

"You said 'we'. How do I know that I can trust you?" Jay finally asked.

"Trust me to do what?"

"I don't know." Jay paused. "Just trust you."

"Well," said Noom rubbing the stubble on his chin, "the fact is you can't. You can't trust me at all. That's one thing people say about me. You can't trust old Noom to keep from changing things around."

"That's not what I mean. I came here to be alone and, I suppose ... well to hunt for something."

Noom's eyebrows raised as he widened his eyes. "And you hunt for this something along rivers?"

ΩΩΩΩ

Long ago, one very cold winter, in a land of sparse timber and scattered boulders, two brothers were hungry. The older brother went to his mother and asked to be fed. Instead of preparing a meal, she told them to go hunting. "Try your bow and arrow," she said. "Perhaps they will feed you."

So the brothers gathered their bows and quivers and set out. Four days they hunted, following scattered animal tracks. From time to time they would catch a glimpse of an animal in the bushes. But then it would vanish and they ran after it until they were out of breath. Finally exhausted and very hungry they wanted to return home, but they were too embarrassed. They decided to go to their grandfather's lodge, half-a-day's distance away. Perhaps he would care for them.

Grandfather welcomed them, sat them by the fire and gave them food to eat. And as they ate they told grandfather of their misfortunes. He listened patiently to each outburst of self-pity. "Hmmm," he said. Finally the boys were full and fell asleep close to the warmth of the fire.

In the morning the brothers felt much better and decided to return home. They thanked their grandfather and gathering their things, prepared to leave. At the lodge door he stopped them. "You catch nothing because you know nothing," Grandfather said. "If you had knowledge you would succeed."

§§§§

"No, you don't understand. I come here because it's a good place to be alone and think about some things."

13

"Good, I like hunting for somethings." Noom beamed. "The same people that say I'm untrustworthy admit that I'm an excellent something hunter. I can read the tracks of a something because I know that something is what it does."

"What?"

"Something is what it does."

¥¥¥¥¥

The air was silent except for the smooth rhythmic lapping of the river's water against the sandy beach. Afternoon light was beginning to cast soft shadows on the watery surface and Jay could feel its heat slowly radiating from the sand under his hands. He had prepared for this trip believing it would be a vacation from his disappointments. The trip was to be an escape from the unexpected, and the last thing he had wanted was to meet someone on the river. Now he was feeling another small cut of disappointment. A cut that would add another thin layer to his scarred hopes. Jay sat nursing his resentment, digging the heels of his running shoes deeper into the sand. Noom noticed the heels were worn down much more than the toes, indicating a preference in direction.

ΩΩΩΩ

"A long time ago," Noom began quietly, "my father decided to buy a car. He was a young man living in a small Nebraska town, and he read about the new contraptions. He dreamed of owning a car, so one day he counted his money and took the train to Denver to purchase one of those wondrous new machines. He went straight to the dealer to look over the selection. This was the first time he'd ever seen an automobile except in pictures, and he looked inside and under the car and sat in it, feeling the steering wheel. Since he didn't really know what driving was like he kept his words to himself. That evening as he walked to the hotel he watched the few cars on the streets as they rattled by and imagined himself driving one. It felt good, and he knew which one he would buy.

"The next morning the salesman showed my father all the levers and knobs used to start the car. They cranked it up and drove around the block.

My father paid for the car and left for home. Home was a long way away, across plains and all by dirt road, so he bought some food and set out. It took him five days to drive home, driving from early morning till dark. At night he would build a fire by the side of the road, cook his dinner and sleep in his car.

"When he returned home he proudly drove the new car along the main street of the little town where he lived. Most people there had never seen a car before, so my father promised to give everyone a ride. The next day he drove his friends and neighbors up and down the road that ran through town. On one of the trips he had a passenger who had driven cars before, and the man asked, 'Why don't you shift?' 'What do you mean?' my father asked. 'Why don't you use the other gears? I've been watching you drive up and down this road all morning, but you never shift.'.

"My father had driven the way the salesman showed him. The passenger explained the gears and how to work them. My father was thunderstruck. He had driven all the way home in first gear. All two hundred and fifty miles. He was embarrassed, but learning of second and third gears was like getting two extra cars for free."

ΔΔΔΔΔ

Many machines and devices have a button or a knob to return the machine to a favored condition. The device has then been reset. When a clock is reset it is returned to a favored condition, and therefore resetting is a way of maintaining control. Generally it is felt that resetting restores order. When things become disordered we attempt to reset them. Certain mechanical puzzles are devised so they can't be reset easily. The whole point of a puzzle is to test one's ability to establish order from chaos.

There are events, which once set into motion become uncontrollable, and these tend to be frightening. The original or correct order seems to have been lost, and a reset button can't be found. These events are called destructive and are dreaded. Decay and degeneration appear to attack order and destroy it. However when a device is reset it doesn't become any more ordered; it is simply returned to a favored order. What is ordinarily thought of as change doesn't actually effect order, it effects what is thought of as

15

favored. As one state of order is lost another is created. Often the secret to resetting is noticing that order hasn't been lost, it has simply moved. If the ability to restore is adequate, the illusion of control is unnecessary. Change becomes an automatic reset button.

§§§§§

"I know unexpected things often get in the way," Noom continued, gazing quietly at the young man. "And I understand you're wondering if your coming here will have been wasted. But you can know you're perfectly free to waste your vacation in any way you want. Only later will you be able to look back and find out. A year from now when you remember the afternoon we first met, you can decide."

Then he focused on a spot between Jay's eyes and very slowly widened his own eyes. Jay's pupils dilated rapidly and Noom knew it was done.

"While we are here," Noom said as he gestured expansively, "you can enjoy this glorious place in a way that you've never experienced anything before. Maybe once or maybe twice, but once will be enough."

After the old man had looked so deeply into his eyes, Jay had the distinct impression of hearing a soft rumbling that seemed to originate somewhere in the depths of his brain. Deep and melodic, almost like prolonged chanting, a sound that was strangely reassuring, as if it were the ageless voice of primal neurons humming as they worked. Like the purr of far away thunder it rolled on and on, capturing the edge of his awareness.

ΩΩΩΩ

It was early September and the first hint of fall eased along the river valley. Noom always liked fall, beginning with the day when the sun tipped just enough to cause the earth to finish its long summer exhalation. To begin a slow inhalation, drawing in its moist breath to save and crystallize for winter. Most people think of spring as the season that begins the annual cycle, but for Noom it was fall. As the days cooled something within him quickened. An excitement slowly building, an excitement that he frugally stored. It would catch his breath at odd moments, reminding him of how seasons continually pump new beginnings into his life. For an old man it was wonderful to feel ageless.

¥¥¥¥¥

Jay's internal dialogue suddenly diminished, and without it his sense of immediate time vanished. The finger drumming stopped and his hands slowly relaxed; his thoughts were released to wander in the twilight. As he gathered wood for the fire he remembered a day in his childhood when he discovered that trout eat insects.

In a small stream near his home Jay happened to see a speckled fish rise steadily from the depths of a dark pool and swallow something on the surface. The lazy liquid movement of the fish fascinated him and he longed to see it again. He waited and waited and in time watched the fish rise again and eat a bug. Then it came to him in a flash, he could find insects and feed the fish, and he did.

He soon learned the fish's preference in bugs and took delight in anticipating the sight of the stream's leviathan rising again. Day after day he returned to the pool and cast freshly caught insects onto the dark still surface. He called the fish Old Trout. He would tell Old Trout what he had in the jar in his coat pocket as he walked along the trail to the pool where the old fish lived. A little boy talking to a fish in his head, telling him what kind of bugs he had and how good they would taste. On days he couldn't find bugs Jay brought a slice of bread. Tearing off small bits, he threw them, one by one, into the water at the head of the pool. This was the spot where Old Trout liked to feed best.

Jay tried to remember what ended the affair, boy and fish, but he couldn't. He must have become interested in other things, leaving the fish to his watery world. Old Trout. Jay hadn't thought of him for a long time; it was a pleasant memory.

One after another, events had led him to now, twenty-eight years old and bending to gather fire wood on a larger stream with an older fish. As he looked back along the events of his life, none stood out as remarkable. Some were larger than others, of course, some were small and hazy, but no one event overwhelmed the others. The remembered sound of the old trout

17

silently breaking the smooth surface of his boyhood stream stayed with Jay as he built the evening fire.

ΩΩΩΩ

While small bright orange flames were growing and started to consume the dry wood Noom sat and stared at the river. "You know, rivers seem to slow down when evening comes," he said. "I don't know why that is. I've wondered about it, and during one period of my life I lived on a river and thought about it a lot. I wondered if while I slept the river slowed down until it stopped. I dreamed that while I slept the river would finally stop, becoming clear. I dreamed you could see every rock. You could see all the white rocks and every dark one covered with moss. The river was so still that the fish dozed and you could watch their gills barely move as they slept. In my dream this was a very special moment, when the river stopped. And then very deliberately the river would begin to flow the other way. It all happened so silently that you didn't notice it at first."

"The water would begin to flow back upstream, so after awhile in my dream I didn't know which was the right way for the river to go. During the day I planted sticks along the bank pointing in the direction of its current. And then at night as I dreamed I'd look for those sticks, but the water always went in the direction that the sticks pointed. I began to suspect that the sticks changed direction with the river. So I would get up and look at the river during the middle of the night, hoping to catch it while it stopped.

"But I never could find it still and clear. It was always flowing in the direction that the sticks pointed. I thought about the problem of knowing for certain if the river changes direction, and how if the river changed then the sticks could change and so on. I realized I was looking for something which was unchanging. Something that I could gauge the flow of the river against. Something that I could measure life by. The more I thought and experimented, the more uncertain I became. I wasn't sure when I looked at the water at night that I wasn't still dreaming. And finally I wasn't sure I was awake during the day when I planted sticks. The only thing I did know for certain was that when I thought of the river stopping it was a wonderful feeling."

Noom paused and cocked his head slightly to one side as if he was listening for a distant sound. "Then one night during the dream when the river stopped, I stopped also. It was startling and I could see clear down into my own depths. In the morning I went and stood by the river and knew that I could look at one side of reality or look at another side of reality. I had been stuck looking at the edge and that's a very narrow view," he chuckled. "You can look at the reverse side, but remember even the reverse side has a reverse."

Noom continued to gaze at the river as the fire settled down to burn in the twilight. Turning to Jay he smiled. "But I still think rivers run slow in the evening."

ΩΩΩΩ

The air had cooled and was flowing smoothly down the valley. Rustling the leaves in the tops of the tallest trees it carried smoke from the fire high out over the water. It was time for beavers to come out and begin their nightly labor, pruning the river's banks. They managed willow thickets and controlled the trees. With teeth, the color of very old ivory, they nibbled and gnawed at the woody growth, keeping it trimmed and flourishing. Untold generations of beavers learned their ways from this river and now delighted in maintaining its bounty. They were its workmen. Sturdy and thorough they patrolled the river's course with nightly vigilance. Jay noticed indications of their past activities while gathering wood. He found sections of limbs with all the bark removed, which had floated down river during previous floods. Wood was left high and dry at flood line, cut to length and ready to burn.

≈≈≈≈≈

Noom retrieved a faded gray canvas sack hidden in the willows. Inside riveted pockets classified his gear. The sack was patched, having been expertly repaired many times until it resembled the ancient pannier of desert trader. Rummaging through the sack he withdrew a small roll fishing line, a hook tucked in the middle.

19

"What are you going to do with that?" asked Jay.

"Supper," replied the old man as began searching for a strong willow to serve as his fishing pole. Cutting and trimming with his pocket knife, he deftly fashioned a serviceable pole and tied his line to the tip. Noom picked a leaf about the size of his thumb and delicately trimmed it. He then wetted the shaped leaf in his mouth.

"What's that for?"

"Bait," said Noom, accurately threading it onto his hook.

After he cast his green lure into the river he sat down, pole resting across one knee. The reward for patience is patience. Noom had heard that adage many years before but now he knew better. The reward for patience would be a fish. He didn't believe in virtue; he believed in results. He knew that events had different rhythms, and one way to equalize them is to wait. He knew there were two ways to proceed: To act and to wait. He had acted and now he waited. When he was much younger someone pointed this out to him. "Noom," he was told, "there exist two ways--doing and waiting to do. They differ, be aware of which is which." He then started to examine his own activity and found that much of his life was lived in between, neither acting nor waiting, mostly fumbling, worrying and regretting. Now he waited, making himself comfortable at the water's edge, crossing his legs with the pole over one knee and his hands folded in his lap to keep them warm.

The old man stopped looking and began to watch. He allowed his visual awareness to expand to the sides and up and down, from his hands to the quickly darkening sky overhead and from far right to far left. He watched a seamless visual field, attending to everything equally. His vision was aimed, but not focused, at the very center. He accepted the movement or stillness of the things he watched. The river, the land and sky beyond began to appear as if a sheet of thin gauze were placed before them. This, he knew, indicated that his waiting and watching was reaching fruition. He could now turn the picture before him in any direction he liked, rotating it at will in his mind. He could watch the river run straight up or straight down, whichever served his fancy. After he completed a full rotation a swallow suddenly flew into the picture at the upper left-hand corner and swooped low over the river. Snatching an insect in its beak it exited out the lower right-hand corner. Noom watched the entire episode without moving his eyes; they remained directed toward the hills across the water. For amusement Noom mentally reversed the scene. The bird entered flying backward, spit out the bug and continued back to where it came from. Then a tremor in the pole diverted his attention; the waiting was over.

Noom landed a plump catfish with a minimum of ceremony. Quickly the fish was cleaned, hook and line were returned to his sack and exchanged for a frying pan. He filleted the fish and soon had it cooking over the fire. "Do you like catfish?" Noom pointed his knife toward the pan. "There's enough for two."

"How did you do that?" Jay asked, amazed at the speed with which things were happening.

"Do what?" Noom glanced up from his cooking.

"Well ... that." Jay pointed at the pan.

Noom was squatting by the fire and he turned on his heels and pointed the tip of his knife toward the river. "The fish was there, now it's here," he said nodding toward the fire.

"Yes I know, that's what I'm asking. How did it get from the river into the pan so quickly?"

Noom meticulously loosened his fish from the pan and flipped it over to cook the other side. "Skill," the old man answered simply.

"Skill?" asked Jay. "What about luck? Or even knowledge?"

"Is there a difference?"

§§§§§

Noom relished the night; it was a time for pondering. Often when he camped alone he would extinguish his campfire and sit motionless in the dark. Long ago he had discovered that while people's minds are blank they see different things. Some people see a screen that is light and for others it's dark. When his mind was blank Noom saw a velvety blackness, so night was a special time for him. It wrapped close around him, extending out into the cosmos. The dark allowed him an opportunity to dive deep within himself and explore a limitless realm. He knew that for many, night was a

21

time of foreboding, a time when the world can be rearranged. For him it was a time to explore because at his very center Noom maintained a beacon. He absolutely trusted this beacon; it always guided him unwaveringly. Exploring in the light was one type of activity, in the dark another; the old man had both his day and his night. Sitting back and looking far up into the night sky, he took special notice of a single star overhead and looked at it for a long time.

"Someday you or someone like you will go to that star," he gestured toward it with his chin, "perhaps far beyond."

Jay followed the line of his gaze. "It seems so far away."

"Yes, it does. If you lean back and see all the sky at once, taking your time, you'll find that star is just beyond the end of your nose."

Jay lay back on the beach looking into the night sky. He focused on the star and slowly let his vision expand, seeing ever more stars. As he watched, the sky quickly seemed to become blacker, the stars brighter and at the same time softer. They blurred slightly and began combining into patterns like white lace held in front of a black background. Jay blinked his eyes and continued expanding his vision until white lace filled the whole sky. After a while he relaxed his eyes and was beginning to enjoy the sight, when suddenly he felt rocketed into deep space. It so startled him that he lurched up onto one elbow and looked into the fire to reorient himself.

"Jesus, I thought I had fallen off the earth," he said, staring at Noom.

"Or that the heavens had fallen on you." Noom smiled and nodded his head upward. "Look again."

Jay lay down again and collected himself. After several tries he could repeat the experience without such a shock. For a few brief seconds he had an impression that he could reach out and touch the heavens. Noom noted a slight twitch in Jay's hand, "Not now, just watch."

§§§§

Staring into the heavens, Jay suddenly remembered his grandmother. He wondered if she could be alive somewhere among the stars, knitting lace to fill the cosmos as she had filled her house and her children's houses. Tears came as he recalled the small old woman humming contentedly to herself as huge galaxies of woven thread steadily sprang from her busy fingers. He hadn't thought of her for a long time; she died when he was still quite young. Jay remembered the chair where she worked at night, an old cat in her lap. An old cat who had long since given up batting at the thread as it unrolled from the basket beside her chair. She called him Thomas Cat. "Thomas Cat," she would say in her small voice, "do you think this looks nice?" She held up a doily for her cat to see. Continued purring she took as an affirmative answer.

Her sewing basket was a mystery to Jay. It contained colored threads, hooks and needles, all the tools that she used to make the things that cluttered her house. Once, as he watched her work, Jay sneezed three times in succession and she asked, "Sneeze three times and you can expect company. Who's coming to see you, dear?" He couldn't think of anyone who would be coming to visit him and in later life whenever he sneezed he wondered who might appear. No one had ever come. And now as he watched the night sky he wondered again about what was contained in that old wicker basket beside her chair. How the threads might be related to creation, to the strings of galaxies which stretch forever.

Turning to Noom he said, "You know, when I was little I used to lie in bed and try to think about how big the universe is. I have an uncle who told me that you could never get to the edge of the cosmos. He said that if you tried you'd just end up coming back from the other direction. So at night I tried to imagine someplace farther than what I imagined the night before. It was so frustrating, never finding the edge, that I would cry myself to sleep."

Jay was embarrassed after telling his story. He had never told anyone before and was surprised at his feelings.

"Yes," replied Noom, "how can the universe be so big and right in front of your face at the same time? It sure is a mystery." He sighed and said, "The only thing I know is that the universe has the first move."

"What do you mean the first move?"

"It proceeds and then we respond."

"But what if I do something first?" asked Jay, interested in the thought.

23

"Like what?"

"Like put some more wood on the fire."

"The universe had a fire for you to put wood on."

"But I built the fire."

"And the universe had wood to build the fire with. You can go back as far as you want. You could think of planting the trees to get the wood to build the fire to put some more wood on, but the universe has seeds and a place to plant them."

Jay wasn't ready to give up so easily, and he tried to think of a way around the dilemma. He attempted to remember his college logic course, but his mind wasn't working the way he thought it should. He found himself more and more relaxed, and it was hard to keep his thoughts in a straight line. They swirled and mixed with the past, creating new directions which led him to still more memories. Times and places in his past came unbidden. Strong feelings returned and rapped at the door of his attention.

"It comes down to this," Noom continued. "The universe is older than you. It came first and you come second." He paused. "You might think of it this way. We are the result of a long chain of responses, millions of years of responses. Here we sit able to build a fire and pile on more wood. When we do that the universe has the first move again and we respond again."

"You make it sound very depressing."

"That depends on how you think of it."

"But you're saying we respond and then the universe responds to us and then we respond to what it responded with and so on. That creates an endless chain which depresses me."

"Well, there is an endless chain of sorts. I don't know which is worse An endless chain or no chain at all. The part you're missing is that the universe has no choice but we do. The universe can't choose its response. If you hold a rock and drop it the universe doesn't have any choice about how to proceed. The fact of the universe having no choice was figured out several thousand years ago by some very wise folks. Most people act as if the universe does the choosing and they wait for it to choose them, but it really doesn't care because it doesn't choose."

Jay was perplexed. "Then how do we know what we should do?"

Noom chuckled. "You think the universe gives you little signs, little hints and suggestions about what you should do?"

"Well, yes, I guess so." Jay hated to admit it but the old man was right. He did believe in some way that he was dependent on others and on circumstances to direct his life. He tried to bend the world to his will but had neither the strength nor resources so the effort left him bitter. Vanquished, he felt weak and worthless. This clashed with an opposing feeling that he deserved the universe's direct concern and compassion, that he merited its special attention because he was a very special person. If he couldn't be king then at least he should be prince.

"The most noticeable feature of the universe is that it proceeds," Noom said. "We change its direction or flow, but we can't stop it. The universe has procession and we have choice. Those are the rules. It always has the first shot, and we can choose our response. That seems like a fair trade-off, don't you think?" Noom poked the fire and continued. "This affair, universe and man, is depressing only when we don't use the full range of our vision. If you do the same thing over and over and it never worked too well in the first place, that becomes depressing. Getting run over time after time gets old. Stepping out of the way or doing the driving yourself or any of thousands of other choices makes life very interesting. What if? And then finding out."

"You make it sound ... well sort of sad."

"You mean that the universe doesn't care about you or look after you?"

"Yes, I suppose so."

"Well, there is a bright side. At least it's not always interfering in your life. It just proceeds, like this river here," Noom said pointing into the darkness. "You can drink from it or swim or fish in it. It's all up to you."

ΩΩΩΩ

In the fall, fat mallard ducks arrive and camp on the river. Some spent the winter on the water, foraging and cavorting. It is only in rare years that ice and cold drive them farther south.

They live in a remarkable world, these ducks, for they have no boundary to their field of vision. Mallards' vision covers a full 360 degrees.

25

They can see where they've come from and where they're going at the same time. Front or back are probably of little interest to ducks. What distance they can see backward or forward is unknown.

It is believed by some that a duck can look into the past or future at will. Others go so far as to claim that time is created and stored in the heads of ducks, that they are repositories of ancestral lore on a geological scale. They believe viewing a duck closely in the wild is to share in an unlimited future. or past.

If ducks do in fact carry an immense impersonal history then the lone cry of a wild duck on the wing has special meaning. This might explain the occasional finding of prehistoric duck-head effigies in odd corners of the world.

However, it may turn out that ducks are only interested in what lies to the side, because in their eyes the river might flow straight back to where it came from. Whatever the case, it is known that a duck is hard to sneak up on. The trick is to watch without being seen, and this is difficult, as a duck is a bird of unbounded vision.

§§§§

Later, as Jay lay in his sleeping bag watching the stars he asked the question that had been on his mind since he first spotted the old man throwing rocks.

"Who are you, really?"

Noom's voice was muffled by the blanket which had appeared out of his mysterious gray sack. "I am what I do. Good night."

ΩΩΩΩ

That night Jay dreamed he was aboard a white starship journeying into the vast expanse of deep space. From an observation bubble by his bunk he could see stars, all the shining suns of a galaxy. The ship's outer skin bristled with a large variety of detectors: Magnetic, gravanometric, optic. Inboard were gyrolocators and particle synthesizers. Information was fed from the detectors into processing units that reported on fields surrounding the ship as it hurtled through space. Screens instantly posted updates of constantly changing conditions. The ship was a very delicate instrument which sensed even the whispers of events long ago. The vessel's primary function was to report and respond to ever-changing conditions during its voyage, to be sensitive and aware. The crew's quarters were in the top forward deck, well located for viewing the dark night of space. Jay spent his time there watching and waiting. A monitor gently alerted him to the detection of a semi-random signal centered in the high infrared band. The signal was extremely weak, straining the sensitivity limits of the ship's delicate instruments. Gliding to the right, the craft slightly altered its flight to align with the source of the signal. Then Jay dreamed he saw small orange flickers of a dying campfire reflected in a sleeping river. A river flowing slowly through the center of a galaxy called the Milky Way.

Chapter Two

Noom opened one eye and from the shelter of his wool blanket watched the early light of first dawn. Methodically he studied the deep purple aurora expanding across the eastern horizon. During the night he dreamed of a place across and beyond the river. Many years ago Noom had been directed to an isolated spring at that place and instructed on how to proceed once he arrived.

Long ago under the steady blaze of an oil lamp an old map crackled as it was carefully unrolled across a rough wooden table. Noom's youthful attention was directed to a faint line drawn on the yellowed paper. An odd hieroglyphic at the line's end marked his destination. His white-haired mentor, sitting across from him, tapped a timeworn finger on the mark. "You will know the place by this sign," she told him. "Go there and listen. Notice what you hear and then listen again." The woman's hands had gathered whole forests of herbs and delivered armies of babies. They had the strength to shoe a mule and the steadiness to thread the finest quilting needle.

"But how can I be sure when I have found the place?" Noom asked.

The finger silenced his questions and pointed to a steaming bowl of stew set before him. With a long stick the woman poked the fire under her kettle and sang an old Welsh gleaning song. Stopping to peer at him occasionally, her airy laughter delighted the crickets who lived behind the woodbox.

After he had finished the stew Noom asked again, "How will I know for sure what to do when I get there?"

"You will," the old woman answered simply. "Child, ask your questions once you get there. They will be answered far better than any words I can give you." The old whispery voice sounded like the soft flame of the oil wick. "Go now." She smiled at Noom, her crooked finger motioned him toward the door. And he went, map in mind.

Noom travelled across the continent to the river crossing and once there followed his recollection of the tattered chart as he walked far into the hills. His memory and legs were both strong and by nightfall he arrived at the hieroglyph and set up camp. Then Noom sat and wondered what to listen for. He had been filled with anticipation and curiosity.

Now at that same river crossing the old man watched dark silhouettes of cottonwood trees. In the early blossom of morning light he waited for green foliage to emerge. Looking with one eye, Noom could eliminate depth in the landscape before him and imagine it as close or as far as he wished it to be. He drew the dark morning in very close and wrapped it around him like a cloak. One of Noom's peculiarities was his habit of perceiving the world in unusual ways, a practice which allowed him to become an active observer and sample different facets of his reality. The old man felt that no one view was superior to another, though a certain view might be more useful for the particular task at hand.

Soon the leaves would assume the glory of fall, but this morning they were still green. The leaves rustled as a timid breeze crept through the canyon. Cool air carried with it river smell, a smell that satisfied some ancient part of his brain. A part that knew of mud, the part that never blinked.

As light slowly increased in the east Noom could see more of the terrain. The first beginnings of color appeared and he distinguished the bright red of rose hips glowing across the river. Clouds in the eastern sky began to burn like sunset, the world of morning was expanding.

Soon dawn moved faster and the upstream rapids came alive. Air along the river was beginning to roll with the warmth of daybreak. Noom could see where the sun would burn through the horizon and illuminate the bright green tops of the biggest trees with a sudden shaft of dazzling light. Morning quickened and the valley filled with rich warm morning sun. Dew refracted the light, sending out sharp sparkles. The river valley erupted with rich color and deep dimensions. When the sun touched the surface of the river and reflected back into the now blue sky, Noom slowly closed his eye. He reviewed the coming of morning several times, watching in his mind's eye the memory of a brilliant river valley exploding from predawn blackness. Each time he ran his memory forward quickly and watched the birth of day in less than a second. The valley created itself in a single instant, engulfing him in vivid sparkling light. Morning had come.

§§§§§

For Jay mornings had always been difficult. In seventh grade he come across the word, prehistory. His teacher, Mrs. Evans, said, "In the prehistory period man lived in caves and ...." It was then he understood prehistory as something like morning, at least his experience of early childhood mornings. He remembered being very young and looking out a second story window into the dark dawn of winter. The stone walls of his house were gray and cold, and in the morning a lone window in his room looked back into time, east into prehistory. The history lesson was forgotten but still he thought of the long ago past as a time before his ancestors had any light or color. Noon to Jay was when history began, certainly not any earlier.

In his sleeping bag Jay yawned and watched Noom who stood at the edge of the river gazing across the water. "You keep looking over there. What do you see?" he called out.

Noom turned and smiled, "Good morning." Returning his gaze to the hills he continued, "I'm just remembering. The first time I came through this country I wandered back in those hills looking for a certain place."

"You've been here before?"

"Sure. The first time I was a little younger than you are, I suppose. It was 1926."

"Why didn't you tell me yesterday?"

"I've been here before, you've been here before, and I'd guess a whole lot of people have been here before. It's a nice place to camp."

It never occurred to Jay that other people would have known of his

31

favorite spot. "What was it like then?"

"When?"

"In 1926."

"Oh, remarkably the same. I didn't have much to do that particular fall so I did some traveling and passed through here." The tip of Noom's fishing pole dipped suddenly and he turned and lifted it from the rock where it was propped. "About the only thing that seems much different is the fishing. It's a lot better now."

Jay dressed and washed his face in the river while Noom prepared his breakfast fish.

"You said you knew what was back in those hills." Jay asked.

Noom set his pan off the fire and rocked back on his heels. "Sure, do you want me to show you?"

ΔΔΔΔΔ

The notions of freedom and security seem to oppose each other. Security originates from the small, particular and definite. Freedom, on the other hand, is generated by the large, general and unlimited.

Any demarcation, real or imagined, which limits someone or something becomes a boundary, and this is the determining factor in both freedom and security. Boundaries may be fences, laws or beliefs. They may be national borders, brick walls or culturally approved behavior. Imaginary constraints, the strongest of all, separate the accepted from unacceptable. The limiting nature of a perimeter creates security by diminishing access so when a home is inviolate it becomes a castle.

The concept of rights, personal or otherwise is an aggregate of the web of innumerable boundaries surrounding us. This web defines which doorsteps we may cross and which thoughts we may think, and so heresy exists only through the process of exclusion. An ability to cut across boundaries results in freedom, and the ability to keep one's boundaries strong results in security. The turtle carries its own compact bony protection while the wings of a wild goose create the independence it seeks.

Notions of freedom and security support each other, from the security contained within a seed, a plant may expand and grow, to live in the sun. Boundaries are meant to include as well as exclude, and with each larger boundary drawn, differences vanish and the need for law shrivels. Inclusion strengthens as there are fewer boundaries to patrol. The size of one's personal periphery depends on the strength of its center, so this center must be firm before a mind can begin to expand. If expansion is too rapid then the center begins to wobble and the entire structure is threatened. To expand is to risk and to shrink is to guarantee.

Living without any boundaries at all is to align one's fate with that of the cosmos. Security is created by marking and maintaining boundaries and freedom generated by erasing and expanding them. A boundary pencil has two ends and they both need to be used.

¥¥¥¥¥

While they ate breakfast, Jay thought about going back into the distant hills with the old man. One part of his mind warned him that he could become involved in something mysterious and possibly dangerous. He didn't know this stranger, and the previous day's events had been unlike anything he ever experienced. Another part was intrigued and interested but couldn't guarantee that he would be safe.

Jay watched the old man chew his food. Something about the thorough grinding made him nervous. The strong square jaw steadily pulverized each mouthful to bits, like a bulldozer crushing everything in its path. Noom's eyes were alert, scanning the far side of the river. Jay knew he would be uneasy journeying into prehistory with this man. What if they never returned, receding farther and deeper into gloom? Living in cave after cave all the way to the final cave, the ice cave, where time stopped and he would watch those powerful jaws grind rocks.

¥¥¥¥¥

Jay Thomas was born in a small town in the Colorado mountains. When he was young the world seemed confusing, and he struggled to understand things and people around him. The only constant was the peaks and they drew him with their unhurried permanence. When he was

33

old enough he began to explore nearby foothills, returning home after dusk. A young boy arriving at the back porch just in time for supper, protected by the soft darkness of evening.

One day, scouting a tiny valley hidden in the folds of the mountains, he found a badger's skull. Bleached white by sunlight it fit comfortably in his hands. Something about the object moved him deeply for as he held the skull the world around him changed. He imagined he had found a hidden place of enormous power and that the skull was the locus of this force. He built a special crypt to hide his sacred badger skull and went home thinking he had found something which would protect him.

The next day Jay returned to his secret valley and retrieved the skull from its hiding place. Again he the feeling of power engulfed him. Taking the skull to a small stream, he meticulously washed it, scrubbing each bony ridge. It was compact and perfect in his hands and he practiced walking slowly with the skull thrust out before him. He believed that by pointing it precisely he could release its full power. Since he knew little of the skull's potential, he proceeded cautiously.

In time Jay developed a special grip for holding his bone talisman. Walking with a stiff-legged cadence, he would point it and blast inanimate objects with an imaginary beam of unlimited energy. Old stumps and gopher mounds were annihilated by the mighty power he wielded. Each evening after practicing he hid the skull more cautiously than the day before, and its power grew.

In bed at night Jay imagined that a wonderful future was very soon to appear. It was one of the strongest and most exhilarating feelings he had ever known, the anticipation of profound revelation. He was filled with a sense that he was close, very close, to the source of something which would sustain him forever. Something, an understanding or a knowledge, which would allow him to feel invulnerable. Armed with his ally, the badger skull, the boy was unafraid while he slept.

Then one evening Jay hid his skull so well that he never found it again. He searched and searched but it had vanished. He could remember the location of the hidden valley and find that as easily as he had done many times before, but once there he became confused. Jay frantically searched all the places he could have hidden the skull. But each was empty. Without his skull there was no magic, and the small valley, drained of its mystical aura, returned to being ordinary. Its light harsh, the trees and rocks stark and lifeless. He felt empty and alone. The perfect white skull had been buried so deeply and so cautiously it would never be found again. It was the greatest loss Jay had known. Gone was any hope of mastering his future. He tried to forget and when he did remember, he was filled with a deep sadness. He had possessed and then lost his refuge, his only connection with power. The disappointment was almost unbearable.

Jay wasn't aware of it, but he was still searching for the missing badger skull and that feeling of mysterious mountain strength. Concealed within himself the vivid experience lay safe and forgotten on an unvisited shelf of childhood. The memory trace still existed. It remained there for him, waiting until he gained the experience of age and the courage to venture back into the secret valley of memory.

§§§§§

Jay was thinking again about the rocks which floated and those which sank. "If I go with you, what will I find?"

Noom took a long breath and looked directly into Jay's pupils. "Back there," he motioned toward the hills across the river, "is a land with no guarantees. I don't know what you'll find. I know what I found and I'm willing to show it to you. This side of the river you already know about. Over there is a different story, a story yet to be told."

Jay thought about what Noom said. Maybe he was judging the old man too harshly, maybe his vacation wouldn't be a disappointment after all. He had to admit he did find the old man intriguing. "Well, okay," he said finally, "I don't suppose it would hurt to go and look."

"I didn't say that," Noom stopped him. "It may hurt a lot."

"That's not really what I meant," Jay laughed nervously. "You're joking aren't you?"

"Not a bit." The old man's eyes never wavered.

The two men cleaned up the campsite and packed their belongings. Jay strapped on his backpack, Noom shouldered the canvas sack and they started to wade the river. Near the middle, in waist deep water, Jay stopped to ask, "Will I be able to return if things don't work out?"

"Sure, you can go back any time you want." Noom's laughter spread over the water and mingled with the ripples.

Across the river Noom found a faint trail and set out briskly. It felt good to travel again after waiting for the young man to come. His impatience had been relieved by sorting rocks in the river. As he walked Noom remembered starting out on this very same trail many years ago, his pants river wet as they were now. He had wondered what the old woman's cryptic instructions meant. "Go there and listen." What was he to listen for? What sound was to be heard at the end of the path? Curiosity had spurred him on.

ΔΔΔΔΔ

Cause and effect is a very fundamental way of organizing perception. When events are organized in time, arranged sequentially, causation is implied. Causation seems most obvious in events which are perceived to be irreversible. In these cases, cause is given meaning by noting the effect. What something does is what it means. And this meaning is ascribed locally because it is forgotten that every event is mediated by all other events. Any single event is a facet through which all events reflect, they can't be separated. The universe can be seen through a drop of rain falling into a quiet pond. Ripples have no bounds, they shake distant stars. Each specific event is a signature of the whole.

In events which are reversible, cause and effect can be switched and as a result meaning changed. If backward is indistinguishable from forward then a concept of sequence is maintained while the illusion of time is lost. In these events the order of sequence is necessary, the order of time is not. Certain transformations have unfavored starting points; either will do. Water can become ice or ice turn into water, the transformation reversible.

Another class of events involves choice. In some biological systems the concept of probability can be raised to a concept of choice. Exercising choice freely is to ascribe meaning to happenings. Since meaning is context dependent, when a context changes so does its meaning. A dipper full of cool well water on a hot day has a different meaning from one on a snowy evening.

Often understanding causation is simply a matter of examining larger events which contain any specific activity which interests us. Every situation has an infinite number of unique meanings, and by choosing one, we establish a specific meaning by eliminating the rest. Through this process of selection meaning is created. To maintain a sense of continuity and relationship in the universe we use the glue of meaning to stick a series of events together in a way that we desire. For some this adhesive never hardens and the world can be rearranged at will.

In honey bees the eye is faceted, in humans the mind.

§§§§

Just before noon the two men approached a large juniper tree and Noom propped his sack against the tree trunk, sat down to unlace his boots and let his feet rest. All morning had been spent walking, walking silently without a break. During the hike Jay thought about the floating stones. They created an unbearable tension in his mind, he was both frightened and intrigued at the same time. He felt that unless the issue were resolved something bad would happen. The river stones created a hairline crack in his certainty and he was frantically trying to repair it before it spread. He felt that if that crack weren't stopped immediately something crucial could shatter. Shatter beyond repair and that he would be lost forever, plunged into a dark well where the universe would taunt him as he drowned.

He remained standing, fingers drumming. "Those rocks didn't float did they? You messed with my mind somehow."

"Well, that's one way to look at it," Noom glanced up. "I don't know which is more impossible, rocks floating or messing with people's minds. What are you asking?"

Jay turned and faced Noom. "I tried it."

"What are you talking about?"

"Last night I threw a rock in the river and it sank just like rocks are supposed to."

37

"Supposed to? How do you know what rocks are supposed to do?"

"That's not the point, I want to know the truth."

Noom looked far into the distance and took a deep breath, letting it out slowly. "There isn't any," he stated.

"Look, either the rocks floated or they didn't, and I want to know which it is."

"Then why ask me? You already told me yours didn't." Noom searched Jay's face for a response; finding none he continued. "Okay, they didn't float and I messed with your mind, I tricked you. Which is worse? Which version disturbs you the least? Both have consequences which are far reaching. Did the rocks float or was your mind clouded? It could be one or the other or possibly both and maybe neither. You'll never be absolutely certain until the day your rock floats."

Jay was angry. "I just want you to tell me the truth," he snapped.

"I told you there is no truth to know."

"Sure there is. There is truth and falsehood. Why won't you tell me?"

"Are there rocks that float and ones that don't?" asked Noom.

Jay's experience didn't match his knowledge. Knowledge and experience clashed in his mind and the conflict made him unsteady. He couldn't choose one over the other.

"Look, I just want some answers from you. Some pretty strange things went on back there and I want to know exactly who you are. And none of those funny answers." Jay unbuckled his waist cinch and slipped off the shoulder straps, setting his pack to the ground.

"Are you usually this testy after hiking a few miles?" Noom taunted.

"No, I'm not."

"Well then, where would you like me to start?"

"In the beginning."

"Okay," said the old man rubbing his chin. He stretched his legs out straight and settled back against the tree. "I guess the beginning was when I was born in 1907 in Homeworth, Nebraska. Well, not actually in Homeworth, near Homeworth would be more accurate. It was a Sunday I believe." He stopped and looked up at Jay. "Did you want me to start before that, about how my parents got to Homeworth?" He watched Jay's blue eyes go cold and begin to narrow. "No I guess not. Anyway it was a Sunday and stormy as I remember and ...."

"What do you mean as you remember? Are you trying to tell me you remember the day that you were born?"

"No, I didn't then but I do now that you're asking me. I can't think of any other reason it would have been raining." Noom paused, a puzzled expression on his face. "It must have been storming."

"You're nuts. Do you know that? You're totally gonzo."

Noom leisurely folded his hands in his lap. After gazing at the young man for a long moment he said in a whisper. "All your life you've been hunting for a whacko like me and now you've found one. Relax, son, sit down. Hitch a ride on the hay wagon, go to town and see the elephant."

"Hay wagon? If you keep talking like that I will start to believe that you are from Homeworth."

"Near Homeworth," Noom corrected, holding up his index finger. "It was about five miles to town."

ΔΔΔΔΔ

Earlier that morning Jay stooped to retrieve a light gray pot shard. It was thumbnail size and painstakingly scribed with fine straight black lines. Long ago a wood fire hardened the clay, setting the black marks. The pot cracked and fell apart in firing; its pieces scattered, one shard waiting for Jay.

Now he drew it out of his pocket and rolled it between his fingers. The sensation from the rough edges brought back a part of his childhood, a wonderful and mysterious time when he hunted arrowheads. He roamed the hills, head down, searching for any bit of flint that peeked out of the dirt. Touching the shard brought back the sense of awe he had felt when he lifted a flint chip to examine it closely. Brought back the fascination with an idea that since arrowheads were created by human hands this marked them as different from any natural object.

Nature proceeds without intent; however, with man intention becomes his signature, his uneraseable sign. Whenever man touches nature it is formed and reordered by his intent. This is what Jay had discovered,

39

human intent clearly and elegantly revealed in an arrowhead. Someone intended the flint to become an arrow point; that intent organized and propelled its creation. Each fragment the boy found held this intent as strongly as it did when the act was originally performed. When intent is exercised it becomes timeless. Intent was the human alteration, a long transparent finger from the past reaching out to touch him.

To touch without intent is to be a part of nature itself; it is to be blown by winds and pass without leaving a trace. Intent must be lived with before it can be lived without. It is the mind aligned and directed toward an imagined event or arrangement and, so intended objects become historical records.

Someone intended the bowl to be hard, to be useful and beautiful. The shard Jay found was a remnant of proof, evidence of the original action which signified directness and strength in the maker's intent. When actions are clumsy and confused they indicate intentions set at cross purposes. But when intentions are aligned they fuse into a single action, honed and polished, moving with the sound of arrow flight.

As a child, Jay never gazed into the smoky eyes of antiquity; a curtain of time hid them from him. He was content to carry his treasures home and deposit them in a special matchbox that held his collection of sacred and long-ago things, a matchbox lined with soft cotton. Sometimes just before bed he would slip the matchbox part way open, push back the covering with his finger, and touch the tip of a cool flint point. It helped him sleep at night.

ΩΩΩΩ

"When I was a kid growing up," Noom said beginning another anecdote, "there was a carpenter in Homeworth. Name of Jack Tibbitts. He did good work and built lots of fine houses. One day when Jack was working, pounding a nail, he missed the nail head and smashed his thumb. The injury was so bad that he couldn't work for awhile, and he got to thinking about the incident between the hammer and his thumb. The more he thought about it, the more Jack's thumb throbbed. The more he relived the event, the more unhappy he became. He had never injured himself before and was determined to find the cause of his accident. Finally one night it came to him, it was the hammer that smashed his thumb. If he only had the right hammer, he thought, that would never happen again.

"Night after night he lay awake and thought about the right hammer and what it would be like and what it would do. He began to go to different hardware stores hunting for the perfect hammer. He would walk in and say, 'My name's Jack Tibbitts and I'm hunting for the right hammer. Show me what you've got.' He looked at framing hammers and sledge hammers. He tested different handles, wooden handles and metal handles. The more he searched the more he found that no hammer was quite right. He would ask people to show him all the hammers they had. And each time he was disappointed because he couldn't find the perfect one. Jack then widened his search and looked at mallets and the small brass hammers jewelers use. None was perfect for what he wanted. His search became an obsession. He began going to other towns looking for the perfect hammer. Soon he wasn't spending much time at home and his wife and family suffered. His wife said, 'Jack Tibbitts, you'll just have to do with what you've got.' 'No,' Jack replied, 'not till I find the right one.'

"He looked at wooden malls for driving stakes and for a time was interested in air-powered hammers, but they failed to meet his critical tests. Jack became an expert on hammers and could speak at great length about them, their variety, manufacture, balance and so forth. He was devoting his life to the search for a perfect hammer. People would say, 'That Jack Tibbitts, he sure knows a lot about hammers.' And then one day I heard that Jack had died. His thumb had healed up just fine, but as far as I know Jack never pounded another nail after that accident."

¥¥¥¥¥

In Jay's mind an old window was opening. A small boy floated out, kept aloft by the scent of fragrant lilac bushes below. The child looked back and watched lace curtains billow as the stale air of winter rushed out to find hummingbird wings.

41

§§§§§

Miles from the river the land was becoming softer as the geology relaxed, rocks changing to a light red sandstone. And the dirt had the same soft red tint. Vegetation was sparse but greener and healthier against the background of red rock and dirt. Jay had an impression that the land was quieter and more dreamlike. He wasn't sure where they were, all he knew was that they were north of the river and traveling deeper into the hills. The light, clear and clean as it reflected from a cloudless turquoise sky, seemed to say, "Hush. Hush."

"So why did you come here in 1926?" The question was all Jay could think to ask. Suddenly his concerns seemed distant and unimportant. Nature has a way of encouraging surrender with its immediacy, and deep down the young man was grateful for a reprieve.

"I don't know that I have a very clear answer," Noom paused, remembering. "I suppose I didn't have anything to keep me where I was. And I ran across a person who effected me oddly. She had this map, to me it was kind of like a treasure hunt." He rose and shouldered his sack. "I suppose it was the first time I did something without thinking that I had to have a good reason for it."

"And you didn't really know where you were going?"

"Not really. I memorized the map, what there was of it, so I had a destination, but not too much else. At the time it seemed to be enough."

"And is that where we're going?"

"Umhuh, we should make it by nightfall. Put that shard back in your pocket and let's get going."

As the two men continued traveling farther into the hills, Noom walked with a slight side to side motion. Each step he took tilted him slightly to that side, like a metronome, and this steady rocking propelled him forward. Following in Noom's footsteps, Jay bobbed up and down. Bouncing, he could momentarily see over the top of the old man's head with each step. And they continued, each with his particular style of locomotion, one bobbing and one weaving.

¥¥¥¥¥

When Jay Thomas finished college he wanted to travel, to taste the exotic and behold the unique. So he went to Europe. Slowly his travels turned from a vacation into a search, and then from search into a troubled journey. His money ran out and he didn't know how to get a career started. After all, what was a humanities major to do, he didn't want to take a job beneath him. But necessity is forceful and upon his return to the States he took a menial job until something better was offered. He wasn't ready to settle down, and in time the world would provide a career which he could find stimulating and rewarding. While he waited he fantasized and wondered who he really was. If he could discover his true identity then he could begin. What Jay didn't know was that the cosmos doesn't conduct talent searches, it accepted him just as he was. He was the only one who was disappointed with his situation.

ΩΩΩΩ

The red rocks wear their great age proudly. True, they aren't the oldest of rocks but nevertheless they are ancient, well entrenched before the ants came. Their age is guessed at in millions of years. 250 million years? Perhaps not a day over 230 million. What's the difference in a few million years?

When they were young, the rocks were lifted up so they could see the wide sky and late summer sun, so they could mark their horizons. As soon as their birth was complete, death began slowly to wear them away. Erosion, that great transformer, played over their surfaces. Adults now, their reddish blush permeates the whole country as they erode into dust.

The soft red color resisted gravity, soothing Jay's sight. A red mist filled the air, giving it weight and depth. What he didn't know was that the particular red quality of space wasn't reflected light, it was rock thought. The rocks north of the river were especially deep thinkers, so their thoughts weren't rushed. Everything was considered, thought over slowly and deliberately. They were good thinkers and talked openly among themselves, thoughts floated easily on dusty air. They were interested in their own beginnings and the country around them.

A people had come to this land and lived for several millennia leaving remnants of their aspirations, including the pot shard Jay found. They came and flourished while the rocks napped one afternoon. Their time in the desert sun had come and gone in a land of red rock dreams. The drama of a civilization can happen while a stone dozes.

For all their deep thoughts these rocks didn't have a very developed sense of humor, maybe they didn't need one. A simple joke would get a chuckle lasting years, just enough to pass the time. They lived their lives at a much slower pace than the rest of the world, knowing of history and beginnings and ends, they had seen much. It is difficult to surprise a rock.

How to know their thoughts, listen to their rumblings? It is hard for most travelers to slow down and listen patiently for a single word. Rock speech comes a syllable per season. It rearranges the meaning of a lifetime when age ceases to be an absolute. To hear rock speech is to relent, to unearth a timeless time, then one can join their conversation. Rocks exist in a time where dawn means something other than morning; for them sunrises flicker by like the tip of a mosquito's wing. They live in a dreamy dance of memories past, recounting myths and legends, gossip at the water hole. Ask a rock politely and it will tell you all it knows. The tale may take a long while but it is a communal story, one all should know, for their names will be spoken in the telling. A planet is known by its rocks, they are the oldest among us.

¥¥¥¥¥

On one of his previous camping trips Jay drove down into a canyon and through the town of Blue, Arizona. It wasn't a town so much as a place. A bar and post office were about all he could remember.

He spotted the name on his road map and was curious. When he left the highway a gentle steady rain started to fall. Through the warm downpour he saw a blue horse ridden bareback by a young girl with blond pigtails. He forded the Blue River and drove on toward the Mogollon Rim.

Earlier that day, the girl had painted her horse red, white and blue with poster paint left over from Mrs. Moore's fifth-grade art class. The red and white paint on the horse's head and neck was washed away when a slow drizzle started a little after noon. As Jay drove by on the muddy road the girl waved, wondering if this stranger was impressed seeing an Apache maiden riding her war pony in such a lonesome place. It was the fourth of July.

ΩΩΩΩ

Years ago when Noom travelled west on his task to listen, he was unprepared for what he found. His 500 mile journey was made mostly on foot which gave him a chance to wander and ease into the desert country. To breathe its air and observe its light until he was no longer startled by dawn. As he penetrated the dry land he began to learn its quick moods and temperament. Unlike others who preceded him to the region, he was looking for a place where his future map might begin as well as where the old paper one ended. Unknown to the young earnest man plodding westward, the wilderness within was already mapped and it was his good fortune to gain a foothold at the edge of the chart.

When Noom first crossed the river he came face to face with a land whose patina was its polish. He worried that he would lose his way and wander aimlessly hunting for the spot marked on the map. But the way was easy and unobstructed. Direction and location were freely given by a land which watched him pass with steady unblinking eyes; it had little else to offer. Noom found the West a good area to pursue mysteries because they lay so close to the surface. With bright light and dry air, little was obscured.

Mist is rare in the West because the moisture and specific inclination to create such things are lacking. In fact the West lacks the inclination to create much of anything. The high desert isn't a builder; its history serves also as its present. Noom found a land that was continually shedding its skin, keeping only bones and letting the fat wash away to distant places where it accumulated. In other places empires flourish, feeding on accumulation. But no empire will last in the western desert, because the desert doesn't accumulate. During his journey in the West Noom learned to travel light in a land that encouraged mobility. A place where essentials came first and there was no last.

The high dry western desert proceeds by desiccation instead of

45

putrefaction. This land practices evaporation in every sense of the word, keeping itself renewed and fresh in the process. It practices erosion not for export but rather to discover its inner heart. It encourages and then finally forces its inhabitants to be migratory, as it is for the most part migratory itself. And of these inhabitants, the oldest gauge their wealth not by what they own, but by what they know. In a place where rations are meager, experience becomes paramount.

And Noom had been sent to experience. Listen, he was told. Uninterrupted experience, lucid and direct, greeted him when he crossed the river. In the desert everything is given freely to those with strength to behold the immediate and obvious. By continuously changing, the land's agelessness is kept forever young. The land is interested only in structure -- most particularly its own. Rendering itself to its very bones, they are displayed with pride. The Southwest is a study in the rehabilitating effects of erosion. Winds keep its surfaces polished and body bright. A powerful mirror is created and maintained which allows strangers an opportunity to develop keen insight and some measure of courage. At times the land imposes a terror which can be great, yet it is unafraid. Unafraid because all its secrets are exposed. Worn openly and given freely to passing strangers, the secrets remain safe. This land into which Noom entered was severe in its gentleness and extended few promises; however, the few that were extended were kept absolutely. All contracts were kept current.

Many believe the Southwest possesses a great magic, but they are disappointed in the end. Its power lies in the fact that the essential is ordinary and the structure of the ordinary is understandable. When he crossed the river those many years ago Noom found a powerful land where the unknown is still known and the unborn expected. In the fall of 1926 when he reached the end of the line on the old map and stood looking at the symbol, Noom didn't know what to do. So he waited and listened. At first he heard wind whispering as it roamed the small canyon, rustling dry brown leaves of oak brush. He listened until he began to hear grass bending as it swayed in the breeze.

By the second day Noom noticed a low pitched rumbling sound that interrupted his thoughts whenever his attention wandered from his determined listening. He searched for the source of the sound along the bottom of an arroyo. It was like the faint sound of buffalo running over an immense plain, always just over the horizon. Noom searched and searched but could not pinpoint any source. Finally he sat with his legs folded under him and waited. The sound began to rise in pitch. Soon he began to discern short words and phrases. The volume increased and then he found its source. The sound was emanating from within his own mind. Old arguments with past friends and strangers had been rumbling just below the surface of his awareness. Critical voices of resentment and bitterness, voices of warning and doom.

Noom never realized how much he talked to himself. After listening for several days to the non-stop rattling, he finally gave his many voices a single tone. A tone that he liked and felt was truly his own, his original voice. The tone began to grow softer and more faint. On the morning of the eighth day he rose to continue his listening but could hear nothing. Listening harder and deeper than ever before, Noom finally heard it, silence. The sound so startled him that he stopped his listening and began talking to himself about it. But by the end of the day he could listen to serene silence for long periods. He knew then what it was like to be free from internal dialogue. He stayed for another week, experimenting with his newly found voice, discovering how pleasing the sound was. He found he could talk to himself whenever he wanted and then stop, listening to his inner silence. It was wonderful, just like speaking aloud, when he stopped silence reigned. No more fearful, punishing, criticizing voices. Noom thought they originated from outside himself, but gradually he realized they came from within. When he finally accepted this the silence came. When the many became one, all arguing ended.

§§§§§

They followed the edge of a red rock escarpment the better part of the afternoon. After sundown the two travelers arrived at the foot of a small canyon and camped. In fading light they could see it winding back through the cliff.

47

"Is this our destination?" Jay asked.

"This is the place. In the morning I'll take you back up that canyon to a spring," Noom replied.

The old man was tired by the day's walk, and after they ate he rested, gazing into the campfire's flames.

He had spoken little since they arrived. Finally he asked, "Have you ever thought about fire?"

"No, not really. What's to think about?"

"Controlling fire is one of man's greatest achievements. It took us a long, long time to understand fire and to begin to use it. Steel isn't possible without fire, or ceramics or cooking or many of the things we take for granted. But it wasn't till we understood that fire wasn't a thing that we began to make some progress in understanding our world and the way it works."

"How can you understand fire?" Jay asked, brushing his dark hair back from his forehead. "A fire's a fire. What's to understand? A thing is what it is."

"And how does one know what something is?"

"You can just tell. Would you have trouble telling if something is a fire or not?"

"No, I wouldn't. But you see it goes a little deeper than that. I know what something is by what it does."

"That's nonsense." Jay shook his head.

"Maybe. But how can you tell," Noom asked pointing toward the flames, "that this is a fire?"

"It burns. What else can I say?"

"There you are. Something is what it does. This fire and these trees," Noom said, gesturing into the darkness around him, "our thoughts and yesterday's clouds. They are all what they do. That's how you know of something, by paying attention to what it does."

"What trees?"

"I'm speaking figuratively. I suppose there is a lone juniper out there somewhere." Noom smiled and looked into the night. "We tend to think of trees as things because they hang around so long. But trees turn sunlight, air and some stuff in dirt into wood and leaves and shade."

"Then you're saying that everything does something?"

"Yes, and it's more than that."

The two men paused, enjoying the fire's company as its warmth protected them against the chill of the desert night. At length Jay broke the silence. "Okay, so what about rocks?"

"What about them?"

"They just sit there."

"Yes, until they do something else."

Jay thought for a while. He was tiring of this 'is-does' business. He was uncomfortable with the 'does' part. In his life the 'is' part he had already imagined, the only difficulty was that no one else had also imagined it and made it come true. When he thought he had figured a way around Noom's argument, he proceeded. "So would you agree that a rock is hard?"

"Which rock?"

"That rock over there," he pointed. "It's hard. I'll go and get it and show you." Jay sprang up and went to get a large rock just at the edge of the firelight. He struggled to lift it and carry it back to the fire. "There," he said dropping it with a thud. "There's a rock and it's hard."

"I still don't understand how you know it's hard."

"Because when you hit it like this," Jay in his annoyance hit the rock harder than he intended, "you can feel that it's hard."

"And what did the rock do when you hit it?" asked Noom pointing to Jay's skinned knuckles. "We can talk about the nature of rocks. We could talk all night about rocks, but only after some kind of interaction can we feel fairly certain we know what we're talking about. Only after your knuckles interacted with the rock did you know of its hardness. Things are known by their interactions, by their doing. Take this fire, we know it by what it does. It gives off a certain light and heat and changes wood into ash. Chemists call fires optically noisy chemical events. When we figured out some of the things fires do and how they do them, fire became friendly and we were no longer frightened by it. Fire is one of the things that distinguishes us as human."

Jay nursed his bruised knuckles. "Okay, speaking of humans, how does what you're saying apply to people?"

"That's one of my best examples," the old man answered with a smile. "Someone is what he does. We do so that we might become, people are what they do. Grass is what it does. That star," he said pointing overhead, "is what it does. Everything is a process and some processes last longer than others and these we call things."

"Then you're saying that people are processes?"

Noom nodded, returning his gaze to the orange flames.

Jay tilted his head back and spoke quietly across the fire. "I don't believe I remember meeting anyone as odd as you."

"Probably not," Noom chuckled. "But you can invent your memories and call them belief."

"When you talk like that I get a funny tingling in the back of my head."

"It's not the way I talk, it's the way you listen that makes your head feel funny. You keep listening to what's already been said." The old man paused and looked up at the night sky. "I once heard a story about someone kind of like you."

"Like me?"

"Well, not exactly like you I suppose, because he was someone else. But I am reminded of you. Anyway he lived in a land which had a road running its full length, and if you wanted to go from one place to another you travelled along the road. The road went through a small village in which lived a curious boy.

"Now this boy did the usual boyhood things and one of the things he did was to watch the comings and goings of strangers along the road. He noticed that some strangers were different from others. Some of the people traveling the road carried large bundles of food to eat during their journeys. Others stepped off the road when they were hungry and picked fruit from trees. This puzzled the boy and he began asking people in the village, 'Why do some of the travelers eat from trees and others carry their food with them?' He always got the same answer. 'What trees are you talking about?' 'Those trees,' he would say. The villagers would give him strange dark looks and walk away. There was muttering in the village that the boy was beginning to see things and that this was a sure sign of madness. People started avoiding him. So he asked the travelers with bundles. 'Why don't you eat from the trees?' 'What trees?' 'Those trees,' he said pointing toward a tree heavy with fruit. The travelers would give him the same dark look as the villagers had and scurry on.

"This troubled the boy and he decided to wait under one of the trees. In time a traveler stopped and after picking fruit from the tree, sat down beside him to eat. The boy tentatively asked the man 'Why do you eat from this tree when the others don't?' The man looked at him and said 'It's simple, son. See this mark on my forehead? Persons with this mark are free to eat along the road as they wish.' The boy had never noticed any marks before, but there on the man's forehead was a pattern of finely etched lines. They were so fine that the boy could see them only if the light was just right. Some of the lines swirled and others ran straight, making a distinctive mark like a delicate web. The man finished eating and continued on his way.

"The boy began watching for travelers with marks on their foreheads. The man was correct, only the travelers with marks ate from trees. When he mentioned the mark to the villagers he got the same stare, and so he went back to waiting under a tree. In time another man came and picked fruit and sat beside him. 'Sir, I know that only those with marks like yours can eat from these trees.' 'Yes, you're right,' the man replied. 'What I would like to know is how does someone get such a mark?' the boy asked. The traveler finished eating and looked thoughtfully into the distance."

Noom fell silent and turned his attention to the fire. Taking a stick he began to rake burning embers to the sides and pushed glowing coals into a small mound in the center. Prudently he separated the burning from the burned. Wielding his stick like a spatula, he smoothed and patted the coals into a small cone. The blackened pieces of unburned wood he arranged in a circle set well back from the cone. When he finished he sat and waited for the fire to cool.

"And what did the guy tell him?" Jay finally asked.

"What guy?"

"The traveler."

"Oh, yeah, I almost forgot. Let me think." Noom scratching his chin. "He told the boy, 'It's not an easy thing to do, to get one of these marks, but I will tell you. You must find a place where you can be alone and comfortable. Then seat yourself and stare into the palm of your hand. Do nothing but stare into your hand and in time you will find the answer to your question.' The man rose saying, 'Good luck to you,' and went on his way."

In the darkness Jay thought about the story. "I don't think that sounds like me at all."

"Now that you mention it, I'll have to agree. It must be about someone else."

"Which hand was he supposed to look into anyway?" Jay asked.

Noom removed the blanket from his sack and was meticulously gardening a soft bit of ground, removing small rocks and bits of debris, preparing to bed down for the night. "Oh, he could look into the right hand or his other hand," Noom mumbled. "I don't know which would be most useful in such an endeavor, I don't suppose there's much difference."

❰❰❰❰❰

In the northern sky there is a star unlike all others. A star so delicately balanced and accurately located that along its axis time stops. This star has been known longer and has been given more names than any other. Its axis is anchored to earth by human hopes which hold it taut, scribing a dependable line, unchanging in a changing world. The North Star's location and dependability give direction and comfort to all who encounter it. It neither rises nor sets; night or day it is there, a constant lonely beacon.

Explorers in the northern hemisphere watched the star's light which assured them of finding a homeward path. True north was the compass point from which to calculate their return. The star was of no help when a traveler ventured forth; whatever lay ahead was unknown. Right or left made little difference voyaging in uncharted directions, but returning was to calculate all the little rights and lefts and to finally arrive at a bearing. A bearing which was as absolute in direction as the North Star itself. From this notion voyagers derived great comfort. At night travelers watched the North Star and it gave them courage.

However in the Southwestern desert there lived a people who also watched the star, for it troubled them. They called the star Awb, the Fearful One, the one who is lost. What so deeply troubled these people was that Awb remained motionless. Of all the dancing stars in the northern sky only one was still and unhappy. Believing that movement was life, these people feared that Awb was near death and took it upon themselves to breathe life into the lonely star. They became guardians of the constant star and had even taken its name for their own, hoping that this would encourage the star to spin and dance again in the precession.

The Awb had no use for the North Star's steadiness because all of them possessed a shining inner beacon which was maintained by the balance of their minds. At night they ate their ground corn and dried squash, calling out to the sick star, "Dance now, we are here." To them stillness was death, and they prayed the star would move before it fell. For the Awb, what was constant and what was not were separated only by time, and of that they had an unending source.

¥¥¥¥¥

Jay lay in his sleeping bag wondering about Noom's story. Surely there must be a difference, he thought, as he held out his hands in the night air. He tried to determine which hand was heavier or warmer, searching for any distinction that would indicate a solution to his dilemma. Jay began to slumber and little by little his arms slowly dropped until they rested peacefully at his sides. Little did he know the Pole Star's keen arrow of light had shone in both his out-stretched palms, annotating them with its own shadow.

ΩΩΩΩ

Coyotes range along the river and some nights they sing. Usually they sing in small groups, but the river has on occasion been rendered silent, listening to a whole hillside of sitting coyotes, singing with muzzles raised.

These songs heard by a wakened ear seem a collection of raucous yips, yaps and barks. But to the ear which listens along that narrow and delicate crack which exists between sleep and consciousness, they are songs almost painful in their great beauty and age. To anticipate hearing a coyote song constrains the mind in such a way that only discordant noise is heard.

However the ear which is alert but unprepared hears. These songs cannot be remembered or imagined, only experienced, heard at night when the air is black and sky heavy and clear. Coyotes sing of bright mandalas formed by neck feathers of pheasants and old golden kimonos hidden away in dark wooden trunks in Kyoto. Songs are sung of spider webs so finely spun they become anvils upon which starlight is cut.

Then the desert dogs trot home to fall asleep when morning comes. A coyote song heard from the inner edge of slumber can sustain an entire land in its wondering.

Chapter Three

¥¥¥¥¥

During the night Jay dreamed he was living on the Kentucky frontier in a little settlement far from civilization. In the morning as he enjoyed the warmth of his sleeping bag he tried to remember his dream, searching back into the darkness of night. The early morning light was gently prying him away from the dream, and he struggled to recover the memory before it dissolved in the sea of nightly drama. He caught a fragment just in time to draw the dream back and put it in order.

He lived in a small log cabin with a mud and stick fireplace at one end. In his dream he had barred the door and gone to bed. During the night a heavy knocking at the door awakened him. He took his flintlock from wooden pegs on the wall and crept toward the door. "Friend or foe?" Jay called out and the heavy pounding stopped. He waited, listening for any noise outside the solid wooden door. "Who's there? Friend or foe?" he called out again. After a long pause a deep and tired voice answered in a puzzled tone, "I don't know. Which are you?" There his dream stopped and Jay now lay wondering who had been at that massive door.

≈≈≈≈≈

Noom had risen very early and quietly stolen away in the dawn light. He went in search of a mountain mahogany tree. Twenty years before he had taken on certain duties and obligations which now as an old man he would fulfill. It wasn't so much a matter of ritual as one of tradition.

Originally he was slightly amused by the rite that would now guide his actions. The custom seemed very primitive and magical and Noom was told, "Yes, it is foolish. However one day you will find comfort in foolishness." His teacher was correct, for now that he was older he was beyond any feeling of embarrassment.

Walking briskly Noom kept a steady eye on the eastern horizon. The materials he was searching for were to be gathered before dawn. Mountain peaks could be seen to the north and west, but the eastern horizon was flat and level. The arbitrary dawn rule turned his search into an adventure as he enjoyed an imposed time limit. The challenge had been laid down by his teacher. "If the light of the sun touches you before your search is completed you will be a toad forever." It was a childish way of testing himself against those who had previously fulfilled this obligation.

He proceeded not out a sense of duty but from a wish to repay the sources of learning which had been freely offered. Noom had only once witnessed the ceremony he was now beginning and he would perform it but a single time. It was his way of acknowledging a continuity of learning and of privately honoring those whom he remembered with great fondness.

When he first experienced it the rite had seemed very mysterious. His objections were countered with, "Why exclude the mysterious, some find great satisfaction in the mysterious. It keeps you and the earth firm. Besides it will get you out of bed before dawn at least one more time."

When Jay arose, Noom was not to be found. The campsite was bathed in sunlight as he dug into the pile of ashes. A few embers were still alive and with the aid of a handful of dry grass a fire was soon blazing. Water was boiling when Noom suddenly appeared.

"Where have you been?"

Noom needed to sit a moment while he caught his breath. "Out racing some old ghosts." He beamed broadly. "What a great morning, after breakfast I'll show you why we came here."

Later as they approached the spring, Noom grasped Jay's shoulder and pointed. "There," he said.

As Jay watched, water seeped from a small crack in the smooth face of the red rock. Water, following the crevice, flowed down across dark green moss and dripped into a small clear pool, hiding in the shade of two large leafy chokecherry trees. From the pool it seeped into the dirt, staining the red earth a hundred feet down the small canyon. The thin strip of damp earth and vegetation growing along its course attracted insects that hovered above. Dragonflies and small gnats skimmed over the surface of the tiny pond.

"In the summer," grinned Noom, "butterflies come here to drink. It's a sight to see when they come in big herds."

Jay was confused as he approached the pool. He could see himself and blue sky reflected on the surface. "Is this what you wanted me to see? We came all this way just for this pothole?" He expected more, but more of what he didn't exactly know.

"Yep, this is the place. See those bubbles?" asked Noom.

Jay looked closely and noticed small chains of bubbles formed by the splashing water. Breaking away, they sailed across the glassy surface to join other strings on the far side.

"See how they join up with the others," Noom continued. "And notice how two bubbles join together to form a larger single bubble."

Two bubbles Jay was watching joined so rapidly that his eyes missed their merging.

The old man crouched down to examine the bubbles more closely. "Have you ever noticed that two bubbles, when left alone, become one and not the other way around? The process only goes in one direction."

Jay vigilantly watched and saw little flotillas of bubbles joining and rejoining until only one large bubble remained. Then the last bubble would pop, vanishing also. A whole legion of bubbles disappeared as if they had never existed. The many become one and then suddenly departed without leaving a trace of any kind. Jay found himself wanting to ask why they had come all this way to look at bubbles but thought better of it. Kneeling beside the small pool he amused himself by waiting till a single large bubble formed and then touching it with his finger tip. In an instant all the ancestor bubbles were liberated in a single fluid blink.

The Structure of Delight

ΩΩΩΩ

The wing of a butterfly may be unmatched in its beauty and variety. Every wing is divided by veins into many cells. These wing veins form rigid struts that separate and support the wing cells. The method and art of stained glass windows were inspired by the butterfly wing.

Wing cells are composed of tiny scales, each a single color. The spatial patterns of these scales enchant the eye with chevrons, crescents and ovals called eyespots. The overall wing is a mosaic of independent patterns, one to each wing cell. To form a coherent whole they all must refer to and be aligned with at least one reference point located somewhere on the wing.

Pigmentation is one of two ways by which scales are colored. The second way of coloring a butterfly wing is structural. Exceedingly fine structures on the surface of each scale refract and diffuse light into individual colors. Row upon row of these miniature light manipulators stand on pole-like rods supporting wedge-shaped receptors which cleave sunbeams into rainbows.

To live for any time at all on the wing of a butterfly requires one to find the single focus of symmetry and to camp near that spot. Otherwise one struggles through forests of light receptors, endlessly ensnared by discarded colors, and becomes confused and lost. The location of this point is a closely guarded secret which no map can accurately divulge. However, it is said that a full day's travel due north from the confluence of the two main wing panels will place one in the general vicinity. At the focus of symmetry the air becomes perfectly still and the ground clear and soft, for here beats the heart of order.

Ancient legends tell of mountain moths, fur-bearing butterflies which were totally silent in flight on wings designed to mimic snow flakes. Their short rich fur was without pigment, and each iridescent hair owed its color to the interference of reflected light. And when the moths flew in great numbers, an observer would become lost in a blinding blizzard of brilliant color. Gliding by moonlight they looked like small war kites, suddenly freed from their tethers, with strict geometric patterns boldly shining forth. Kingdoms were traded for a single pelt.

§§§§§

Noom was good humored, relaxing beside the desert seep. Earlier during breakfast he had told Jay stories of growing up in Nebraska. He obviously enjoyed returning to a place that meant so much to him, and he breathed deeply, smelling the air to refresh his memory. This was the spot where his youthful journey terminated, where he had camped and listened.

It seemed to Jay that the old man was smelling some hidden fragrance, a fragrance which made him livelier. He sat on a rock, under a piñon tree, looking pleased and inhaling deeply.

Noom drew a stick about six inches long and as big around as his wrist from his coat pocket. Opening his clasp knife he painstakingly examined the blade's edge and when he was satisfied, began to carve. Jay watched as Noom's knife cut slowly and evenly into the wood, raising long curling shavings. While Noom carved he recalled his past and laughed while telling stories. Jay scrutinized the bubbles as they trekked through their evolution. From a foamy beginning their size increased while the number diminished. Using a grass stem, he punctured each master bubble before it erupted on its own. During a pause between stories he asked, "Noom, I want to know the truth about the rocks in the river."

The old man stopped his carving and looked up. "I told you there is no truth to know."

"Sure there is. There is the truth and falsehood," Jay insisted, setting his grass stem aside.

"Explain that to me."

"It's like an onion, if you strip off all the layers then what's left is the truth."

Noom raised his eyebrows in mock astonishment. "The inside of an onion?" Then he resumed working his piece of wood.

"No, I'm not talking about onions. You know that. It's just a metaphor of the way I see the question of truth."

"Then using your example, what are the layers that were stripped off?"

"The false part. There is either truth or falsehood and when you strip away the false part all that is left is the truth."

"That's one way of looking at it," Noom said as examined his handiwork.

"You keeping saying that. When I asked you about truth yesterday, you said the same thing."

"Yes, I do. I said it yesterday, I'm saying it today and I'll probably say it tomorrow. There are a lot of different ways to look at any question." Noom waited before continuing. "You see, I don't understand how there can be false events. Events are events, neither true nor false."

"That's not the point. I'm not talking about events I'm talking about what happened."

"In your head or in the water?"

Jay was crestfallen. The old man wouldn't say whether the stones really floated or not. And now he was indicating that there might even be different types of events, those actual and those mental, both with equal importance. Jay knew that his original question was getting hopelessly snarled. A crack of doubt was slowly expanding and Jay felt powerless to stop it.

Noom closed his knife and shoved it into his pocket. He rolled the stick back and forth between his fingers examining the carving he had completed so far.

"Let me explain it this way," Noom began. "Some people have a library in their heads and in that library is a solitary book. This single book is called The Truth, spelled out in big gold letters on the cover so you can read it easily. What's in the book is also called the truth. That's how you can tell if something is true, just look it up in the book." He glanced at Jay to see if he was listening. "Now then, one-book libraries are guarded very cautiously, because new information and experiences are always trying to sneak in. Sneak in and be entered in the book of truth. I suppose the world is untrustworthy in this sense, it's always trying to expand and interact with your brain. One must take precautions or you can pick up curious notions. Notions that may be delightful and interesting and even a little crazy. Notions which might fill a hundred books, maybe a whole library." Noom paused, watching a train of bubbles on the pool's surface.

"Anyway, people with one-book minds avoid any danger of becoming contaminated by monitoring which experiences are allowed in, and as a result they are seldom confused. However, they're also pretty narrow."

"So, you're saying that I'm narrow?"

"No I'm not. I'm saying that an experience has slipped through your inner defenses and it doesn't match what's in your truth book. And this mismatch is making you cranky. You can't throw the experience out and yet you can't keep it, because it doesn't fit. Son, there is a part of our brains that's merciless in demanding that accounts balance. I'm saying that truth is not a property of events or experience, it's a filing system in our heads. We only have confidence in our perceptions if they have been entered in the book at a previous time. We only see clearly if we already know what is going to happen. Children are born with books which are largely empty and events are entered uncritically. As they get older and their log of experiences grows, the number of new experiences allowed to enter diminishes. It's this phenomenon which gives rise to the concept of truth. You can't teach an old dog new tricks, but you can teach a young dog new tricks its entire life."

A small pile of shavings and wood chips rested in his lap as Noom continued. "The closing of the book is the end of learning. When new entries stop being made learning ceases. Learning is storing new impressions in the mind," he said tapping a finger to his temple. "If you limit this storing by concepts of truth, you end learning."

"I don't see what you mean. You should try to learn the truth, isn't that what we're here on this earth for?" Jay asked.

"You know," Noom chuckled, "learning the truth always seemed a paradoxical phrase to me. Learning and truth don't have much to do with each other. In a way, the idea of truth is necessary, it keeps our universe in order and gives us a sense of continuity from one day to the next. But the continual guarding of one-book minds also does something else. It's called defending one's point of view. What's inside is the truth and what's outside is false and must be guarded against. Anything allowed in already matches what's in the book and is taken as further proof of the truth. It's a self-perpetuating system. What's registered in the truth book is called belief and so beliefs have boundaries. Boundaries to what we do, boundaries to our behavior. Boundaries to be defended. People have to fight for their beliefs don't they?" Noom smiled as he wiped wood chips from his lap. "How disturbing would it be to think of truth as an arbitrary distinction?"

Jay was sitting on the ground with his hands clasped around his knees. "So what are you saying?"

"I'm saying that if you drop the inner distinction of truth and switch to a distinction of use then you won't be cranky so often."

"Then you're just saying to use what works. You're saying that ends justify the means. But when you do that you've just lost your integrity."

"No, no. Following your argument, one protects his integrity and nobility by limiting means and I think that is a mistake. When you limit means you restrict resources which are available to you. Limiting means doesn't guarantee anything, let alone truth. If a carpenter limits his tools to a pair of pliers and a stringline, he's not capable of doing much damage. But neither is he capable of building something really wonderful." Noom stopped to let Jay absorb his words before he continued.

"Now I want to be very clear on this point. I think that defining outcomes, defining ends is the act of integrity. A clearly and exquisitely defined outcome automatically constrains means. Switching from a distinction of truth to one of use, in fact, makes you more responsible. It makes you ultimately responsible. Most people who worry about their integrity are unwilling to take the final responsibility for it. They want a system of values which will guarantee that others think them noble. Notice that when I talk of use I leave out the concept of values. That's because I think it's the responsibility of the individual to create and accept the consequences of his own values. And also notice that I stress the word consequences instead of the word create. If you code information and experience as to its usefulness, its effectiveness and efficiency, then the only questions are what and when. Useful for what and useful when. You have to be responsible for the integrity of your outcomes. Dropping any distinction of truth eliminates conflict in a single stroke and what remains is delightful."

"That's nuts."

"Probably," Noom laughed. "Would it be useful for you to believe that some of the rocks I threw floated and the one you threw sank?"

"But then I wouldn't know the truth."

"You're right. Technically events are experiences, so I'll just say truth is not a property of experience."

"But if I think about an experience being useful, then I have to think for what. Useful for what?"

"That's right."

"And then I'd have to think about when it would be useful."

"You've got it."

"You're making things a lot harder, I just want to know the truth. Why won't you tell me?" Jay pleaded.

"Then you're asking if your experience on the river matches some other experience in your one-book library. Does it?"

"No. Not that I know of."

Noom stood and stretched his arms. "Then I can tell you without hesitation that your experience of seeing some of the rocks float is false. Not true. Nada. Like the man who went to town and didn't see the elephant. He saw the non-elephant."

"Why do you talk that way?"

"I guess I just don't know any better." Smiling broadly the old man nodded, pointing beyond the spring. "Come on, the non-elephant has passed this way, let's follow his non-tracks and see where he didn't go."

ΔΔΔΔΔ

Belief is the formalization of meaning, belief is meaning fossilized. It becomes the rock on which a personal fortress can be built. However, a shelter constructed out of ever-shifting understanding becomes a magic carpet, leaving the earthbound behind.

Whenever meaning is spoken the moment is lost, stored forever in an untouchable past. While meaning remains fluid, each moment lingers near the infinite. And so the unnamed kitten of a litter enjoys the risk of becoming a lion.

§§§§§

Beyond the spring and almost at the head of the canyon was a smooth rock wall protected from weather by a high jutting ledge. Pecked into the surface of the stone was a formidable collection of petroglyphs made by Indians who lived in this region hundreds of years before. Jay had seen ones like these during his camping trips but never in such quantity.

Depictions of horned water serpents crowded a herd of mountain goats. Fields of jeweled corn plants had been painstakingly incised under multi-leveled rainbows. Eight-foot ghost figures holding feathers in their hands guarded one end of the wall, while snake symbols wriggled across the base of the rock.

"This was here the whole time!" Jay exclaimed. "Why didn't you tell me?"

"Yes," Noom smiled. "Isn't it wonderful?"

As Jay stepped closer to examine the petroglyphs, he spotted one that intrigued him. It was about the size of his hand and looked like the letter H with its crossbar replaced by a zero. The red sandstone for several inches around this one mark was empty and clean.

"Look at this," said Jay, feeling the incisions in the rock, "it looks almost like part of an alphabet."

Noom nodded his head. "It's the mark of the Hawkeen."

"The what?"

"The Hawkeen."

"What's the Hawkeen?"

Noom leaned back as he gazed at the petroglyphs. "Well, they're difficult to describe, there are so few of them."

"Them?"

"Yes, it's a group. Kind of a club or maybe more like an order or perhaps a cult." He thought for a moment, stroking his chin. "It's a group of people who share some common interests. And that," he said pointing to the wall, "is their mark, their sign. In English it's called the Ho because it looks like a combination of those two letters."

"How come I've never heard of them?"

The old man chuckled. "Son, there's a lot you've never heard of. I wanted you to see this sign, it's very rare."

The mark was cut deep in the rock. Unlike the others it had been engraved with metal tools. Its edges were sharp and clear, the indentations smoothed, almost polished.

"The Hawkeen have existed for a long time." Noom continued. "I don't know much of their ancient history, but during the last couple of centuries they have spread throughout the world. It's a guess, but I'd say all together there are several hundred Hawkeen, maybe over a thousand or two. I don't know that anyone has a very good idea, not even the Hawkeen themselves."

"And how did the mark get here?" asked Jay, still fingering the indentations.

"From the looks of it I'd say that a Hawkeen put it there a long time ago. It marks this place as sacred. One of the source points."

"You mean it makes this rock sacred?"

"No, it more properly marks the spring."

"I think it should mark this rock wall as sacred, the spring doesn't amount to much. Don't these petroglyphs mean this is sacred ground?"

"They also mark the spring. I don't know but what the word special would apply here more than sacred," Noom grinned. "When I say sacred you get a lot of fanciful visions in your head. The Hawkeen are late-comers to this region and they found the spring to be special for a variety of reasons, the same as the people who lived here before them."

"Tell me about the Hawkeen, what are they like?" Jay asked, his interest piqued by the mysterious nature and fine workmanship of the sign.

"Well, again that's kind of hard, because they're all different. Some are loners, outlanders, and some are very public. Men and women of all ages. I think one thing which distinguishes them is they're all a little crazy. With some you notice it more than others. They think differently from most people."

"You mean they should be institutionalized?"

"Maybe, but they have already done it themselves. That's one of the things the Hawkeen is for," Noom chuckled. "They think a lot of different ways and get together occasionally to share new thoughts and understandings. Some of them think a lot about thinking and some of them don't think at all. I suppose you could say the Hawkeen is a guild of the mind, formed by people who enjoy plying those particular arts. Usually it's just a few, but I have heard of as many as fifty getting together in one place. That doesn't happen very often because a large group will usually have a very good time and get into a fair amount of trouble. It's like fifty wizards having a party, the countryside just can't handle it."

Noom shook his head in amazement as he remembered the only big gathering he attended. It was in the Austrian Alps and the combined laughter caused avalanches. The citizens of a local village took such a dim view of their proceeding that they drove the whole troop away.

"So how come you know so much about them?"

"Because I'm a Hawkeen."

"What? You're a Hawkeen?" Jay had imagined a very strange and exotic collection of people. He was momentarily stunned as his fanciful imagination was suddenly reduced to the simple old man standing before him. "Do they mark themselves with this sign?" Jay said, pointing to the rock wall behind him, hoping for at least one small piece of exotica.

"No, the Ho locates this place, identifies it as the source. The Hawkeen say if you ever drink from the source you'll never be thirsty again." Noom smiled at his young companion's temporary confusion.

"You mean if I drink from the spring I'll never need to drink water again?"

"No I didn't say that. You'll always need water and drink it, you'll just never be thirsty."

"That's crazy, feeling thirsty is what lets you know when to drink."

ΩΩΩΩ

Noom sat down on a rock, enjoying the morning sun. "When I was a kid, there was a man in Homeworth who was a drunk. The town drunk. When he was on the street, people would walk real fast as they passed him. His name was L.C. Just initials. I don't even know if he had a last name. Old L.C. always talked to us kids, telling us of being in the Civil War and how terrible it was. He walked with a limp supposedly caused by a

Confederate bullet. We knew that he was making the story up but we liked it anyway. I suppose he talked to us because none of the adults wanted to be around him. He was held up as an example of what would happen to you if you didn't eat your vegetables or learn the multiplication tables or anything else people wanted you to do. In a strange way the people of Homeworth needed L.C.," Noom mused. He had always felt a faint kinship with the old war veteran and it was only in his later years that he understood why.

"Well, anyway, when I was nine or ten he told me something that's stayed with me. He said, 'Noom, people are always talking about my drinking. I hear about it everyday. They ask me why I drink and tell me that if I would only stop drinking such and such would happen and so on. They always talk about my drinking but never about my thirst.' So you see," said Noom looking into Jay's eyes and then pointing to the mark, "Hawkeen are unusual people. Many places marked just like this exist all over the world and they're all called the source."

"You mean springs all over the world that are somehow connected?" Jay asked. "That's impossible. Springs can't go under the oceans."

"Like I say it's an odd bunch, very odd."

Noom suddenly lost interest in the mark or any more of Jay's questions and wandered back to the spring. He found another sunny spot to sit and continue his carving. Left alone, Jay began exploring the rest of the canyon, looking for more of the fantastic petroglyphs.

ཙ ཙ ཙ ཙ

After Noom was born his father named him but could never explain the meaning of the name to his son. "I could tell you in Swedish but I don't know the words for it in English. It's a very old and powerful name from the time of the Vikings." The best his father could do was to show him how to write the name using runes. "There," he would say after scratching the word in the dirt, "that's what it means."

Noom's father was born in a small settlement on the eastern coast of Sweden. In the village a one-eyed blacksmith taught him the runic alphabet and special Viking hex signs, drawing with a birch twig in fine ash beside the cooling pit. The smith, with his one eye flashing, whispered as he imparted secret lore of a people who had stalked the world in longboats. The distinctive writing, illuminated only by glowing embers of the forge contained a strength which carried all the way to Nebraska and ignited its dust.

Noom would stare at the scratchings and try to comprehend a homeland of which he knew nothing. As a child he carried his name like a secret, a shiny and powerful thing.

His father would sing Swedish songs as he drove the spring wagon to Homeworth and back. During the evenings he played the violin. Noom's mother worried about sin and Swedish being spoken in the home. A strange boy with a strange name.

Shortly after his fifteenth birthday Noom's parents were killed in a railway accident and he left Homeworth traveling alone. One rainy afternoon, a month later, a tiny old woman riding a mule found him huddled under a bush by the side of the road near the little town of Birch Tree, Missouri. The woman stopped and with clear hazel eyes peered under the foliage. Strands of white hair escaped from her oil cloth rain slicker. "My goodness Boondoggle, who have we here?" A mule, with rain dripping from his chin, gazed at the wet urchin and was not impressed. She took the boy home and after drying him out, fed him full of hot stew.

Derry was 67 years old and contented. She lived alone in Shannon county plying the arts of midwife and herb healer. Attending to the pains and fears of her neighbors, she and her faithful mule Boondoggle traveled the region's narrow dirt roads. Called a Granny Woman, she was much sought after because of her healing skills and knowledge.

Born in Wales in 1854, Derry sailed to the United States at the age of 12 in the hold of a spice-trading ship. The memories of those strange aromas stayed with her the rest of her life and were used whenever she came across a plant that was unknown to her. She came to develop an olfactory sense of any plant's medicinal uses.

In Kentucky she married a miner and they raised four children, two boys and two girls. When first married, the young couple moved to some level acreage on Hollow Creek and lived for a while in a tent while the land was broken up with a single-footed plow. After crops were planted, a small log home was built and they were snug and secure by Christmas.

Derry took an interest in the region's plants and was soon collecting mints and oswego, pennyroyal and pigweed. She learned about spicebush and sweet birch, nettles and toothwort. Black mustard and charlock were cleaned and dried, stored until needed. There the couple lived, on Hollow Creek, adding a new room each time a child was born.

About the time Derry's children were grown and leaving, she and her husband moved to Missouri. They bought a small farm with a stone house, a good well and big fine barn. There he died when the great influenza epidemic of 1914 passed beyond the Mississippi River. Left by herself, Derry devoted all her time to the wild plants she so dearly loved. She made chickasaw plum pie and pinchcherry jam. Thorn apple relish and riverhaw preserves filled her ample root cellar. And for children Derry prepared a tonic called persimmon beer. Made with persimmons and locust pods, it kept scurvy away during winter. But her favorite plant was wild ginseng. 'Sang' she called it and encouraged Noom to watch for the plant wherever he went. "Look in places where the sun hardly hits at all," she told him.

The Granny Woman cured croup and colic, dysentery and dropsy. Heart trouble and headaches were banished along with chigger bites and pneumonia. Much of her healing was done by faith because she knew that belief was the strongest and most unifying medicine she could ever prescribe. When she spotted a child with warts out of her bag would come a mysterious red box. "Child," she said tapping her box with a long finger, "I collect warts and I don't figure I've ever seen such fine specimens as you've got there. Would you sell 'em to me for a penny each?" To be selected for the Granny Woman's mysterious wart collection was a high honor. And after the bargain was struck and the money paid she would gently remind her small customer, "Now I know you're honest and you'll keep your word, but in a week I'll look right inside my box to make sure all them warts been delivered." No child ever reneged on his end of the bargain and the wart box, of course, was never opened.

Noom stayed in Missouri with the Granny Woman for three years, chopping wood and hauling water, keeping Boondoggle's barn clean.

Boondoggle was a large mule standing 15 hands tall. In truth he wasn't a mule at all, rather, a less familiar hybrid called a hinny. This meant his mother was a burro instead of his father. Although referred to as a mule it was a point of dignity with him to ignore the speaker's obvious ignorance of his ancestry. He retained all the many mule qualities plus a few more.

When Derry moved to Missouri he came with the place. He was born there and there he would die. Boondoggle was self-willed to the point of unreasonableness and in the beginning there was a contest of wills. The mule won, getting his name in the process. The battle was over whether he would wear a bridle. Boondoggle never had worn one and saw no reason to start in mid-life. They finally came to an understanding when Derry realized he responded to verbal instructions. Being a mule, his hearing was very acute and he didn't like to have his ears touched or handled They were his primary form of expression. Having made his point, the mule carried her through storms and knee-deep mud with only gentle words and an occasional pat on the neck for direction. His loyalty to her was unbounded, and it came as a great relief to the old woman to be able to mount her mule at night after delivering twins and simply say, "Home now."

Boondoggle was proud of his abilities. At the stream where a log crossing was provided for foot traffic, wagons or cattle were required to wade, he always chose the log. Even at night in a driving rain he kept his feet in a steady line and walked its length without incident. Though he was hard of hide and sure of foot his robust body housed a sensitive spirit, and he wouldn't accept injustice or irrational treatment.

When Noom arrived Boondoggle was his senior by thirteen years and master of the barn. Right at the beginning, Noom poked the mule with a pitchfork and was confronted with a week's worth of revenge. Only after the boy delivered a heartfelt apology was the incident dismissed. From then on Boondoggle refused to conceal his contempt for the job of teaching a slowwitted youngster the etiquette of feeding and caring for a mule. Most of the time when he and Noom were alone in the barn he would lay his ears back against his neck and groan. When he was disturbed or upset in any way he would refuse to eat, causing Noom great exasperation. "Boondoggle," he would plead, "please eat something, a mouthful, one stem, anything." But the mule always won and only later when things were going as they should would he become more carefree. Boondoggle loved to roll, and Derry repeatedly instructed the boy always to allow him the opportunity whenever he was unsaddled, otherwise a hunger strike would ensue.

The mule had a definite sense of how to proceed, and he was humorless in dealing with anyone he thought to be a fool. Boondoggle felt only a minimal amount of attention was needed for most tasks and he insisted it be given without interruption. Noom was wrong to think the mule single-minded, for his many years trained him to be extremely mindful, quietly alert to his immediate surroundings.

¥¥¥¥¥

After searching along the canyon walls for several hours, Jay was unsure what he was hunting for. The old man's words disturbed him. Perhaps he was searching for something that would rekindle his sense of certainty. The last couple of days shook his belief in any particular order of things. He remembered a time in his life when he felt certain.

He was traveling through Arizona in an old pickup. On an Indian reservation he spotted someone squatting beside the road. When he pulled to a stop he saw that it was a woman sitting on a watermelon waiting for a ride. Inside the cab she placed the melon between them and nodded up the road saying, "Keams." Jay took this to mean Keams Canyon which was marked by a small dot on the tattered road map now held down securely by a fat green melon.

Uncomfortable with silence as they drove, Jay began trying to think of things that he and the woman beside him could talk about. Noticing ominous clouds on the horizon, he asked, "Do you think it's going to rain?"

"Oh," said the woman, "we can't ever tell."

Jay realized the woman took his question as a request for a prediction of the future instead of a speculation, so he rephrased it. "Sure looks like a good rain is coming."

71

"Oh," said the old woman in a high bird-like voice, "we can't ever tell."

"What do you mean?"

"Well, we won't know until after it's over."

The self-evident nature of the statement silenced Jay as he struggled for a way to start a conversation.

"Well, I think it will rain," he finally suggested.

"Oh, you white people," the lady giggled, "you always think about what's comin'. Rains are good by the way they end, not by the way they begin. When I was a little girl I watch the clouds buildin' in the west and wonder if I have any puddles to run through. And my grandmother she see me and she ask, 'What are you waitin' for?' and I say 'Puddles, I'm waitin' for some new puddles.' So one time after a rain she take me out into the corn field and showed me a single leaf on a corn stalk. 'Look just at the tip, see where the water drops form?' I counted the drops one by one. All around the field I see drops of rain fallin' from the tip of every leaf. 'This,' she say 'is how to know of rain, watch the drops. A lot of drops make a lot of puddles.'"

When they stopped at the store in Keams Canyon the old woman bounded out of his pickup, slamming the door. "Maybe puddles today, maybe tomorrow." She waved and Jay drove on.

A hundred miles down the road he noticed the watermelon had been left with him. It was the sweetest he ever tasted.

§§§§

That evening after sunset closed the small canyon, zipping it up for the night, Jay looked deep into the fire as he thought of the symbol cut into the rock. Remembering the smoothness under his fingers, he asked, "Tell me more about the Hawkeen. You've got me all interested now."

Noom turned his head slowly and gazed into the night sky. He shifted his weight onto his elbow and returned his eyes to the flames, remaining silent for a long while.

"The Hawkeen are masters of belief," he began finally. "They collect beliefs and trade them, sell them or give them away. They invent them and bargain for them or steal them. Hawkeen will believe anything you want them to. They will believe everything and its opposite also. They know that beliefs are what make your head work, that a belief is what it does. Another belief of theirs," Noom chuckled and shook his head at the thought.

"The Hawkeen have a belief that the more beliefs one has, the more choices one has. Most people want fewer beliefs, they want their list to be short and correct so they can commit it to memory. Religions seem to be that way. But the Hawkeen are different and some say just plain stubborn. They can believe anything to the point where it's the same as believing nothing at all. I suppose fundamentally they believe that there is nothing not to believe, if that makes any sense."

"Well, at least if they believe everything they can be sure of being right," Jay stated.

"I suppose so," Noom replied. He got up to put more wood on the fire. Placing small branches across the flames he waited till they caught fire before he spoke.

"When you ask about Hawkeen belief you're stepping into quicksand. Beliefs are valued as to their usefulness in any particular situation, and situations change. They figured out a long time ago that much of the conflict in oneself or between people or nations has to do with colliding beliefs. So they decided to save themselves a lot of grief and believe everything. It's like the bubbles you saw at the pond this morning. All the small bubbles of belief crowding against one another join and rejoin until there is just one giant bubble. Then some Hawkeen take delight in popping it. No bubble, no boundary."

Jay took the pot shard from his pant's pocket and began to roll it over and over, like a coin, between his thumb and index finger. He thought of the pond back in the canyon and how each time he pierced one of the bubbles, it surprised him. He had tried to poke them more slowly, hoping to see a bubble deflate. But each time the collapse seemed instantaneous and the speed with which it occurred gave him a start, almost like a small electric shock.

"You know," Noom continued, "people have a terrible desire to be right. Many people will sacrifice their own happiness and that of those around them. They will sacrifice their lives and everything dear to them to be right.

Being wrong seems to create an unbearable tension. Many people's opinions of themselves and the world are more important to them than the results the opinions bring. Being wrong hints of losing one's bearings, losing one's mind and going mad, or worse. It's a natural fear, this being wrong and a great one, often greater than the fear of death, because many people will die before they will be wrong. But it's interesting to contemplate being wrong. What if you were wrong about yourself in major ways that would benefit you?" Noom asked. "Sometimes great problems can be solved easily by being wrong. Often it's a very simple choice--would you rather be right or happy?"

¥¥¥¥¥

After Jay Thomas returned from the Europe he toyed with the idea of becoming an artist. He took some drawing classes and purchased equipment. He subscribed to art magazines and attended gallery openings. He had intense and lengthy discussions with his friends about the importance of art. But he never finished a painting.

A girl friend concluded that his art career wasn't getting off the ground because he lacked inspiration. So he attended several workshops designed to furnish him with the spark of artistic creativity. But his paints and canvasses ended up in the closet and he got a job at a small bakery that specialized in English muffins. That too wasn't really what he wanted, it was just something to pay the rent while he waited.

≈≈≈≈≈

Both men were silent as they watched the flames dance. They were warm and comfortable by the fire and neither felt the need to speak. Noom slowly closed his eyes and let the pictures of the day's activities swarm before him. In his mind he reviewed them and then sent the images far into the distance where they became very small and finally vanished from his optical fabric. A very small speck marked the point of departure and Noom drained his mind through that point. The pictures came slower and slower as his memory of the day was carried away and filed somewhere beyond the mental molecule. Noom waited patiently for the next scene and then the next to depart. The clutter of his mind diminished and soon just fleeting bits of memories sped through his visual vortex. These last images he called junk pictures. He knew that when the junk ended, when the last of it left, all would be quiet and he could serenely watch just the single speck in his mind.

Many years before, a Hawkeen taught Noom about the spot and its uses. "When you have reached the speck," the man explained, "wait and watch. If you wish to know something from another place or time, wait till the speck vanishes and observe what enters from that place."

Noom's visual field was now seamless and even with one small dot in the center. He always enjoyed a deep sense of calm and relaxation that came from watching this silent point.

The Hawkeen told him of other uses of the particle. "If you want to direct a future event, let that speck expand into a picture of what you want to occur. Let it expand larger and larger. Let it expand until it fills the cosmos, until the picture is so large that you can see no part of it and it vanishes. Practice this until you can do it very rapidly. But be careful," the man cautioned, "picture making works something like cosmic want-ads. Your picture's strength will depend on how specific it is. Be sure to add all the details and richness to your image that you want to have happen. Weak, incomplete pictures bring weak, incomplete results. You will get what you imagine."

Noom practiced until he mastered strong, clear and complete pictures. One of these had lured Jay to the river. At last the speck disappeared and the information he wanted came in long rapid strings of intense imagery.

"I thought you were asleep just now," said Jay breaking the silence. "You looked like you were dreaming."

"You've heard of dreamless sleep?" Noom smiled as he roused himself. "I was having a sleepless dream."

As Noom slowly opened his eyes he retained the memory of seeing an old wise trout swimming deep into the flames, a bright bug in its mouth.

75

ΩΩΩΩ

When Noom left Missouri to follow his map, he traveled through Texas on his way west. He was out of money and getting a little thin so he stayed in Texas for a while, working for a sharecropper. He learned how to pick cotton and make adobe bricks. As a young man he was very good at arguing. He could argue one side of any subject and then for the fun of it he would switch and argue the other.

"Moral victories don't count," the Texas farmer kept telling him. "They don't get the crops picked or the bricks made."

But Noom always had more words. He was young then and thought he could bend the world to his will. Being quick and clever, he felt he could make up for his lack of power and knowledge with words. It was a hard lesson to learn that cotton sacks fill bit by bit, a cotton boll at a time. Long rows of soft white blooms awaited his finger tips and he dragged a cotton sack, working until his hands were raw and cracked. Rows of corn and beans enjoyed his words but were unbent, remaining straight and true like the brown mule who trudged uncounted miles to plant them.

Slowly the land seduced Noom. It was forgiving and didn't care if he talked. The Texas dirt was so old that it didn't get upset with his sharp words and short temper. It was good at waiting, not having anywhere to go or anything else to do. The dirt waited through a long cold Panhandle winter and in the spring encouraged the young man to plant.

Noom had never thought much about seeds before. But in the wooden barn behind the house, Hubbard squash awaited him, dozing, old now in the winter of their lives. Plump, they spent the previous summer learning songs of the soil and rested now, firm with that knowledge. Tough rinds held chants in their flesh. In the darkened barn, words were repeated for the seeds within. Experience was being passed from the old to the yet unborn. "Your time will come and with it a life in which to grow." The horn of plenty had sounded for them and the squash rested, quietly reciting the lessons of their lives.

Throughout the barn other voices mumbled, entertaining the sparrows who lived under the eaves. Strong dry burlap sacks stacked in corners held chattering corn seeds. They were a lively bunch and spent the winter telling genetic jokes. The beans, however, were a serious lot and sang seemingly endless, spiraling choruses over and over. They worried more than the others that the information contained in their hearts would be forgotten once they were planted, and so they recited their long history again and again. Murmurs filled the interior of the dusty barn, summers being retold in botanical tongues.

When it came time to plant, Noom became dimly aware that seeds knew something. Contained in each small kernel was a history and lineage much older than his own. The smooth hard seeds seemed definite in the dependability of their past. He rode the planter behind the old brown mule, smooth leather reins in hand, listening to the clicking of the planting plates as they metered out eager seeds in long straight rows. Seeds who learned their winter lessons well, and soon young bright green shoots began opening to the sun. Noom was happy watching the crops begin to thrive. He found much to his surprise that he remembered snatches of Scandinavian songs which he sang when he wasn't boasting of the ample crop he envisioned.

Then the Texas hail came, smashing corn and cotton. Noom stood under the barn's tin roof and watched as all the young plants were destroyed in just a few minutes by hard cold stones. Water ran down rows carrying foam and bits of green leaves as the hail thundered on. The pounding shook the earth underfoot. Then the storm stopped as fast as it had started, and Noom ventured out to walk through muddy fields, astonished at the damage.

When he returned to the house he shook his head and said, "It's a strange world."

"Compared to what?"

"What do you mean?"

"It's a strange world compared to what?" the sharecropper asked again.

"That's a good question," Noom stammered.

"Yes, it is. Give me a good answer."

At last Noom was at a loss for words. They stuck in his throat as tight as cotton to the plant. An unbending hail had pounded his words flat. It

77

was time for him to go.

The sharecropper accompanied him to the road and said, "Remember, boy, you can use it or be abused by it."

"Use what?"

"Your mind. You can use your mind or be abused by it."

Noom left Texas with a dollar and four cents in his pocket and another lesson from the Hawkeen.

∾ ∾ ∾ ∾

When Derry and Noom gathered wild plants he carried the sack and followed behind as she explained how to locate and identify different herbs. He was at least a foot taller and could easily see over her head as she pointed out plants of interest. When the sack was full she would stop to rest, enjoying being among her botanical friends. At these times she talked of concerns that seemed to drift in and out of her mind like a bee working a honeysuckle blossom.

"Child," she might say, "sometimes when when we think bad things are gonna happen we git scared. But at those times, if you notice real careful like, it's not them events that scare the wits out of us. What we think them events is gonna to lead to is what scares the wits out of us. If a person was walkin' along a mountain trail you might hear a big loud crash and look up to see big ol' boulders rollin' down the hillside toward you. Do you think the sight of them big ol' boulders rollin' down toward you is what scares you?" Tilting her head to one side, she kept a sharp eye on Noom to see if he was following what she was saying.

"Oh no, it's them head pictures of our bodies bein' all broken up that frightens us. Them tumblin' rocks are already known about and accepted, the pain of injury is what we fear. If we get banged up by them fallin' rocks, then that is accepted and our head races to picture what our injuries might bring. We get to thinkin' that we might die and we get real scared. Again, it's somethin' that we anticipate. We only fear what's in the future and what's in the future can only be pictured in our head, can only be anticipated. We're scared of what we imagine will happen, not what has already happened. There is nothin' to fear in this world, child. What is known ain't feared, folks can only fear the unknown, the imagined, the pictured. Our fears are of our own makin'. Often we're real wrong about what's gonna happen. If you doubt your skills and knowledge, if you doubt your ability to get by in most situations then you begin to fear your future. Scaredy cat like. Then we begin to imagine what we can't do, not what we can. We get to thinkin' on them skills which aren't around for us and the knowledge that plumb escapes us. We think we know what we lack and picture that lack. In that instant," Derry said snapping her fingers, "we lose whatever skills and abilities we do have and are reduced to bein' helpless. That's the way the future becomes even more threatenin'. It's kind of like them Chinese puzzle boxes, there ain't no fear in what has happened or what is happenin' but instead what will happen. When I tend to folks I can't change what has happened or what is happenin', but, Lordy, can I change what they think is gonna to happen."

Noom was young at the time and only later did he begin to understand the simplicity and power of the old woman's observations on pain and disease.

"Child, don't say what you can't do, it's of no use, it don't exist," she continued shaking her head. "Armed with what you can't do, tomorrow will be real scary. Instead picture what you can do, what skills you got now, just like what we have here in our sack. And finally imagine what you would like to be able to do. That's where hope lies. Dwellin' on what you can't do leads to fear and knowin' what you can do brings courage. Picturin' what you would like to be able to do rekindles hope. And with hope, learnin' is easy. Without hope learnin' is like gettin' kicked in the head by a mule, real painful like. Rememberin' our skills and abilities brings us joy, for they are our wealth. Can you tie your shoes?"

Noom was always surprised at these simple little questions at the end of her monologs. "Well yes, I guess. Sure."

"Then you might begin picturin' what else you might learn to tie and untie. Always begin with what you can do. What you can't do ain't of no use at all."

"But tyin' my shoes isn't hard," young Noom argued.

The tiny old lady then smiled sweetly and continued softly. "Maybe not, but tell me, how many ways do you regularly tie your shoes? What you dwell on creates who you are. If you dwell on what you can't do then you turn into an awful mess. Everyone who is alive can do somethin'. And the somethin' we can do now is get back to old Boondoggle, he's probably gettin' impatient for supper."

Picturin' was for Derry a mighty activity.

§§§§§

As Noom roused himself from staring into the fire, Jay asked, "What were you thinking about just now?"

"Well, I'm not sure," Noom mumbled. "I don't think I was thinking about anything."

"You had to be thinking about something." Jay suspected that the old man was just being difficult.

"No, it doesn't work that way. Thinking isn't about something, it's the thing in itself. I know what I'm saying sounds funny, but I'm pretty sure that's the way it works. When you think about what you're thinking about, you've just lost it."

"But I can think about anything I want. I can think about my childhood or my travels or for that matter my shoe," he said pointing to a worn running shoe.

"It's hard for me to explain." Noom scratched the back of his head and looked into the fire. Seconds ticked by and Jay was becoming impatient. "Okay," Noom said at last, "I think I have a way to explain it. Do you know how to think about butterflies?"

"Well I suppose so. I've never thought about it before, but I'm sure that I could think about butterflies any time I wanted."

"Then go ahead right now and for a few moments think about butterflies."

Jay conceived several pictures of butterflies. He finally settled and watched an orange Monarch fly gracefully in an imagined garden. Its wings would flutter and then spread for a silent glide. "Okay, I'm thinking about butterflies. Now what?"

"Now," said Noom, "I want you to think butterflies."

"I'm not sure I ...."

"Of course you're not," Noom stopped him, "just imagine what thinking butterflies is like."

Jay tried to ask again but Noom stopped him. "No, don't talk. Just do it."

Jay wasn't used to doing things right off, he wanted to talk about them first. By talking he could usually receive assurances that his failure wouldn't be held against him. He held a deep seated notion that doing was always for someone else, not for himself. But because Noom refused to let him speak he had little choice other than to think butterflies. When he tried he was struck by an odd sensation. He suddenly knew exactly what Noom meant. He could imagine gliding through the garden supported by soft air currents. Through most of the day a buzzing noise in the back of his head was just on the edge of his awareness. It would take up the rhythm of any natural sound he heard. At the spring it seemed to follow the sound of splashing water, and whenever he became directly aware of the music in his head it would vanish. He now understood. Whenever he would think about the sound it would change. When he thought butterflies now, the buzzing followed his flight and musically kept him aloft. Jay's face began to relax and almost glow as he experimented with the buzzing. He found he could think fire and the sound would follow. He had dreaded the tone during the day and wondered if it would ever go away. While exploring the canyon he worried that he would be stuck with the sound for the rest of his life. And now suddenly he was afraid he would lose it.

"What if ...."

One of Noom's large hands sprang up to stop him. "It won't," the old man said. "You have control and now know the difference between thinking about butterflies and thinking butterflies. The difference is vast and is the answer to your question of what I was thinking."

Later when they settled in for the night Jay asked, "Would it be possible to dream dreaming instead of dreaming about something?"

"I don't know, tell me in the morning."

81

The Structure of Delight

ΩΩΩΩ

In this arid region the spring serves as a watering hole. Animals and insects come to drink, but not nearly so often as might be imagined. Many species native to the Southwest have, through ingenious evolutionary methods, reduced their need to visit a stream or waterhole on a daily basis.

During very dry years the spring is reduced to a seep, but this hardly lessens traffic. The small pond serves primarily as a place for the community to meet, leave notes and exchange gossip. Jay had read some thousand year old gossip, as fresh today as when pecked into the red rock's smooth surface.

Mule deer nervously approach the spring on quick feet after sundown. A jack rabbit occasionally stops by for a deep draught. Kangaroo rats bound in to find out the latest news. As they rarely drink, these rodents only purpose at the oasis is to spread rumors. Morning doves arrive in the evening to sip and coo while dragonfly eggs hatch at the pond's edge. Water, of course, is one attraction, but a stronger reason for coming is to retain a sense of belonging. It is for this reason Noom camped away from the spring, minimizing any disruption to the desert community.

The Hawkeen speak of all springs being connected, for a spring's function is to maintain connectedness. And so this is the very place they left their calling card chiseled in stone, to prevent it from being erased inadvertently.

In a new land, the first thing to locate is the waterhole. Occasional visits will keep you in touch.

❨❨❨❨❨

A chant for blessing waterholes includes the words:

From a far place we come to mend that which is asunder.
White butterfly speaks with old man toad,
Pleasant it has become again for the deep-water people.

Chapter Four

¥¥¥¥¥

In the morning Jay was rummaging through his pack for dirty socks when he suddenly yelped and jumped backward. Grabbing a stick, he poked at the pack and waited cautiously until a large brown furry spider crawled out and scurried off into the rocks. "What a way to wake up," he said trying to regain his breath.

"For you or your friend?" laughed Noom. "She thought she had found a home for life. Now her future isn't what it used to be."

"Not in my pack it isn't." Jay took a deep breath trying to calm himself.

"Wow, that was a surprise," he said as he began collecting his scattered socks.

Beside the pool, as Jay washed his socks the spider scare faded and he found himself thinking again about the peculiar symbol cut into the rock wall. He was intrigued by the mark and Noom's description of the Hawkeen. The fact that such a group existed he found oddly comforting.

When Jay was a child he suspected that he wasn't really a part of his own family. He would watch his parents and brothers and sisters, silently feeling he wasn't one of them. He imagined being adopted, imagined being conceived in another place and by different parents. In grade school he discovered the word 'ilk' and knew immediately that the word provided an insight to his true identity. He imagined an entirely different race of ancestors, the Ilkians. Jay developed an interest in geography, scanning maps for a clue to the location of the Ilkian homeland. He leafed through the entire set of The Book of Knowledge, all twenty-six books, searching for any picture or scrap of information. But the Ilkians remained elusive and in time he forgot all about them.

The nagging worry stayed with him. Like the spider, when he thought he had found a home it turned out to be someone else's. In a way, Jay's life was a search for belonging.

△△△△△

The sack Noom carried had been made by a sailor at Wyndham, a port on the northern coast of Australia. Constructed from sail canvas, it was hand sewn and reinforced with brass rivets and leather, fashioned to Noom's specifications. It served him well during his years of travels, patched and repatched, a journal of his itinerary.

Whatever the old man needed was contained in that sack. While walking behind Noom on the way to the spring Jay tried to guess what the sack contained by looking at the bumps. He was sure of a blanket, frying pan and an old blue enameled coffee pot because he had seen them. There was extra clothing, canned goods and buried somewhere inside, fishing line and hooks.

At the river Jay was struck by the urge to rummage through the sack if he got the chance but restrained himself. When they left the river Noom looked like an immigrant carrying all his belongings on his back. For all Jay knew that's just what he was.

To be an immigrant means crossing a boundary into unfamiliar territory. An immigrant is one who doesn't yet belong. Belonging requires the formation of a new identity consistent with the new territory and most immigrants proceed with this change only to a certain point. When they reach a balance between old and new, beyond which they feel incapable of proceeding, they will say, "That's just the way I am." With that phrase any further change is ended. We can be immigrants in our own countries or families or even our own bodies. It isn't culture or language or national borders that makes us immigrants but boundaries of the mind.

To belong means to exchange one boundary for another or to enlarge our personal boundaries to include whatever we are trying to adopt. Some people with a recurrent illness will say, "That's just the way it is." With these words a boundary is created within the body which divides the parts which are strong from those which are weakened. The illness has been changed from "I" to "it", changed from belonging to not belonging. The mental resources needed to make the necessary leap that includes all parts are lacking.

To be an immigrant in the universe means to be a stranger forever or an outcast wherever one goes, and of course the converse also follows. When a large enough boundary is maintained in the mind, the question of belonging is forever settled. One belongs everywhere.

Noom owned many objects which referred to different times and places of his past. They were all stored in his sack.

ΩΩΩΩ

A family of barn owls lived near the spring. At the base of a piñon tree, burrowing deep into a dirt bank, the parents had first nested many years ago. The belief that owls hunt using keen sight is common, but for the barn owl life depends on hearing. At night these creatures are able to find prey with sound alone. They do this by comparing any differences between the sounds in each ear. An unusual symmetry exists in an owl's ears, the right ear is directed slightly upward and the left downward. This anatomical arrangement allows barn owls to locate the source of sounds, both vertically and horizontally, better than perhaps any other animal in the world.

Surprisingly, human hearing is as accurate as an owl's in sensing direction but lacks the owl's ability to determine elevation. The brain of a barn owl maps space with great precision, enabling the owl to locate its prey in total darkness with deadly accuracy. In their nocturnal journeys these owls range farther perhaps than any other bird. The nine species of barn owls differ enough from other owls to warrant being classified as a family.

The most striking feature of a barn owl's anatomy is a feathered facial ruff, which plays an important role in the location of prey. This forms a very efficient reflector of high frequency sounds. Two troughs run through the ruff and funnel sound into ear canals. Like a hand cupped behind each ear these troughs amplify sounds. The ruff feathers have special sound dampening properties and filter noise into bands of high and low frequency. Low frequency sounds give clues to direction and high frequencies to elevation. Each bird has a small comb on its middle toe with which to maintain its ruff.

When small rodents forage by night, they are nearly invisible. Hunting from the air makes the task even more difficult, since owls must determine the location of their prey in three-dimensional space instead of two. The immobile eyes of barn owls, set in the skull much like head lights, are always aimed in whatever direction the owl is listening. The bird compares the quality of sound from two independent sources, one for each ear, with special brain cells that are activated by specific frequencies. Perhaps barn owls possess a whole keyboard of neurons. To them, the night world is known through the variation of noise. Maps coded by sound are assembled and maintained. Their hunting terrain is charted with the geometry of music and when the night air is still they fly out to search its melody.

In the Southwest lives a tenth specie of barn owl, discovered and known only by the Hawkeen. The primary difference between this specie and others is that the tenth purrs softly while it sleeps. It dreams in sound and these purrings are the auditory equivalents of visual dreams. Those who have learned the language of owl dreams can listen when the owls sleep by day and learn of their nightly journeys. To the Hawkeen these owls are much more than novelties, they serve as a library of regional maps.

§§§§

After he returned and hung his socks on a small tree branch to dry Jay asked Noom, "Will you teach me about the Hawkeen?"

The old man leaned back and observed Jay with a long gaze. "That's a dangerous thing to ask for."

"Dangerous how?"

"Dangerous in the respect that if you really understand their ideas you may not be able to return to the world where you think you now reside. Learning is a risky business."

"Oh, come on," Jay joked, "you make it sound like learning is going to another planet."

"Well, in a sense it is."

Jay nervously brushed his hair back from his eyes. "You're serious aren't you."

"Very serious." Noom was scanning the horizon. The peaks of distant mountains held his attention. "Very, very serious. There were times when I first began that I wished I could go back and forget it all. And I tried, I went searching for Homeworth, but it was gone and I found that I was alone. At that point I didn't have any choice but to go on." His eyes continued to scan the horizon.

"Homeworth's gone?"

"Yes." Noom nodded. "I was never able to find the place again." He swung around and tilting his head slightly looked at Jay. "There came a point when the road behind me vanished and while I searched for it the road ahead of me vanished. And I was alone. From there, a step in any direction was a step into the unknown."

"So what did you do?"

"I looked around. I looked all around me and headed for high ground." Noom scanned the peaks again. "Like that, in the distance," he pointed, "some high ground."

Jay's eyes followed the line of the old man's finger. "That's quite a ways."

"It always is."

"You're not really thinking of going there are you?"

"I am if you want to learn of the Hawkeen."

Jay gazed at the mountains in the distance. "How do I know that ....," he started to ask.

But Noom stopped him. "You don't; there are no guarantees. The other way is back to the river. Choose."

Jay remembered with anger the times he had turned back. He was now sitting somewhere in these hills, he wasn't sure where, with a crazy old man. He was annoyed at the abruptness with which Noom placed before him the dilemma of continuing or returning. He wanted information about the Hawkeen, not to participate in their training. His learning had always been about something, the surface not the substance. And so he was

87

forever knowing about everything instead of really knowing anything. Inner substance is more sustaining than outer symbol, but Jay feared sampling beyond the symbol. He didn't understand that a symbol only has meaning through use. Many times before, he had been caught in his lies when he claimed his skills were more extensive than they really were. He asked Noom to teach him about the Hawkeen and the old man took him seriously and insisted that he expend effort. Jay wanted mastery without calluses. For him knowledge was a form of entertainment, not something to be hunted and devoured and finally digested into the fabric of his being. He was only dimly aware that for Noom learning and changing were identical. To learn was to change and to change was to learn, there could be no learning without change. To remain unchanged was to remain forever without knowledge.

Jay's fingers drummed faster and faster and then suddenly, as if he had exceeded some internal speed limit, a sense of calm began to spread through him. Some invisible internal membrane had been punctured and all the tension came out in a huge sigh. "I don't want to go back," he said simply.

Years later he would remember the morning he washed his socks at a spring and realize just how important that decision had been. Much later, he would understand that the importance of his decision wasn't whether to go forward or back, but simply to commit himself to proceeding. Looking back, Jay would consider that morning as the beginning.

((((((

When the Awb danced, as they often did, they danced with purpose. It was their way. Part of the dancing was elaborate and perfect, the rest was endless repetition on a dusty afternoon. But therein lay the magic, the power of ritual. Careful and methodical repetition of the mundane insured that a way would eventually open for the special, the spiritual. Through repetition the ordinary would become extraordinary, and this, the Awb believed, would allow them for a brief moment to bridge the narrow gap which separated them from other worlds. Members of the village would join to build, condense and finally purify a force which, if strong enough, could arc across that gap. Snap. Contact.

Then it would be completed, the transmission made. It was a gap they believed none could cross except in spirit. The other worlds remained always just one small spark away, the other side of the mirror, that close. It was a short jump that all Awb would make, each in his or her own time. However, when they needed to make contact before their time, the Awb danced.

One fall, before the year of their fourth migration, a special dance was held, a dance that existed only in the memories of the oldest among them. Their religion was a monument dedicated to the generation of spiritual sparks, to the creation of small blue lightning bolts of clear pure thought. All experimentation had been completed long ago by their ancestors, and the Awb carried with them the experience of thousands of successful dances.

During fall equinox the courtyard in the center of the village was meticulously cleared and the dirt packed. Masks were made and daubed with ocher in special designs. Fans and feathers were cleaned and straightened. No detail was left unheeded. Preparation and practice continued until all were satisfied that it was time for execution. After four days of rest and fasting, village feet commenced shuffling on the spiritual carpet, and when the force was again concentrated, a transmission would be made. Snap. Contact.

In the late afternoon the head priest, a crippled ancient, tottered along the ranks of dancers, blowing smoke over them from his blue clay pipe. Other worlds, so close and yet so distant, were alerted to prepare for communication. A great leather drum stood anchored in the center of the plaza. At the moment a blazing autumn sun touched the western horizon the priest dropped a single white feather. Before it touched earth the sound of one enormous drum beat propelled the intentions of the entire village across the void in wingless flight. Snap. Hello.

§§§§§

Jay stared at the mountains. When he turned he asked quietly "How long will it take to get there?"

Noom smiled. "If we leave by mid-morning, we'll be there late tonight.

89

But before we go there are some things you should know."

He took out the stick and knife and sat down to carve. "The Hawkeen usually begin their teaching with perception, and perception is full of paradoxes. In fact you might say that perception is paradox. Certain philosophers claim that the world doesn't exist and that our perception of it is all that exists. Others claim the world does have an independent reality and go about kicking rocks to prove it. So the first paradox is that both views are useful."

"But how can they both be true?"

"I didn't say they were both true, only that they are both useful." Noom stopped his carving and blinked at Jay. "This business you have about truth keeps you from really understanding very much. I think it should be clear right at the beginning that the Hawkeen aren't very interested in attempting to discover any type of true nature for reality. Fundamentally they doubt that it's possible, and moreover they think it's a waste of effort to try. They instead have chosen to collect different world views. To experiment with the unique properties of each. I don't expect you to agree with the way the Hawkeen think, but I do expect you to accept it as their view point. Do you understand?"

Jay nodded silently.

"A second paradox is that sensation and thinking are the same thing. Ordinarily we imagine that we sense and then think about those sensations."

Jay found a spot to sit and drew his knees close to his chest. "So what does happen?"

"The Hawkeen are interested in the five senses, but since ordinary thinking doesn't use taste and smell very much I'll set them aside for now. We are left with seeing, hearing and feeling. I'm saying that thinking as we know it is only the interplay of our senses, especially those three, nothing else. Maybe I should be more precise and specify conscious thought, because it's possible that there may be other types of thought and senses that we aren't conscious of. So the idea is self-proving, we are only aware through our senses; therefore, any thought we become aware of is sensorially based. The test is to try and think anything without seeing, hearing or feeling it."

Jay placed his chin on his knees and started thinking. As he worked he would alternately smile and frown as if to try harder. Noom waited patiently until finally Jay laughed and said, "Well I haven't found a way yet."

"If anyone does I'm sure it will be you," Noom laughed. "And as you try you will eventually try to convince me that you have thought of something using no sensation whatsoever. However, while you're alive your attention is always somewhere. Maybe that's what life is, attending." The blade stopped momentarily as Noom savored his thought. "Anyway, attention is something like your finger, it's always directed somewhere. Whether outstretched or closed into the palm of your hand, the tip is always pointing in some direction. During any event, when you're awake and alert, your attention is always active, directed toward something. It is important to understand that this functioning isn't a matter of will. The only willful part is choosing between the senses. For instance, you can change from watching a river to listening to it. We can direct our attention but not turn it on or off. If you think so, try sometime to turn it off."

"In general, attention has four modes: External or internal, and wide or narrow. Beginning with the first two, the important thing to notice is whether you are attending to internal or external sensation. Many people attend to internal information and assume that's what going on outside. In effect, they hallucinate an external world because the sensory information they base their notions on doesn't originate from the outside. Let me start by directing your attention outward. Think of your skin as the boundary. You have a choice of three senses and a further choice as to whether they will expand or contract. You can look at that twig," Noom said pointing with the knife, "where your socks are. It's beyond the boundary of your skin. Now you can see just the branch or you can see the whole tree with the twig as one of its parts. The same is true of your hearing. At any gathering of people you can listen to one person speaking or listen to the noise everyone is making, so your hearing also can be broad or narrow. When you skinned your knuckles the other day you paid attention to your

91

knuckles to the exclusion of the rest of your body at that moment. You can focus your attention on just one of your knuckles and the sharper your focus is, the less you sense the rest of your body. When you widen your attention, as you did the other night while watching stars, it changes your perception. For the most part, people use focused attention in their daily lives. When shopping in a supermarket they attend to individual cans and boxes and seldom see the store as a whole, all at once. Do you know what the ceiling of your supermarket looks like?"

"I don't know that I do. Why would I look at the ceiling?"

"To find out what it's like, to use the ceiling as a starting point to perceive the store differently. If you can view the ceiling all at once then you can move your vision down and begin to see the store as a whole. Now let's talk just of feeling. Within feeling there is an important distinction to know and it is this." Noom stopped carving and blew some small shavings off the stick.

"Feelings can be divided into two parts which I'll call primary and secondary. A primary feeling would be the warmth you feel from the sun on your face or perhaps a pain you might feel in your stomach when you're sick. Do you understand primary feelings?"

"Do you mean anything I feel inside my skin?"

"Well, not quite. Secondary feelings are what we normally call emotions. We feel them also, but they differ from primary feelings in that they are responses. They are responses to what's happening in our heads; not so much what we think but how we think. Emotions give meaning to our thoughts and hence the world. Emotions are meanings. An example would be the feeling you have when your dog dies for instance. That emotion you experience is the meaning of your dog's dying. It's a great mistake to confuse primary feelings with secondary ones. The first is the world, the second is about the world. The second is what the world means to you and your opinion of it. This is the difference between what we call objective and subjective experience. However, when people say, 'You're not being objective,' they usually mean, 'You're not accepting my subjective experience as reality.' To base your ideas of the world on secondary feelings is a mistake, because those feelings are a response to the world, not the world itself nor what we can know of it. By and large, people don't disagree over primary sensations. Primary and secondary feelings can be understood as the difference between the statements the rock is rough and the rock is ugly. The trick is to be aware of the difference between primary and secondary information. Both are necessary, but different. In a very strict sense, the outer world can never be known exactly. For that matter the inner one can't either, but the appropriateness of information can be improved vastly by noting whether it's primary or secondary.

"Now, let's talk of internal attention. In general it's the same as external, you again have all three senses and they can be wide or narrow. Internal sensations are the world of memories and imaginings, what is ordinarily called thinking."

"I don't quite understand about feelings in the body. Is a muscle cramp inside or outside?"

"It depends on where you draw your boundary. You can define your body as being part of yourself or it can be part of the world. In the sense I was originally speaking of, a cramp would be inside. But what I want you to understand is simply because it is internal, that discomfort shouldn't be confused with an emotion."

¥¥¥¥¥

When Jay was young a dog came into his life, a small furry black and white pup named Tyler. The dog was strong and curious and wagged its tail while trotting about on puppy feet. Tyler slept with Jay and they went fishing and exploring together. Boy and dog began to grow up happily.

Years later there came another dog into Jay's life, a handsome thoroughbred. And Jay was entranced with his new dog and played with it endlessly. Tyler mourned the loss of affection and slowly became withdrawn and surly. He would lie by the porch and growl when the other two went off on adventures of their own.

Tyler began to chase cars on the road that ran near the house. One evening Jay heard the screech of tires and ran out to see a car speeding off leaving a motionless mound of black and white fur in the road. When he reached his old friend, Tyler was quiet and watched him with steady eyes.

93

Then the eyes began to cloud and slowly close. During the time it took for the old eyes to close Jay understood what he had done. He buried Tyler that night by flashlight and in the morning was a child no longer. Later when someone explained suicide to him, Jay knew instantly what the word meant.

Only recently had Jay become old enough to own a dog.

ΔΔΔΔΔ

You have your yes and you have your no.

In a sense that's all there is, yes and no. Waiting is another matter.

What, when, where, whom; you have your yes and no.

All choices.

When yes and no dance together who leads?

A question remains.

Find what can be answered all yes or all no.

All stories start from there, in the beginning ....

§§§§

"As I said, by and large, people don't disagree over what they perceive. They do, however, disagree over what those perceptions mean," Noom continued. "The major difference between primary and secondary feelings is that secondary feelings, or emotions, are meanings. And meaning is where people disagree. You might say that all sensations reaching the brain are messages. It's important to understand that such a message is the event and our response gives it meaning. We think that these messages are about something. We think light from the sun tells us about an event going on in the sun. But the light reaching our eyes is the event, the sun is what it does. We think any particular behavior someone displays tells us something about what is going on in that person, but the behavior is the event. The behavior is the person. How we respond gives their behavior meaning."

"You mean that how I respond to how you responded gives your behavior meaning?"

Noom nodded.

"Then there is no end to it. If I respond to how you responded which was a response to what I did before that, then this thing could go on forever."

"Hopefully."

"But that's even more confusing."

"Think of it this way. Have you ever given someone a compliment and they took it as an insult? Or even the other way around?"

"Sure."

"And what you intended to say wasn't the way that they took it."

"Sure, what's your point?"

"Then what did you do?"

"Well, I tried to say it a different way."

"Precisely. You changed your behavior until they responded the way you wanted. Their response defined the meaning of your behavior regardless of your intent. It takes two to tango. If you really want to communicate with someone then it's up to you to keep changing your behavior until you get a response that matches your intent." Noom paused as Jay looked perplexed. "Information isn't about something," he said slowly. "It's the thing itself. When you smash rocks together you hear a certain sound, That sound isn't about rocks smashing, the sound is rocks smashing. Sensory information isn't about the world, it is the world. If it were possible to stop all attention the world would vanish. It would no longer exist. Deep sleep is like that and so is death. We respond to every message in some way, however slightly, and those responses create meaning. If you don't respond then you're dead, that's the definition and test for death. Responding in different ways gives the world different meanings. If you have a choice of responses then you have access to different worlds. Many people think that the world is the way it is and sensory information is about that world. But information is the world, and your response gives it meaning, creates the world, as it were, beginning fresh each second. So if you don't like your world change your responses and, as if by magic, you enter a new one. Our every action or lack of action creates in the moment."

"Elaborate a little more on the part about different meanings."

"All right. This morning when you found a spider in your pack, your behavior indicated that a large hairy spider is ominous and dangerous.

"Well, sure, it scared me," Jay said defensively.

"But you weren't scared by trees or rocks or by your sleeping bag. If you were hungry and from a spider-eating culture then your behavior might have been different. A big fat spider might then have a different meaning, namely breakfast. A change of responses changes big spiders from being dangerous into tasty morsels. Take coyotes for instance. Coyotes are omnivores, they'll eat most anything. To them the whole world looks like a meal. Opportunists are like that, they see their world as endless opportunity, and so it is."

"So what would you have done with the spider?"

"About the same as you," Noom chuckled. "I'm not from a spider eating culture either. Knowing that your attention is always somewhere is the first step to gaining mastery of perception. We can perceive the world using all three senses simultaneously. When you waded the river you could feel and hear and see the water at the same time, making your experience much richer. You can start learning attention by noticing where it is at a particular moment. After you have gotten fairly good at noticing where your attention is, and in what mode, then you can begin to switch. For instance, when you hold a rock do you get most of your information concerning the rock from feeling it? Or do you get it from seeing the rock or hearing any sound it makes as you turn it in your hand? Whatever your favorite sense for rocks is, try the other two. Shift your attention to the others and find out what they're like. The next step is to change consciously the width of your attention. As you look at the landscape, expand your vision as far to the sides and up and down as you can. Then narrow your vision to one particular point and notice the difference. Try the same with hearing and feeling. Wide and narrow, notice the difference. After you've practiced for a time you'll notice that paradoxically the extremes seem somewhat similar. Very narrow and very wide have a strange relationship to each other. They meet on the other side."

"The other side of what?"

"I don't really know," Noom shrugged. "Like I say, it's a paradox."

"There certainly seem to be a lot of paradoxes."

"Well, I'm certain of how it works but not why. Don't let the existence of paradoxes stump you. A paradox is just another way of saying that you haven't figured it out yet. Anyway, you'll find that switching attention from internal to external involves something of a jump, but wide and narrow remain separated only by degree." Noom paused, marveling at the strangeness of the idea. "In any event, one state isn't better than other any state. However, one may be more useful in a given situation. With three senses and four modes that makes an even dozen ways to perceive. The Hawkeen call this the twelve states of attention."

"And they sit around and practice this stuff?"

"Some practice until it becomes automatic and then they forget about it; others play with it their entire lives. They say it adds sparkle to the world. When you were in school you occasionally heard a teacher say, 'You're not paying attention.' The fact was that you were paying attention but not in the way your teacher wanted. When someone says 'Pay attention,' they usually want you to focus your attention externally. Some tasks require several of the twelve states in combination. To gain mastery you must train yourself to stay in any single state for long periods. When you can do that then practice rapidly switching through all twelve. It's not a matter of will but a matter of training. The practice of meditation, for instance, is the training of attention in a very specific way, usually internal and narrow. If you set out to learn to meditate you will be amazed at how quickly and easily attention can move to other states. So the primary training meditation provides is the ability to hold attention in a single state for long periods.

"That's not so hard. Why do you make it sound like such a big deal?"

"Very well then." Noom opened his eyes widely before issuing his challenge. "Look at your thumb nail for one minute. Find out what happens to your attention."

"Just look at my thumb nail for a minute?"

"Yes. You said 'just'. Find out how big 'just' is. Can you direct your attention for a single minute?"

Jay positioned his legs under him placing a hand in his lap. Closing his fingers with his thumb on top, he began to peer at his nail. Noom watched as every few seconds a slight contraction in Jay's brow indicated he had caught his attention wandering. Seconds ticked on.

"That's long enough. Now tell me how big 'just' is."

"Bigger than I thought," said Jay sheepishly. "So how can I keep attention on my thumb?"

"There is a way to quiet yourself. You can use it in preparation for thumb viewing or anything else you want. Sit comfortably as you are now and slowly let your eyes close. When they have closed, begin to imagine one of the bubbles you played with on the pond, growing larger and larger. Inhale a little deeper then usual and as you slowly exhale say the word 'thorough'. Say it like this: Thhhhhhhhhhhhrough."

Noom demonstrated by taking slow breaths and stretching the word out to match the duration of his exhalation. "Speak so the sound is just barely audible and let the bubble expand until it fills the world at the end of your breath. When you inhale, start again with a tiny seed bubble. If you like, you can imagine that your breath is inflating the bubble. One bubble with each breath. I'm going to stretch my legs a little now and you can practice." He thoughtfully closed his pocket knife and brushed wood chips from his lap.

≈≈≈≈≈

The old man in Texas had shown Noom this exercise one hot afternoon after hoeing cotton. They sat in the shade of a big tree by the house drinking well water and gazing out across the fields.

"Sometimes I wonder what the point of hoeing is," Noom complained. "It seems like the weeds will never end."

"It's a fact, weeds sure do grow." The old sharecropper nodded his head. "Let me show you something that might help."

When Noom first tried the exercise his bubbles would only expand to the diameter of his outstretched arms and he was disappointed.

"Be easy with yourself, son," the old man told him. "When each bubble is inflated let it quietly float off and start on the next. They will grow in size as you get better at it. There are plenty of weeds in this world and a person needs as good a hoe as he can find."

∿ ∿ ∿ ∿

On a hot Missouri summer afternoon it was easy for a boy's mind to wander, especially when the mule looked like he was asleep. Bluebottle flies would buzz around Boondoggle's head and land on his long gray outstretched ears. His lower lip would begin to droop and one would think that the mule's mind was completely empty, however it was just idling. Boondoggle wasn't a kicking mule, he was a biting mule. The other unusual thing about him was that he never slept.

Early in life Boondoggle developed a habit of relaxing while standing. His eyes would glaze and his ears would flop to the sides until they stuck out straight to the sides. In this state the mule would be noticing nothing in particular and everything in general. He found that he spent most of his time waiting on humans and Boondoggle developed a deep patience. There were many who thought Boondoggle an imbecilic with his glassy eyes and sagging ears but they were mistaken.

In the beginning Derry warned Noom, "There are two things about Boondoggle," she said petting the mule's neck, "he's the most dependable critter I've ever met and he'll bite you if he gets the chance. Watch out for this mule because he's always a-watchin'."

Boondoggle took delight in biting the boy. And it was only after Noom began to remain alert to his surroundings that he could avoid the quick teeth. The mule seemed to have an uncanny ability to tell when Noom's mind was wandering and used these lapses to land another well placed nip. Most of the time the mule seemed sleepy and detached, but between those long gray ears an ever watchful brain crackled.

The worst times, Noom was to learn, were when he thought Boondoggle was beginning to sleep, which was actually when the mule was most alert. He came to understand that Boondoggle didn't hold any particular thought in his head. When he relaxed he paid attention to everything, and that included any opportunity to bite. Dogs and adults throughout the county gave this mule a wide berth.

The Structure of Delight

It was a mistake to imagine that Boondoggle ever slept or daydreamed. Daydreaming was not something he approved of, especially when there was a task at hand. And he didn't think anyone or anything around him should be off woolgathering. Late in life the mule stopped sleeping altogether; standing in his barn with dropping ears, he just waited for morning. He spent most of his life in this very relaxed state. He sensed everything around him, and if anyone was nodding off he brought them back with a sharp reminder. When someone's attention began to slip, it gave the mule an opportunity to strike and strike he did. Noom still carried a faint white scar just over his right kidney and if you examined it closely you could make out the mule's signature. His strong front teeth left a mark that Noom would carry his whole life. The boy usually had several welts where he was bitten, and Derry would comfort him with liniment and words. "Child, it's just his way. You've got to watch out. That mule is a stickler for keepin' your mind on what's at hand."

"Well, why doesn't he ever bite you?"

"We've got an understanding."

It wasn't so much an understanding that Derry maintained with Boondoggle as that she remained alert. Derry didn't know any other way to live life than to be alert to her surroundings, and this was the reason she and the mule got on so well.

Noom began to feel that turn-about was fair play and attempted to sneak up behind the mule whenever he seemed distracted. But every time Noom was about to deliver the blow he dreamed of, Boondoggle would slowly turn his head and eye the youngster suspiciously, baring his strong white teeth.

For the first year Noom's pride was dented with the red welts of mule bites. Then he began to wake up and stay awake. Of all the lessons the boy would encounter in his long life, some of the most powerful and enduring came from the Missouri mule, Boondoggle.

§§§§§

When Noom returned, Jay was examining his thumb nail. "Did it seem to help?" he asked.

"I don't think I did it for a full minute."

"Be easy with yourself. There are plenty of minutes in this world. Now I want you to consider something a little different. Thinking, as we commonly know it, is the use of all the states and the transfer of information from one state to another."

"I don't understand. What do you mean by the transfer of information?"

"To be more precise, maybe I should say translate instead of transfer. Any information in a sensory mode can be translated into another. For instance, you can look at the sky," Noom gestured upward, "and see all the blue. What feeling is associated with that color? Now look at the red of the rocks. How is the feeling of red different? With hearing you can notice what a blue sky sounds like, that sort of thing."

"You mean to make up a corresponding sensation?"

"Well, it's not so much making something up, although in the beginning it will seem that way. It's more noticing the transfer of sensations. Your brain already transfers automatically, that's what thought is. When you become better at noticing what your mind does, in effect you're amplifying its processes. Your might say that this whole business of training attention is less a matter of will and more a matter of just noticing. Noticing differences, whatever they might be, is to be the key."

As Noom talked Jay's attention kept jumping to his thumb. He had a difficult time keeping his gaze from compulsively returning to examine the minute irregularities of the nail's surface.

"So as you notice that your attention is always in one of the twelve states, you begin to understand that exit from one state is entry into another. Each change of attention is a door into another, that's what thinking is. Your thinking and to some degree your intelligence is limited by the number of states you have mastery of. More mastered states mean more choices and richer experience. If you are limited to a few states you

101

will find that you burn your bridges before you come to them and that's a sad thing to contemplate. As your mastery of attention is limited, so will your world be limited, because the world is created and maintained through the functioning of attention. If you're unhappy with a situation, the first thing to try is shifting attention, you may be in the wrong state. Most boredom is relieved by shifting attention."

"You make it sound like a dance."

Jay's statement momentarily returned Noom to his childhood and a large room at the rural school where people danced on Saturday night. The oil lamps which lit the room were high above the heads of the dancers, and Noom was fascinated by people's appearance. He was used to having the light source sitting on a table so at night people's faces were lit from below. "It's like a square dance," he smiled, "only rounder."

¥¥¥¥¥

One afternoon when Jay was young, he was running along the south edge of an east-west Colorado road. It was a dry summer and small puffs of dust sprang up behind each foot as he ran. He ran slowly and evenly, delighting in his body. The afternoon sun was lazy and its slanted light gave him a steady field to journey through.

Left and right, left again, his bare feet beat out a steady rhythm running along the road. Passing by some bushes he surprised a red-winged blackbird, and Jay was startled by its sudden flight from the roadside. The jolt of bright color froze him and he floated along the roadway hanging easily in mid-stride. In very slow motion his next foot touched the ground and pushed him back into the air. He floated another fifty feet before slowly coming to earth again. He entered another time frame, one-tenth that of the surrounding world and he soon figured out that his breath was the key to continuing this magical running. If he breathed very slowly he could continue to float as he ran.

One day when he was older Jay realized he had lost his ability to defy gravity. It remains the province of small children. However with imagination he could still run and float for miles at a stretch.

ΩΩΩΩ

"I once knew a Navaho," Noom said. "He's probably dead now, but he was an amazing man, an expert tracker. His name was Thomas Chee and he taught me some of his skills. The hardest part of learning to track is shifting attention rapidly. Chee said that when he was a boy he would track people for the fun of it. Find a set of tracks and follow them wherever they went. He would get down and look very carefully at a track and run his fingers lightly over it, touching the edges gently to test the dirt. He would notice the way a person walked. How long was the stride? Was it long or short for that person's size and weight? Then he would shift his attention inside and form a hypothesis about the person, where he was going and what he looked like and what he was thinking. Tom Chee would switch his attention to the outside and expand it to monitor the weather. He noticed what the whole sky looked like, what any breeze felt like on his skin. He instantly calculated the distance to the rumbling thunder on the horizon. Then back inside to imagine how his quarry would respond to the changing weather. Back outside and focused to notice whether the right side of a track had more pressure than the left. Constantly shifting between what he noticed on the outside and what he created on the inside. Shifting between the big picture and details. Each new clue gleaned would change his internal representation of his prey. Tom noticed the signs around him and constantly refined his internal impressions. Tracks told him a surprising number of things. He said that tracks tell a story and it was a tracker's job to find out the whole story.

"The task of a tracker is to amass vast amounts of external information and then create internal conclusions which are constantly analyzed and refined. Tom Chee wouldn't spend more than a few seconds in any one state before shifting." Noom shook his head at the memory. "Wide, narrow, outside, inside, see, hear and feel; he was a master of attention. Sometimes he would track people backwards just to find where they came from. Where they were going or where they had been was equally interesting to him. When you were around him you slowly realized that he was tracking your mind. An old mind tracker living at the heart of his people; there wasn't much that escaped Thomas Chee."

¥¥¥¥¥

Jay remembered a Navaho trading post in one of the more desolate parts of the reservation. The cool interior of the stone building was a place made for whispers. They lay on the concrete floor and piled up high in the corners, talk of wool prices and rumors of witches. Old dusty words listened to the hum of the electric motor in the meat case. Dried blood from mutton ribs stained the butcher paper. A high small window scattered light on saddles, halters and horseshoes. Bridles stopped where the tools began, metal wash basins rested beside wood stoves. Fat rolls of bright velveteen hung over the edge of a case filled with pawned jewelry. Canned tomatoes crowded boxes of powered milk. Tiny echoes hung from rafters and food stamps were accepted. Mail was stacked above names printed cautiously on masking tape. That is where Jay had seen the name Chee. Several of them, all with different first initials. He thought he had forgotten but the memory was just waiting to be triggered by the right word, the right name.

Whispers scurried across the floor, sniffing his boots when he stopped at the trading post to buy gas. Pocket knives and wind-up watches. A Monopoly game and some Handy Man jacks. He opened the glass door of the cooler and icy air greeted him with a handshake.

Drinking root beer on the steps of the creaky wooden porch Jay stared past the gas pump and beer cans littering the ground. Across the road, in the distance, a band of sheep grazed on a low ridge. There should have been a hawk in the sky, riding thermals, waiting for something small and furry to move. But it had drifted over to Cedar Springs that morning. Flies circled as he flipped through a weathered issue of *The Western Stockman*. Whispers crowded at the door, curious about this stranger. The day was stilled by slack thoughts. Summer edging into fall, last of the heat until next year. The sun would yawn and pack, heading south.

"What's your name?" asked a voice from the interior.

Jay was watching two flies crawl across the magazine page. They stopped and between them were the letters ..elmo.. "Elmo. Elmo's my name."

"Where you from?"

When he looked back to the page the flies were gone. They had been investigating an ad for lariats made in Oklahoma.

"Belmont, Oklahoma."

"Belmont?" the voice continued, "Don't they have a big rodeo down there?"

"Yeah. And they've got a big lariat factory, too."

Jay never finished his root beer. It was the loneliest place he had ever been.

ΩΩΩΩ

When mittens are turned inside out they change their handedness. A left-handed mitten can be changed to a right just by turning it inside out. Two singles can be changed into a pair if one is reversed. Mitten-making peoples of the Far North have known this for many centuries and construct their mittens accordingly. The mittens, made from fur, have no preferred handedness. To the seamstress a mitten is a mitten. If it fits, it will fit either hand. And so right and left don't oppose, they are the reverse of one another. A mitten is designed for the hand at hand. Left and right or inside and outside cease to have much meaning, because in an instant they can be changed.

Arctic mittens have little understanding of left and right. For them it's all the same, only different, and they are hard pressed to explain the difference. Each mitten begins its life undefined and cares little if its wearer has two left hands. But it is important to a mitten that both states, right and left, be experienced. Mittens have a saying that goes: "You can be one or the other, and both." There exist other mitten sayings but they become more complex, involving words like symmetry, rotation and enantiomorph.

Mittens of the North are masters of topology and have invented innumerable string games and puzzles to amuse themselves during long dark winters broken only by the Northern Lights. Close by the warmth of a seal blubber lamp they speculate on internal properties of non-Euclidean slip knots, unmindful of the howling wind outside.

§§§§§

"Attention is a major interest for the Hawkeen. For some it's the only interest."

"You make it sound like a sacred cow."

"No. But I do have a theory about cows. In fact it's my Lost Cow Theory." Noom grinned, "I read a story one time of a kid who was sent out to round up the cows and bring them home. He went into the mountains to find the stray cows and drive them back home to the corral. Following their tracks, he searched and searched, but didn't find hide nor hair of the family cows. He did, however, find an ancient dwelling built of stone. When he returned at dusk he told his dad, 'Pa, you should have seen it. It has little rooms and doorways and everything.'"

And his dad asked, "What about the cows?"

"It didn't have no cows, just little rooms and ...."

"I'm talking about the lost cows, our cows, the cows you were supposed to be looking for."

"Oh. I guess I forgot about them."

"And indeed he had," Noom said. "The boy found something far more interesting. After I read that story I got to thinking of how lots of myths and legends are based on the search for lost cattle. How the mother lode was found or a secret place or anything that seemed of more value than cows. So I got to thinking. What if, when you have a problem, you buy a truckload of range cows, because they tend to be wilder, and turn them loose? Then you set out after them and maybe, searching for them, you find the solution to your problem."

"But what if you really find them?" asked Jay. "What are you going to do with all those cows?"

Noom narrowed his vision and looked directly into Jay's eyes. "On the other hand, if you think there's much danger of that, I'll give you my special Lost Cow Theory. Skip the cows. Pretend you've lost some and you'll get the same results."

"Search for imaginary lost cows?"

"Yup. The lost cows will eventually come home because the cows themselves were never lost. They knew what they were doing the whole time. Why don't we start getting packed."

ΩΩΩΩ

During the morning two red-winged blackbirds stopped by the spring. They were scouts for a large flock preparing to migrate for the winter. The two birds were investigating routes that the group could follow on their way south.

The scouts perched high in a chokecherry tree cocking their heads from side to side. They were determining the suitability of the water hole for a stopover point. They listened to the news at the water hole, trying to gauge the availability of feed and shelter.

Whenever the band is ready to move it sends out scouts. This outrider team is composed of an older bird, who has the knowledge and experience of scouting, and a younger bird perhaps on its first assignment. On this, the first of many missions, the younger bird will learn from the best of all possible teachers, personal experience. In scouting, more than in any other task, the unforeseen and unexpected often occur. Each bird depends on its quick wits alone to save itself should trouble arise. The younger scout bird learns to become observant naturally.

Necessity compels the scout birds to train themselves to use their eyes and to remember what they have seen, to become observant. For observation is a scout bird's particular job. A guide bird must be steady and carry out missions with dispatch. The bird develops foresight, common sense and self-reliance.

The two birds, younger and older, will separate from the flock and set out to blaze new trails for it to follow. To be free on the wing and explore regions beyond the boundaries of most red-winged blackbirds is exciting as well as dangerous. Pioneering new directions for the flock to follow, the scouts are free from most of the constraints the band imposes.

The two birds sat close together on a slim branch craning their necks this way and that. Then within an instant they were back on the wing, climbing hard and fast, flying like small falcons to return with a report.

§§§§

As they packed Noom continued. "Much of thinking can be classified as one of two mental processes. I call them defining and exploring. Defining seems to be more concerned with internal states and exploring with external ones. This isn't always the case, since you can explore your thoughts. Let's say exploring is gathering information without regard to its making any sense. Defining is the ordering of that information. We gain an ability to make judgments through the use of both methods. The trick is to switch back and forth between the two. If you are stuck exploring you become confused by the mass of information, you have trouble reaching conclusions and making decisions. If, on the other hand, you keep defining and defining, your view becomes narrower and less elastic. Define is a map and explore is the territory. It's important to know that a map or a belief is an abstraction. That's what defining does, it turns information into abstractions, and those abstractions are arbitrary. Without a good map one gets lost in the territory. It's a paradox that a useful definition creates the freedom and confidence to explore further, to gather more information to use in refining and updating your mental map.

"You make it sound hard. What about the natural rules and laws that govern us and the universe? Once you have them figured out they should last forever. Why can't someone just get it right and that's that?"

"Because there is no right to get. Every time you think you have it figured out some fool comes along and throws rocks in your river. The natural laws you speak of are arbitrary. You make it sound like the world is a result of legislation. Would you be happier if there were a secret and you could find it out?"

"Yes, I suppose I would. If I could understand the world then it would be simple."

"Well, then, I'll tell you. The secret is that there isn't a secret. There are maps and models and hints and tips and techniques. They can be very helpful and useful. They can all aid in navigation, but you still have to tend the tiller. The world is continuous, life is ongoing. The most fascinating aspect of the universe is that it changes. Where did the bubbles go when you popped them with your finger?"

Jay was at a loss for words. The best he could do was to open and close his hand.

"That's right they go and live with the non-elephants at the broken bubble burial ground. Much of what we think about the world is arbitrary. We get so used to it that we believe it is fact. Names and numbers for instance are arbitrary. Nature does not have a concept of number, Mother Nature can't count. Counting is a human invention and distinction."

When they were packed and ready to leave, the men walked to the spring. Jay knelt down beside the pool and taking water in his cupped hands drank deeply. Then he filled his canteen as Noom waited.

"Aren't you going to drink some of the water?"

"Nope, I don't like the taste with all the bug shit in it."

((((((

One morning, long ago, in the Southwestern desert, a strange cloud appeared on the western horizon. The Awb studied the cloud and were quiet for its appearance had been foretold. Their time of vigil was to be ended by the coming of a dark fog, so they prepared to leave.

A bracelet existed among the Awb which foretold of this event. It had been passed down through many centuries, and each owner was called the End Wearer. On the inside of the bracelet was inscribed a prophecy of the coming of the fog and instructions on how to proceed once it appeared. The arrival of the cloud signified that their efforts had culminated in a very slight movement of the North Star, and the Awb were finally released from their duty.

The star watchers, those among the Awb with the keenest sight, believed they detected, during their nightly vigils, a very tiny movement of the star. As soon as the Awb moved it off center the slightest amount the North Star would begin naturally to generate its own orbit. The cloud's appearance filled the village with joy because it signified their efforts had indeed been successful. And so their work was completed. They had given the star hope and it would continue to pursue that hope. It was lost no longer, as movement created courage. The stone observatories were

109

abandoned, the task finished.

Before the coming of the cloud, the sun lifted ample crops from their small rough fields. The village was happy and healthy. The people survived and grew in their high, clear stronghold. The Awb were a people of destiny and so the day the West wind moaned, they raised their heads to hear.

The End Wearer was pressed into service, for the singing was to be led only by her. When the sun reached its zenith all were assembled, packed tightly into the tiny courtyard at the village's center.

Fragments of the song still remain:

My mind restore to me the left hand of darkness.
This, the name the Holy People gave ....

I wish it to be (unknown) riding easily home on his shoulder
The (light) it is slanted with me.
They live on dust and ... the Beaver People, bringing home.

It is becoming, unfailingly it is spreading.
When the sun was dipping low, a prelude to its daily death.
Now I, being the never-tiring (hopping?) .... I walk around the edge of over there.

It has become so,
Offering a ring of timeless comfort in which ....
The middle it points to ... and all things (belong) to me.
All is well again.

Walking steadily, urging their children across the wide expanse, a human migration swelled until the last of the long procession stepped through the sunset into obscurity. "Come," the wind said, "come, it is time." A full moon rose to find the fires dead and canyons empty of nightly singing. And the Awb were gone, leaving behind only traces of how it was in the slow dreamy dance of memories past.

The land and all on it slept well that night.

Chapter Five

When Noom was in his twenties he graduated as a mining engineer from a university in South Dakota. As a student, he had demonstrated a unique blend of practicality and imagination, a gift for dreaming and the ability to make those dreams happen. This rare talent was noticed and nurtured by an old professor of mechanics, Frank Sherman.

Before he attended the university, Noom spent a summer working in a small gold mine. It was a shaft mine, meaning the entrance to the mine was straight down. All materials and workers were lowered in an iron cage suspended at the end of a long cable. The first morning Noom descended into the dark hole he found himself thinking of the saying about putting all your eggs in one basket. His stomach kept waiting for a sudden plunge as the huge pulley at the top of the head frame creaked ominously when the hoist operator released the brake. The cable played out slowly and the cage sank into the darkness, gaining speed as it dropped.

The mine was called the Longfellow and 417 feet below ground level the cage splashed into sump water and stopped with a thud. Everyone stepped out of the cage wading, through waist deep water. Soft yellow light from their acetylene head lamps reflected back from the ripples, and Noom breathed the musty humid air. His first impression was of stillness. The sounds of voices and the splashing of water were muted by the blackness. Each lamp created a soft quiet world which extended fifteen to twenty feet around the wearer like a halo. Noom expected echoes but there were none and when he waded through the water his halo travelled with him, illuminating the silence wherever he looked.

The shift boss soon had the pumps started and the water level began to drop rapidly. In short order, the tunnels to the right and left were clear and everyone set off to work. The water was so acid that copper nails were used in the ladders since iron nails would corrode and break. Water dripped throughout the mine. When Noom looked up to examine the rock overhead a corrosive drop fell into his eye. The eye burned and teared profusely for several minutes, after that he was more cautious.

Noom was hired as a hand-trammer. He filled one-ton ore cars and rolled them a quarter-of-a-mile to the bottom of the shaft where they were hoisted to the surface and dumped. At the bottom of the shaft an empty car was waiting for him in the cage. After exchanging cars he jerked the bell cord, signaling the hoistman on the surface to draw up the loaded cage. The tunnel he worked in, called a drift, was graded slightly so he only had to push one way. After filling a car at the ore chute he removed the set blocks from in front of the wheels and rode back to the station. It was mule labor, a half mile per round trip, and he put in many miles every day.

When Noom could find time he explored the rest of the mine, going up into the stopes where the other men worked. He was curious about drilling and mineralogy, and asked so many questions that finally someone lent him a copy of the *Mining Engineers' Handbook* by Robert Peele. Evenings he read about block-caving and bullwheels, cinnabar and placer claims, dip-faults and draw bars. He puzzled over geology and explosives, drainage and underground transport, ventilation and assaying. When he got all the way to Young's modulus and zirconium he knew what he wanted to become and in the fall of 1928 Noom enrolled in the School of Mines.

The world underground was different than that above. The underground world had a special meaning for the young man, a place where he felt close to something indescribable, and Noom was driven to discover what it was.

ππππ

Frank Sherman was tall and gaunt with thinning brown hair combed straight back. His large clear eyes roamed behind thick glasses while he spoke. They roamed over the listener and the room and sometimes Noom wondered if they roamed in dimensions known only to Frank himself. But when Frank listened his eyes remained fixed on the speaker's face as if he were watching the workings of a delicate watch. His breathing would diminish until he seemed frozen in an intensity of listening. This habit reduced many of his students to stuttering and embarrassed confusion, but Noom found it reassuring. The man was paying absolute attention to what a student was saying, and for the first time Noom began to comprehend what the word respect meant. Frank Sherman's natural way of showing respect was to extend his undivided attention, because he was interested in what others thought. Noom flourished under this special form of concern. To Frank the world was a vast machine, and he marvelled at its arrangements and connections. He tried to impart this sense of wonder to his students.

"Keep your eye on the movement," he would tell Noom, "not the mathematics." Stabbing the blackboard with a stick of white chalk, he would continue, "The equations are just the language, the sound things make when they move. It's a special sound, one that can only be heard in your mind." The right side of Frank's head would become covered with small white dots where he tapped his temple with the chalk. "Listen for it. Some say it sounds like music."

Professor Sherman took special care with Noom and in the second year began assigning him imaginary mining problems. They all involved movement. How best to pump water out of deep shafts or how to move ore along high tension tram lines. "You need to see it first," he would counsel. "See it in your head." Chalk dust would gently drop to Noom's shoulder as Frank tapped the young man's head. "See it in here. When it looks and sounds right, begin the calculations and then bring them to me." The assigned problems slowly became more difficult and Noom was rewarded for particularly ingenious and simple solutions. "Yes," Frank would exclaim, "you've seen it. Isn't it beautiful?" On those occasions Noom left the office unmarked by the ever-present stick of chalk.

ΩΩΩΩ

In Nevada, not far from the Truckee River, a mining district developed. It was named after Henry T. P. Comstock and was a place of unparalleled mineral wealth. The ore-bearing rock, however, was soft and crumbly, and the veins were so wide that cave-ins were a constant threat. This placed the miners in a quandary. The unstable nature of the rock brought their efforts to a standstill. The treasure, just at their fingertips, eluded them.

In 1860 one Philip Deidesheimer, a young mining engineer, appeared at the Comstock and surveyed the problem. Within a month he had invented a scheme for shoring up the mines with logs, a method called square-set timbering. His idea allowed excavation to proceed, and the Comstock soon swallowed whole forests to release its silver and gold. The mines' appetites for trees were immense.

The craft of the timberman became a necessity. Huge wooden structures hundreds of feet high were constructed underground to shore up the mountain when the ore was removed. The new timbering scheme was elaborate. Trees, squared to a foot, were notched at the ends to form special joints where six or more of these mammoth logs could meet. Square-set timbering soon had many variations, special arrangements of the lumber to meet strains from any direction and in all types of mining conditions.

Deep in the mines these timbers still stand, holding mighty loads. The skill of the timberman has survived the constant test of gravity. Building refined structures with massive timbers, these craftsmen were paid premium wages because their skills were so crucial to the safety and profitability of the mines. With axes and chisels, fine-toothed saws and native ingenuity they fashioned stulls and corner posts. Girts and caps were fitted like cabinetry. As the rate of compression was not the same in all parts of a joint and settling was often irregular, the joints were made with very clever arrangements of tenons and tongues. These timbermen combined the very fine and the massive to steady trembling mountains.

Throughout the mines wood was also used in chutes and cribbing, in ladders and stope-lagging and the all important wedge. Many of the timbers were held together without nails, wedged tight within the mountain. Without wedges whole structures could fall apart. With wedges, timbers could be tightened till they rang when struck, making a timberman's ear as important as his eye. So much timber was used in the enclosed underground spaces that timber gas became a hazard. Fungal growth on the decaying timber emitted fumes that had to be vented or working conditions became unbearable.

With the spread of timbering skills, other mines began to incorporate these new ideas. Brunton bevel sets were used in Butte, Montana; step-down framing in Anaconda, and special stope sills in Bisbee. The western mines began to exchange immense offerings of wood for metal-bearing ore. Trees were buried deep in the earth to placate the god of gravity until the ore could be mined safely. Whole mountains now stand hollow, propped up internally, their veins removed.

ππππ

By his third year at the university, Noom's eyes began to roam like those of his instructor. Whenever he was thinking about a problem they seemed to follow the line where classroom walls met the ceiling. When he heard the special music he would commit it to paper.

Just before graduation Professor Sherman called Noom to his office. "You're the best student I've ever had and I've recommended you to a large international company. You can find out if any of this works."

The two men sat across the desk from each other, both scanning the ceiling molding. They knew the nail holes by heart.

"After I'm out of school do I have to move my eyes like this any more?" asked Noom.

Frank Sherman was genuinely surprised by the question.

»»»»»

They were walking northwest, toward the mountains. The climb before noon was steep and now the peaks seemed closer. Jay could begin to make out individual trees that grew on the upper slopes. At the higher altitude the air became thinner and clearer. Noom chose a sunny spot, and as they ate a late lunch Jay wanted to talk about the incident on the river again.

"Why did the rocks float?" he asked.

Noom was eating dried apricots and took his time chewing. "Are you asking why or how?"

"I'm asking why."

"Then you're asking a theological question and from my point of view a fruitless one."

"Why is that?"

"Because a 'why' question doesn't lead to information which is very useful. 'How' on the other hand lets you begin to know how something proceeds, its structure and processes, and that knowledge can be acted upon. Ultimately a 'why' question can only be answered by the word 'because', which leads to another 'why' and so on. 'Why' is a question of religion, 'how' is a question of science, or at least the type of questioning that science is based on. Religion is obsessed with thinking about meaning, and science is obsessed with understanding action." Noom finished eating and cocked his head to the side. "Who says they floated anyway? Maybe you were fooled, remember?"

༅ ༅ ༅ ༅

One day Derry offered Noom a large slice of freshly baked apple pie. Just as he began to take the first bite she stopped him.

"Child, while you eat your pie, you might think of what's at each end of your fork. Forks join what's at their ends, you know. What happens when them two get together? Do they both get big or do they both get little? Does one get big and the other little? It's a curious fact, but forks always seems to stay the same. Forks can do some mighty interestin' things."

"Now," she smiled, "eat your pie."

§§§§§

"When you ask a 'how' question you've entered the realm of science," Noom continued. He closed his sack preparing to continue their march into the mountains. "And science, physics in particular, is sensorially based. The fundamental quantities are time, space and what you might call weight. That's what the whole thing is built on. There are some odd numbers mixed up in it, but the quest in physics is to understand the world in terms of those fundamental quantities. To understand how they interrelate."

"You're saying physics has to do with the senses?"

"Sure. Space, time and weight are representations of seeing, hearing and feeling. Our sense of time is deeply involved with our ability to hear and our ability to speak, and of course the idea of space is built on our ability to see. Weight is the manifestation of our feeling sense."

"What about smell and taste?"

"Smell and taste had a great deal to do with the origins of chemistry. Ancient chemists used those two senses to guide them in their investigations. One of the easiest ways to tell if you're near a chemistry lab is to sniff. Science, in a way, is the externalization of our senses. We know the world around us through our senses. So it isn't too odd that we would formalize these investigations and call them science. Our science and our world will, of course, be constructed in the way in which we think. There's no other way it can be done. The history of science is an interesting account of human thought, the formalization of magic. We've been so intrigued by the magic and mystery of the world that we've created institutions and disciplines to study it. And when we understand a little bit of magic then we want to control it. We delight ourselves with our ability to determine where and when this magic occurs. We don't create it, you see, we just direct it. The universe acts on its own, we just snap our fingers and point. All our knowledge and machines are tools toward that end. We constrain the universe in certain ways." Noom gripped the air with his hands trying to explain his thoughts. "In a sense, we captured lightning and now use its fire in our light bulbs. Knobs and switches, handles and valves are some of the instruments we use to direct what we have constrained. This constraining doesn't have to do with our will. We move bits of the universe around. You might say that by altering the arrangement we constrain. That's what making and building is, altering the arrangement of the material or process you're using. Pipelines or penicillin, it doesn't matter, the universe continually acts on itself and we can direct that action."

"I'm not interested in constraining it. It will do what it will do. Can't we just sit and enjoy it?"

"Of course. That's what the twelve states are for. The world is alive when magic is afoot. When we use the magic of our attention we can begin to know the world in all its wonder. When perceived more fully, the ordinary becomes extraordinary. What you do with that wonder is entirely up to you. You can use it for your enjoyment or your work horse. That's the difference between the pure and applied sciences. It's all choice." Noom's eyes widened with his explanation. "There is a nursery rhyme that goes, 'If wishes were horses, beggars could ride. If turnips were watches, I'd wear one by my side." He paused, smiling, and reached for the sack. "The essence of being human is turning wishes into horses. Your skill at that trick is the measure of your life. It's all a question of how."

¥¥¥¥¥

Jay Thomas had a way of tilting his head back whenever he was at a loss. His eyelids would lower slightly and he would assume a faint smile that he hoped was mysterious. It was the profound look that he developed during his art period. The stance became a habit and very much impressed his friends. But the world at large found the behavior annoying, and people became impatient while waiting for him to respond.

Jay thought the look implied that he accepted his own suffering as the groaning of the universe. To others he appeared as if he were on drugs. One day his boss at the bakery had had enough. "Are you in there?" he asked looking deeply into Jay's eyes.

"Yes!" Jay snapped, slightly angered at his supervisor's insinuation.

"Good. Since you're home maybe you can tell me what you're doing in there?"

Jay struggled and struggled for an answer but nothing came out, because he really didn't know what was going on in there. A week later he quit his job, the strain was too much.

"Do you remember seeing ducks flying along the river?" Noom asked as they paused in a clump of Juniper.

"No, I don't. I don't remember seeing any ducks at all."

"Mother ducks call all their ducklings together just before they are old enough to go out on their own and she speaks to them. 'Come, come, little ones gather around. I have something to tell you,' and the little ducks swim up close to their mother. 'What?' they ask. 'What are you going to tell us?' The mother duck gets the little ones calmed down and then she tells them, 'I am a duck and each of you is a duck. And there are many things for a duck to know in this life. I've taught you all I can teach you except for one thing.' The little ducks become very interested and they get excited again. 'What? What is it?' they ask. 'Now I want you to listen closely and listen well,' she tells them. 'Every day and every hour and indeed every moment of your lives you have a decision to make. If you don't make it, it will be made for you. Your decision is this: Do you want to be a duck or a dinner?' After the mother duck speaks the little ducks usually become silent and stick close by her."

Noom stood and stretched his back. Swinging the old canvas sack onto his shoulder he said, "Well, we better get going if we're to make it by night." He pointed into the distance. "See that peak? Just at the base of it is a cave. We'll sleep there tonight."

The peak Noom pointed out was the highest and the farthest from them. As Jay shouldered his pack he tried to imagine what the cave would look like and wondered if the Hawkeen had marked that place, too.

They soon fell into the walking rhythm of the morning, short in front and tall behind, traveling toward their destination.

¥¥¥¥¥

Years ago a boy wiggled quietly through the brush at the edge of a small pond. Inching forward on his stomach, he kept his shotgun beside him. The boy could see several mallard ducks swimming in the pond and feeding in the failing light of the cold winter afternoon.

Slowly he drew the gun up to his shoulder, poking the barrel through the willows, aiming at the green feathered duck closest to him. The duck paddled a little, moving slightly from the line of sight. As the boy twisted to compensate a stick cracked. The ducks were instantly on the wing, as if they had been propelled from the water's surface, their wingtips slicing the air. None even glanced in the direction of the sound. Up and off the water they flew honking. The boy jumped to his feet. The reason for stealth had just flown away.

He watched the birds as they flew in loose formation, finally disappearing far to the north. Shouldering his gun, he began the long walk home, thin shoes breaking through the frozen crusted snow. It would be dark by the time he reached the lighted windows of home.

No matter, Jay thought, the ducks will return, and tomorrow after school so will I.

His mining degree in hand Noom boarded a steamer in New Orleans. With a single trunk he departed for the job in Australia arranged by Professor Sherman. Inside the trunk were all his belongings, his clothes, mining books, drafting equipment and a favorite rock, worn and polished by the Sand Hills of Nebraska.

After passing through the Panama Canal, the ship set a course for the distant continent. By day, the young engineer would stand by the railing and watch the ocean's flat horizon. At night he would lie in his cot and listen to the engines deep in the boat's hull, pounding out the long miles.

Noom, born and raised on the central plains, felt a strange affinity for the Pacific prairie which expanded to the edge of his sight, broken only by occasional whitecaps. The ocean exhilarated him as he imagined embarking in a new land and testing his engineering skills.

When the ship landed in Melbourne Noom and his trunk transferred to a train. He spent days sitting by the window watching for kangaroos and listening to the clicking of the iron wheels over rail track joints.

Finally, near the middle of Australia, Noom settled in to begin his mining career. At a white wooden boarding house he had a room to himself. Bunk beds, a drafting table and wash basin composed the furnishings. When working at the table Noom sat on his trunk. Many nights he went to bed late with the trunk's floral design embossed on the backs of his legs. The mine was having difficulties, and its future depended heavily on the new young head engineer.

An old aborigine cleaning lady took a special interest in the newcomer. When Noom passed her in the hall the woman would cease mopping and stare searchingly into his face, watching his eyes.

Normally his eyes were brown but when he worked long hours in the darkness of the mine one eye began to acquire an emerald green cast. The metamorphosis was slight and usually no one remarked on it. Noom became aware of his changing eye some years before at the Longfellow mine. At first it startled him but soon he correctly attributed the green color to lack of sunshine. After a month and a half in the Australian mine, the green tint reappeared.

The woman, Asha, also noticed his green eye and one day stopped him in the hallway. She placed her thumbs under his eyes, looked deeply into one eye and then into the other. "You have Night Eye," she told him. He asked her what she meant. "Is good thing, Night Eye," was all she would say. "Very good."

One afternoon returning from work he found a single red pebble in the center of his drafting table. For the next few months he would occasionally find similar small objects, perfectly aligned, in the center of the table. One afternoon Noom approached Asha with the latest small gift in his hand and asked, "What can I give you in return?"

The tiny wrinkled old lady dug into her dress pocket and produced a cloth-wrapped object. Carefully opening it she pointed to a clear and perfectly terminated quartz crystal. "You get more?"

"Yes, of course," he nodded.

Noom wasn't so sure when he thought about it later. He had seen very few crystals and they were of poor quality, but if there were crystals to be found he would bring them to her. He watched for clear, well-formed crystals underground, and just when he had given up hope he found a small vug in a new section of the mine. Eons ago geological forces created a crevice in the rock where the sharp sparkling stones had grown. Taking his mineral hammer Noom meticulously broke them loose and filled up his jacket pockets.

When he showed them to Asha she held her small hands over her mouth and drew a quick breath. "Yes, yes," she told him. "Seeing stones."

Noom suspected the crystals were to be used by the aborigines in some ritual fashion and was glad to be able to provide something which Asha seemed to value. In the kitchen she thoroughly washed and examined each one and when they were dry, wrapped them tightly in a clean white cloth. When she left that weekend the bundle was clasped to her bosom.

ΩΩΩΩ

The Hawkeen maintain a loose network throughout the world. It cuts across national, racial and cultural boundaries, maintaining a diversity which gives them a unique vitality and outlook. Often Hawkeen are bonded by friendship, but the real cement is their intense interest in the properties of the mind.

Within the Hawkeen a certain amount of ritual is practiced, not because it is necessary but because it pleases them. In their investigations they have discovered the sustaining power of ritual and so have included it in whatever they do. It can be said that their highest goal is the fulfillment of personal curiosity. Their public influence is for the most part covert. They prefer it that way.

If there were a principle which guided the Hawkeen in their endeavors it would be the concept of context. They feel all events and activities, human or otherwise, are entirely context-dependent. Events arise and proceed differently in different contexts and this they study. To the statement, 'It's all in the timing,' they would reply, 'It's all in the context,' knowing that timing is but one small element of context. And so they believe that the notions of truth and reality are context dependent and therefore changeable. It could be stated that ultimately they are interested in the context of contexts. The Hawkeen have little interest in content, because content only arises and is given meaning through the magical properties of context.

Theirs is a particular cosmic view which gives them great pleasure, peace and an analytical viewpoint from which to arrive at understanding. The Hawkeen are interested in processes instead of products and encourage diversity as the stuff of context. Outcome is the fuel that drives their energetic lives.

When Noom arrived in Missouri he came to the attention of the group and unknowingly passed through Hawkeen hands for the next twenty years. Only when he was around the age of forty was he apprised of their existence and invited to join. And later, at sixty, he was chosen to be a Region Master. The Hawkeen have divided the world into eighty-nine regions and each Master monitors the activities of his particular region. Regions are about as close as the Hawkeen come to any form of bureaucracy; they don't have the temperament for it. Three members of the Hawkeen are enough to conduct official business at any time or place. There is no hierarchy or authority within the Hawkeen except that gained through the respect granted to ability. Each member answers only to himself.

On average each region covers a little more than half a million square miles, and if they were squares a region would measure about 253 miles on a side. Within each region dwells the HO, marking the figurative center at an auspicious location. The responsibility of a Region Master is to carry on the rituals particular to that region, to coordinate Hawkeen activities within the region and to teach. All duties are carried out within the personal preferences of individual Region Masters. Other than teaching, the function of a Master is largely ceremonial, intended only to keep the Hawkeen in existence.

Derry was the first Region Master that Noom met, although he wasn't to learn of her identity until much later. Because of his occupation and personal interest Noom had known over a quarter of the Masters in the world, each interesting and unique. The patience and wisdom he gained from his travels he then dispensed from his own region in the Southwest.

Hawkeen discoveries continue to filter slowly into the mainstream of mankind's affairs, where they swim steadily upriver to spawn.

Asha told Noom folk stories, many of which involved something she called dreamtime. She would nod at his odd eye and tell him, "A fellow like you need to visit dreamtime." At first Noom imagined dreamtime was a special place where the aborigines went on secret occasions. Then he understood it to be something like heaven, peopled with aboriginal creatures and deities. When he asked Asha and others about dreamtime they seemed perplexed that a Night Eye wouldn't have an immediate understanding of it. Asha would slowly expand her arms as she watched his strange eye. "It's all about, when you go to the dream circle, only dreamtime." She moved her arms in great arcs indicating that dreamtime was as prevalent as air. "Truth is, we all in dreamtime. Always. Only some wake up and know it."

Noom considered Asha's stories examples of interesting folk culture and aboriginal religious thought. He enjoyed thinking about dreamtime and its creatures but felt the experience was unavailable to him as a non-aborigine. Then one night it came to him in a blinding flash. He was staring at the bunk above him, using the springs to solve a surveying problem that was troubling him. The even grid formed by the springs made an ideal place to visualize the trigonometric calculations. The actual grid was too small for the size of his problem. He realized he had mentally expanded it to fill all space as a convenient way to keep track of the location of various points while he calculated. His insight was to understand dreamtime as a particular state of mind. It didn't really have to do with a location or a time long ago but with a peculiar way of thinking of things. He understood that dreamtime wasn't a place or a thing but instead a process and he could participate in that process as fully as any other human, aborigine or not. Later Noom came to understand that dreamtime involved more than his startling flash originally revealed; however, it was in the right direction.

When Noom began his visits to the aboriginal gatherings he was enchanted. A long wooden musical pipe with its low droning helped to guide him into his first explorations of dreamtime. After his first understanding Noom never felt alone again, because separateness didn't exist in dreamtime. Surveying took on a whole new meaning for him. It wasn't measuring the distance between points but was calculating the connectedness of them. He decided that Euclid must have had a Night Eye also. Noom's excursions into dreamtime began to give him knowledge that he would later come to understand as the twelve Hawkeen states.

§§§§§

"We have the idea that space is a place to put everything, whether it be tulips or galaxies." Jay was perplexed at the old man's statement. They had been trudging uphill for hours, Noom's free arm gesturing the whole way.

"We have the idea that space is empty, inert and sterile. We use the idea of space as a place, a place for things to happen. And the manifestation of this idea, in science, is the concept of a vacuum. Matter occupies space and most people think that's about the end of it. But I think they miss a large part of the action. Matter is a manifestation of space. Objects don't just occupy space, they are created by it. Space has properties and is very dynamic. It supports and empowers everything whether it be sunlight or clouds or tree stumps. Matter is created from and by space, so there is an equivalence between space and matter. Not just an abstract relationship but an actual one. Under certain conditions space transforms into matter, and under other conditions matter transforms into space."

"You make it sound like water and ice."

Noom stopped and sat down. The climb and his talking left him out of breath. When his breathing slowed he continued in a normal tone, "It's a little more complex than that, but you have the general idea. When space is transformed into matter a small part of space vanishes, and the rest is stretched slightly as a result. Space can be thicker or thinner depending on how much has been turned into matter. We know that matter has the potential for tremendous amounts of energy. What isn't understood yet is that space has the potential for tremendous amounts of matter. Vacuums are thought of as being places which are dead and lifeless, but I think it's just the opposite. Space is teeming with properties and energy and possibilities." Noom rubbed the stubble on his chin. "I suppose I think of space as the prime mover. The idea of a vacuum will soon be replaced. One

125

of the problems with science, as with everything else, is seeing the lens through which we look."

"What lens?" Jay asked. He was glad to stop and rest and so used any opening to continue the conversation.

"I'm talking about the lens of the mind. We think with models and beliefs that become deeply embedded, and these tend to direct the nature of our thoughts without our being aware of their guiding presence. Every thought is a feat of association at some level, and many of the levels aren't readily apparent. You only see something well when you know in advance what is going to happen. That is the inherent difficulty in learning. What I've seen before is what I recognize, because my lens has adjusted. Seeing something new, now that's the trick. However mysteries aren't necessarily miracles."

"So how can you come to understand something new at all?"

"There are several ways." Noom stretched his back and Jay could hear his spine popping. Then the old man looked straight into Jay's pupils. "But one that has worked for me is to empty your mind and eat time."

"That doesn't make any sense at all."

"I know. But it seems to work." Noom rubbed his chin again and stared into the distance. "You know, there is always a moment in childhood when a door opens and lets the future in. The shock is enormous when a child's universe suddenly explodes. Some people never recover from that scare. It's much like being born. Children react to the future differently. Some treat the intruder with caution and mistrust and some begin to explore it as they would a new toy. The latter children seem to have a better time of it because the future to them looks like an endless procession of new and wonderful toys."

One morning, shortly after his arrival at the mine's boarding house, Noom woke suddenly to find a large fat brown dog staring him in the face. As soon as his eyes were open the dog's thick tail began to wag slowly from side to side. Then it turned and trotted out of his room.

Noom inquired about the dog and learned that it belonged to Asha. When he asked her, she said. "Oh yes, he fine dog."

"What's his name?"

"I could say in my language, but the word is very long." She stopped and wrinkled her brow. "In English his name would be like Fat Tail Wagging."

Fat Tail Wagging lived at the boarding house and returned home with Asha on weekends. He was fat and sleek because of the availability of the boarding house kitchen, which was where Noom discovered he could grin. Squinting his eyes, the dog would pull up the corners of his mouth and wag his tail whenever he was delighted, which seemed a fair amount of the time. Soon Fat Tail Wagging took up residence under Noom's bunk with his collection of old and favored bones. He just appeared one evening with a mouthful of bones, wagged and moved in.

§§§§

At sunset the two were still traveling. They followed an alpine trail through spruce and pine forests interspersed with small glades covered with skunk cabbage and mountain mint. The summer's wild flowers had gone to seed and some of the aspen on the higher slopes were just beginning to flash the first of their golden fall colors. Jay liked being in the mountains. "I've been thinking about the twelve states you talked about," he commented.

"And?"

"It doesn't seem like I go from one to the other. I just kind of end up in a different place. I'm not sure I understand how they work."

"What don't you understand?"

"Well, I've tried some of the different states as we've been climbing, and some are much easier for me than others."

"Umhuh," Noom answered noncommittally.

"I guess it's that I'm a little scared of what will happen if I get lost in one of the states and not be able to get back."

"That's a pretty natural concern when you contemplate doing anything new. There is a part of all of us which is wary and it should be. It

127

saves us from disaster a lot of the time."

"Well, I was thinking, isn't that why some people go mad?"

"I'm not sure that I follow you."

"Don't some people start thinking some pretty strange things and then get trapped by them."

"And that's when they get crazy?"

"Yeah, I guess that's what's worrying me."

"If anything, I think you have it backwards. Think of it for a moment. People whom we ordinarily think of as being mad are those people who have a limited range of attention. We notice them more by what they can't do than what they are doing."

"Explain that."

"Let me take the case of people who suffer from long dark bouts of depression. While depressed their attention is limited to a very few states. This is the primary way for anyone to identify depression and depressives cycle endlessly through those few states. If they ever leave their depression we notice the mood shift by a change in their attention. I say you have it backwards, because what we normally think of as madness is a contraction of attention, a limiting of the possible states. Health comes from expanded attention. So although your fears are real, they remain unfounded. If you sail uncharted oceans you won't go off the edge. The world isn't built that way. You will find still more interesting uncharted waters and one day you'll discover you're back where you started from, ready for another journey. Navigating uncharted waters is safe and interesting from a certain point of view. The twelve states of attention mirror the world. They are both round." Noom paused and smiled at Jay. "However, if you lock yourself in your basement and endlessly count the lumps of coal in the coal bin, others may find you quite mad."

"You make it sound so simple."

"It is. Always take precautions when you explore the range of your mind. That's good practice when you explore anything, but ultimately the mind is the safest place you can be. We have a funny term, being out of one's mind. That just can't happen."

ΩΩΩΩ

A method called fire-assaying is employed to determine the concentration of gold in ore. Fire-assaying harks back to the days of alchemy and many of its procedures are a result of the attempt to transmute metals. During the process smoke, heat and poisonous fumes abound.

An assayer who is experienced can work all day before a blazing furnace without protection. Skin surfaces are kept continuously in motion. Rhythmically, the assayer turns and rotates so he never stops and take the full blast of the furnace heat. An unhurried dance allows him to walk in fire. When all the skills of fire assaying have been absorbed it becomes an art. The art of reaching into fire and withdrawing precious golden metal.

The work of deciphering the inner secrets of rocks is precise and repetitive. All rocks have secrets to tell and on rare occasions the assayer may discover a sample from a fabulously rich lode, the treasures of which are beyond belief. These moments keep the assayer at his work, for to discover and reveal hidden inner riches can be the most exhilarating work of all.

§§§§

"And here's another point you should understand." Noom seemed to be speaking to the forest as much as he was to Jay. With his free arm he made grand sweeping gestures. "To participate in religious thinking one must assume a central role in the universe. You must become the point around which all revolves or is directed toward. You enter a state of being where things happen to you, and the type of things and degree to which they happen defines the quality of your life. Goodness and virtue are measured in this way. If bad things happen to you, you must be a bad person, and if good things happen to you, you must be good and so on. This is a type of magical thinking, the belief that the operation of the universe is a report or a judgment on our worthiness. The belief includes the idea that I can alter the course of the universe by how close or far my behavior is from some arbitrary code of conduct. If I am a good person then the flood will

129

not rise and sweep away my home. If I am a bad person then the waters will rise and I get what I deserve. It is an interesting hypothesis in which the basic operating principal of the world is virtue. This gives rise to watching for signs and portents as an indication of how well one's doing, a kind of advance judgment. Central to religious ideas is the belief that the universe is an extension of oneself and exists to provide judgment of one's state of being. It makes one feel included, to the point of being responsible for the world and therefore constantly judged by it.

"Science is different, however. It uses the point of view of a spectator. This belief holds that the universe proceeds on its own, fueled by known and yet unknown laws. From the spectator's point of view one can participate or not according to one's desire. We can interfere with the natural order of things if we have the inclination and knowledge to do so. The river will continue on its own until I build a dam. The central concept of science is one of action. We can act upon the cosmos at our choosing and thereby alter its direction and nature. Science removes the burden of constant judgment and by doing so removes the individual from the intimate participation with the world provided by religion. When using science we don't feel responsible for the universe, we feel alienated and relegated to the bleachers, alone, a spectator."

Jay was starting to feel that the old man was talking about him. The part about the world passing judgment hit a little to close to home. Jay knew that he had a tendency to believe that the weather changed just to spoil his plans. When it did he took it as an omen that he was being punished. He tried to remember that other people were also being affected, but he usually took it personally.

Noom was enjoying himself. Switching the sack to the other shoulder to rest his arm he continued, "Religion, then, directs one's attention inward. One becomes a hostage. Science directs one's attention outward. One becomes an aggressor. Both directions are an attempt to influence the world around us and both leave us feeling unsatisfied. The first leaves us resentful and the second leaves us detached. One trick to get out of the dilemma is to combine the two modes. Go outside to influence the world and then return inside to find out how that change influences yourself.

Constantly oscillate back and forth, external then internal. People who have mastered this oscillate several times a second. Your nervous system is built to accommodate just such a rapid alternation."

When Jay tried to imagine such an oscillation he found that his head was moving forward and back. Forward to engage with his surroundings and back to find out what he was feeling. The rapid movement started to give him vertigo, but then he noticed that when he extended his attention far into the distance to look at the sunset the vertigo vanished.

"If your thoughts don't influence your body then you can consider your body as external. Anything your mind can't effect is external. This is the origin of the mind-body split. As babies our authority doesn't extend even to our own bodies. But slowly as we establish influence with ourselves we become more secure within our sphere of command and it begins to extend. Perhaps to others, perhaps to neighborhoods and so on. The first step is to gain influence with ourselves. Can we influence our moods, health, our well-being?" Noom turned and glanced at Jay, but before he could answer the old man continued, "Influence starts at home, the center must hold. Retreat to a point where you know you have influence, however small that point may be and then begin. Science and religion both fail in that they abandon the self. They give up the notion of self-influence and when the notion of self-influence is lost the possibility of peace becomes distant. Without self-regulation peace is possible only in a perfect world, an endeavor that science and religion have failed to achieve and will fail to achieve."

Following behind, Jay was slightly bewildered. "So how do you get influence with your mind?" Before the words were out of his mouth he knew the answer. He realized he was using influence as he kept his vision focused in the distance. Jay experienced a small wave of pleasure when he thought of his accomplishment in keeping the vertigo away. Maybe it was as easy as Noom claimed.

"When you can consistently influence just one type of thought then the seed of peace has been planted and you can begin to extend that peace throughout yourself and beyond. Start with the simplest and most elementary type of thought you can imagine, master how and when you think it and the rest will follow."

Jay never before seriously considered that he had anything to do with the thoughts in his head. They just seemed always to be there, ebbing and flowing. Even though he had just demonstrated to himself that he was capable of influencing his mind, Jay found himself saying, "But my thoughts just come and go as they want."

"You make them sound like they are controlled by rays from the planet Xenon."

"No, I don't think that. It's just that they have a life of their own. There are chemicals, neurotransmitters and the like, and what can I do about them? That's the question."

"Yes, that is the question, exactly," Noom agreed. "And you answer your own question by becoming a victim. Your attitude is, I'm a victim of my own brain chemistry so what can I do?" He paused. "Of course there is brain chemistry."

"So if you acknowledge that neurotransmitters run things why do you expect me to be able to do anything about it?"

"If you really believe the operation of your mind is beyond your control then why have this conversation? That you want to convince me of your helplessness makes me think you don't totally believe you have any control over the way your head works. The existence of neuro-whatevers doesn't take you out of the picture. If anything it puts you more firmly in the driver's seat."

"I don't see how."

"What controls the production of these chemicals? Sure, we know chemistry is involved in thinking. Chemistry has a great deal, maybe everything, to do with thoughts. The key is, what do thoughts have to do with chemistry? The body is intensely chemical. Iron in the blood, oxygen, proteins. It doesn't matter if molecules or alligators do my bidding as long as it is my bidding."

"That's the point," Jay stammered, trying to defend his line of reasoning. "How do you know if it is your bidding?"

Noom stopped in his tracks in the middle of the trail. Slowly he turned around. "Son, can you open and close your mouth when you want?" he asked softly. "Can you open and close your eyes when you want?"

"Sure, what does that have to do with my brain."

"Everything." The old man smiled. "Can you remember the most horrible day of your life and then remember the most pleasant at will?"

"Well, I don't know about the most horrible."

"Okay, then a horrible and a pleasant day."

"Sure."

"Then do it for a moment."

While Jay thought back to find two examples of what Noom was asking for he was unaware of the weight of his pack or the fatigue in his legs after the long climb. "Okay, now what?" he queried after remembering two experiences.

"How can you tell them apart?"

"It's easy. Remembering the horrible day feels bad and the pleasant one feels nice."

"Precisely." Noom gestured with his finger. "If we had the knowledge and instruments we could have measured the change in your brain chemistry just now. And for the sake of simplicity we can call the molecules you created, feel bad and feel good. By choosing which day to remember, you controlled those molecules. It doesn't really matter if there are two compounds involved or two million, the results in this case are the same, feel good or feel bad."

"Well, sure I can do that. What do you want me to do, go around pretending the world is nice when it isn't?"

"What would happen if you did?"

"Well, I'd feel like a fool and I suppose slightly sinful."

"Sinful?" Noom's voice rose in astonishment.

Jay blushed slightly. "I know it sounds kind of funny but I would."

"And if you felt good then you wouldn't know the true nature of things? Is that what you're saying?"

"Well, I suppose something like that."

"It sounds like you think the world is a rotten, screwed up place, and that any nice feeling is only temporary at best."

133

"Well, I have to confess, that's kind of what I think."

"Confess? Sinful? Heavens," Noom laughed, "what if the world is a pretty nice place and any bad feeling is only temporary?"

"How can one know which way it is?"

"You can't, because it isn't any way. The game is Pick Your Molecule."

"Pick your molecule?"

"Sure, the molecule you choose gives the world meaning. It has no meaning of itself. You've already demonstrated that you're capable of choosing brain molecules." Noom turned to the side, gesturing widely. "Meaning Through Molecules. A nice slogan don't you think? Or The Molecule of Meaning. Maybe Through a Molecule Darkly. We could invent some sort of card trick. Pick a molecule, any molecule," Noom chuckled. "It's always seemed strange to me that the people who pick dark unhappy molecules think they have the corner on truth and profundity, and people who pick light cheerful molecules are treated like idiots. But maybe you're right," he shrugged. "Maybe the world does have a true and terrible nature."

"So how can I know? How can anybody ever really know what the world is like?"

"Don't ask me. I don't have any idea what the world is really like."

After the sun dipped behind the peaks to the west the air was beginning to grow chilly. Noom pointed with his chin. "It's not far now and most of the uphill work is over. Let's get going."

ᄿ ᄿ ᄿ ᄿ

One hot Missouri summer afternoon while Derry and Noom were herb hunting, she noticed the boy was bored. Boondoggle's lower lip was particularly slack that day and a heavy cloud of flies swarmed around him.

"You can imagine things to be any way you want," the old woman told him. "You can make up all kinds of worlds that could be possible. This isn't the only one, let your imagination soar, child. You can imagine that round things in this world cast square shadows. What would that be like?" she wondered. "And the square shadows only come in shades of pink and have ruffles on their edges, like some kinds of flowers."

The mind being what it is, on several successive nights Noom dreamed he lived in the shadow of a square sun which shed huge clouds of radiant, pyramid shaped grains.

"You can imagine anything and its opposite also," she laughed. "Imagine sugar being spelled with a q."

ππππ

When Noom was half way through his freshman year Frank Sherman called him into the office. "Sit down, son," he said, "I want to tell you about something called an algorithm."

Finding his seat, Noom by this time knew the professor and his ways well enough not to ask any questions. This would throw Frank off-balance and he would have to start all over. So he waited and let Professor Sherman marshal his thoughts and get them all in a line.

"An algorithm is a process you might say, a step-by-step procedure for solving a problem. Mathematics has incorporated this idea with great success, but it has larger applications." By now Frank's eyes were beginning to flicker and roam. "For instance how do you find the area of a circle?"

"Well, I can think of a couple of ways."

"Give me one."

"You could multiply pi by the radius squared."

Frank quickly wrote the formula on the blackboard. "There," he said, sitting back and looking at the chalk marks, "area is equal to the number pi multiplied by the radius squared. That's an algorithm. It's a procedure, written in mathematical language, for solving a certain kind of problem. Formulas are algorithms written in special codes. Recipes for apple strudel are also algorithms. Algorithms are maps which tell us how to get from here to there; they are procedures. A good instruction manual explaining how to tune your car is an algorithm. This algorithm," he said tapping the board, "tells you what you're searching for. It tells you the information you need to get there and it tells you what to do with that information once you have it. This particular algorithm is a general one which will find the area of all circles. You can write an algorithm which will find the area of a fifteen foot circle and it will be specific to that circle and all other identical ones." He paused, rolling the chalk slowly between his fingers. "Now the

135

chemistry and physics and mechanics which you will be studying all employ the use of algorithms. And it's important to understand that most of the formulas which you will learn, and get sick of, are all algorithms. They are precise descriptions of how to solve certain problems. They are not, however, descriptions of the events themselves." Frank tapped his forehead to emphasis the word 'not' and sat staring at Noom. They sat locked, eye to eye, until Noom couldn't stand it any more and started to speak, but Frank continued. "The equation to find the area of any circle has very little to do with circles. A great many students make this mistake, and I don't want you to be one of them."

"Explain that to me."

"Well I think you could be a very good engineer and I don't want you to ...."

"No, I mean the part about equations and circles."

"Oh," said Frank, and then he tapped the board again for emphasis, "this equation, this formula, this algorithm is a coded instruction to your brain to obtain certain information and perform certain operations in a certain sequence in order to arrive at a numerical value for something we call an area." He waited for Noom to absorb his words and then continued. "Algorithms are like little machines. They're beautiful little critters. Elegant algorithms are like quick and nimble mink slipping through the underbrush, the tip of each hair shining as they dart and turn without a sound." Frank momentarily lost himself in his mink metaphor. The hand he was using to imitate the sinuous animal remained frozen in air as he remembered boyhood excursions in the Wisconsin woods. "Where'd you say you grew up?" he asked Noom.

"Nebraska."

"That's right, Nebraska," Frank repeated. "Anyway, algorithms are usually about events but aren't the events themselves. Now the point I want to make is this. Consider what I've said about algorithms not being the event they describe and then consider the event of the algorithm itself."

Noom was silent as he thought. "You mean something like a frame of mind?"

"That's it exactly!" Frank was very pleased. "An algorithm frames your mind. An apple strudel algorithm frames your mind and directs your activities toward making apple strudel." He paused, organizing himself for another thrust. "Now, I'm going to tell you about students. They come in one of three types: Those who learn facts, those who learn algorithms and those very few who learn the algorithm to invent algorithms." Noom glanced at the three fingers Frank held up, hoping he was the third. "An algorithm organizes facts. When you change your frame of mind, you change how you organize the facts of an event. What may seem terrible in one frame of mind may seem funny in another."

"Then you're saying that what we call a frame of mind is really just an algorithm for the brain?"

"That's it exactly! You can call it a frame of mind or a point of view, but it's really just a way of directing the brain so it can organize information. You see, son, to find out anything, anything at all, you need just two things: The correct algorithm and the information it calls for. Your brain will do the rest automatically. That's all you need and in fact that's all you can ever get. I call it gears. Each algorithm or frame of mind is a gear and if I'm feeling stuck or frustrated I shift gears and keep shifting till I find one that works the way I want it to. Frames of mind are equations for the brain. If you use the equation for finding the area of a circle to compute the area of a square you get a weird answer. If you use inappropriate brain gears you get weird moods." Frank stopped. Motes of white chalk hung in the air illuminated by late afternoon sun. "And then," he said quietly, "there is the algorithm of algorithms."

Noom considered Frank's ideas for a week and then returned to the office. "Professor Sherman, I've been thinking over what you said about algorithms and frames of mind and so on, and if what you say is true, then the particular algorithm or frame of mind anyone uses determines his reality."

Frank leaned far back in his chair and glanced up at the white tile ceiling. "That's it exactly," he whispered.

§§§§

As they approached the base of a cliff in the gathering darkness, Jay could just make out a dark opening. Noom dropped his sack beside the entrance. "This is it."

The rough opening was circular, about as wide as a man's outstretched arms. Jay cautiously peered into the cave trying to make out its size while Noom set about gathering materials to start a fire. With a handful of dry grass and leaves he strode inside and knelt down to compress the mass into a small-cone shaped pile. When he set a match to it the cone burst into flames. Stepping back from the fire, Noom turned to his right and from a waist-high rock bench gathered small twigs to load on the flames. Only after they were burning and the cave fully illuminated would Jay enter.

"How did you know there would be wood in here?" His words softly echoed around the cavern.

"When you find wood here, you always stack some more for the next person when you leave. That way there is always dry wood to start a fire when you arrive late like we did."

"Other people come here?" Jay asked suspiciously.

The cave was large enough to accommodate a dozen people comfortably, with a ceiling vaulting high above the dirt floor. Somewhere in the vault, cracks opened to the outside and the smoke rose and vanished. Soon they were settled in and Noom was heating a can of pork and beans. He was hungry after the day's march.

Later after he had eaten Noom returned to his carving. He split his stick in two lengthwise and was hollowing out both sections. In one of the sections he drilled holes with his knife point and trimmed a small mouthpiece at one end. When he held the pieces together and blew, a high squeaky sound filled the cave.

"You're making a flute. I've been wondering what you've been working on." Jay exclaimed.

"I guess you could call it that," Noom beamed holding it up. "A small one at least."

He continued working on the finger holes and mouthpiece, trimming and testing until the notes were in tune. Noom dug through his sack until he found a small ball of amber pitch and set it on a rock at the edge of the fire to warm. After a few small adjustments Noom seemed satisfied when he played short songs of four or five notes. He held one of the wooden halves above the coals to heat. When it was just beginning to smoke he withdrew it and began rubbing the ball of pitch along the rim of its cavity. The resin ball quickly coated the edge with thick shiny sap and then Noom held it over the coals again. The pitch became hotter and began to boil, filling the cave with a pungent scent. Quickly Noom pressed the two halves of his flute firmly together and hot resin sealed the crack, bonding the two halves. After the instrument cooled, Noom trimmed away the excess pitch and examined the bond to make sure it was air tight. Now when he played the flute the reedy quality was gone and clear clean notes resounded throughout the cave. Noom was pleased with his handiwork and passed it to Jay. "Here give it a try."

ΩΩΩΩ

To beat a drum from the inside is to live in the midst of the creation of sound. Stretching the end membranes tightly forms a cavern which amplifies even the slightest acoustical rustling. When one lies within a correctly dimensioned drum, the sound of a beating heart is greatly magnified.

Sleeping inside such a drum returns one to the creation of a primal stirring in the universe, the time when music first sustained itself. The time when the word first travelled, suspended by its own thunder.

Chapter Six

≈≈≈≈≈

Noom rose before dawn. Rummaging through his sack he transferred some belongings to his coat pocket and scribbled a note, which he left on the flat rock beside the fire pit where Jay would find it when he awakened. Then, flute in hand, Noom silently slipped out of the cave.

Walking uphill he could see the morning light starting to pierce the eastern horizon far off to his right. In a while it began to illuminate a peak to his left. At a small shrine near the mountain top many years ago he listened as a man played a small flute much like the one he now held in his hand. The song went on and on as the notes danced up and down the mountain sides. When it was finished the man lifted a flat rock revealing a small chamber below. He placed his flute into the crypt where it took its place with the many other hand-carved flutes left there. The other flutes were old and gray and some had begun to turn to dust as they waited in that stone box high on the mountain.

Noom began climbing slowly toward the shrine. The legs that had carried him through his life, in and out of mines around the world, were now much older. And as he climbed steadily, his old knees began to whisper. Rumors started spreading through his joints. They were tired, particularly after the long march the day before. But the old man silenced his knees and directed them steadily upward.

It was summer when Noom first accompanied Asha to her home for the weekend and there met her oldest son. He led Noom out into the scrub with Fat Tail Wagging following along. Sitting under the shade of a thorn tree he thanked Noom politely for the crystals. Twice Noom's age, Eldest Son's hair and beard were shot through with gray. There was economy in his movements, and his gestures revealed the confidence of an older man comfortable in his surroundings. The furtive nervousness of youth was behind him. His deep-set black eyes gazed long before blinking. Time was the one resource he had plenty of, and he managed it well. During an extended silence he watched the heat waves shimmer across the desert, and then, almost absent-mindedly, he began to speak.

"Music belong my people. Go back long, long time," Eldest Son began. "White fellow call 'em dreamtime. We call 'em time of dreaming. The words for our songs, for the special dances they be handed down from father to son, mother to daughter. Over and over, from before time, many thousand of years. Corroboree is the word used to call that time when my people come together for singing and dancing. Very good time that one. When we tell the dreamtime story to our children, they learn of the spirit ancestors.

"Now them spirits made this land you know. The rivers, mountains, the rocks and trees. These spirits teach us how to live. Lots of them songs special, you know, only men initiated to the tribe can listen. Some of our music is for playing, you know. For everybody, around the campfire. Ahhh, good fun." He smiled. "Other people they got their own dreamtime story, but we all got the same time." He paused looking at the land around him. "When this place been flat, like a table, no mountain, river, tree, nothing, just flat, then from right inside the ground and from the sky come the dreamtime spirit. They move across the land and they make all things that we see here today. Now, we believe that the track left by the big caterpillar spirit, he make the mountains. The dreamtime spirit make all of you and me, people." Fat Tail Wagging was sound asleep, lying flat on his side in the dust. He would occasionally twitch an ear to keep the flies off.

"There are many story, told over and over at night, 'round the campfire," Asha's son continued as he slowly rolled a short twig in his hands. "How the kangaroo got him tail, how the big frog been thirsty, drink all the water and all the land been dry up like a desert. We still got them desert from that frog now. There's the story of how they make the stars, the sun and the moon." His fingers caressed the twig's surface as he spoke.

"Night time 'round the camp fire, we sing and dance and tell of the hunt. Which way some bird or animal live. How they move. How they sing. We say the most important thing we got is our voice. Our music we use to tell stories of life and all around where we live. Sometime we use click stick when we sing, most of the time we play the didjeridu. We make 'em the didjeridu from the branch of a tree, hollow tree, eaten out by the termite. They eat 'em out like a tube. We cut 'em 'bout this long." Eldest Son indicated a length a little more than half his height. "Clean 'em out, paint 'em outside, with a clay. Ochre, you know. White, red. When you blow 'em didjeridu, play 'em like a horn, but little bit different. You don't stop blowin'. Fill your cheek up with air, then breathe in through your nose, quick one. And same time blow air from your cheek, like breathe in and out at same time. A good didjeridu player, he can go on for ten minute. No stop, same sound. Clever didjeridu man can sound like a bird or dingo. Our people got no write 'em down language, we hand 'em down by our story. We tell 'em on a rock, paint 'em on a rock, in a cave, you know. And tell 'em in our song, in our dance. The song man make a noise like a honey bee or might be like a mosquito. Then the song start proper, half-talk half-sing, you know. There is all-time sing, man and woman make 'em that sing from their life or of bird or animal or maybe the song of what been happen now. Or song from long time, long time. The song man use stick for keepin' time. The song man important in any place he is. Different song man got his own certain song. And he sing, nobody else. They sometime travel very far, even through country belong to their enemy, so they can go to corroboree long way away, and them enemy don't hurt 'em, because they got special stick. The stick, it allow for them to pass through. The song man, he sing it at special place. Then by and by they sing play-song 'round the campfire. They sing of love, they sing of war or hunting or of the dreamtime. Or sometime of death."

The two men stood as Fat Tail Wagging roused himself and grinned broadly. Asha's son gently grasped Noom's shoulder. "You come corroboree, plenty for all."

And Noom had gone. There in the light of a night fire he saw and heard the didjeridu, the spirit tube, played. It reminded him of the drone of a bagpipe, though, the sound was much stronger and deeper. The droning buzz was something like the chanting of a deep male voice. The players would speak words or make animal sounds while they played, and these were modulated into the drone, varying its tone. The musicians used a billy-can to splash water down the inside of the tubes, keeping them wet so they would vibrate with a mellow, liquid tone.

By the fire, deep in the Australian bush, Noom found his mind wandering to an immensely distant past, the time before proper words.

❨❨❨❨❨

The Awb's legal system was set in verse and every four years they would gather to sing the law. The members of the tribunal were the ones who knew the full range of the songs and would sing them all, from beginning to end during Wootiki, the time of rule singing. And the people would listen. If anyone for any reason wanted a change in the law, they would compose new verses and sing to the assembly. The old version and the new version were sung back and forth until the people could decide which was the more beautiful.

The Awb felt it very important that the laws which governed their lives be beautiful, and they were cautious in changing any rule that might disrupt that beauty. Only after they were all in agreement would any rule be altered. The high desert dwellers experienced very little disruption in their lives because their laws were intrinsically beautiful and brought them happiness. Their legal system complimented instead of restricting and directing them.

The Awb language contained two verb tenses: What had happened and what was happening. The first wasn't a past tense. It instead referred to what was complete and the second tense referred to what was incomplete. This simplicity becomes apparent as one changes perspective. The word 'wootiki' meant completing and the word 'wootika' meant complete, so a day in one's life could be wootika, while one's life would be wootiki. This interchangeability of tenses gave the language two contradictory but useful points of view. All events are wootika, complete simply by their occurrence and all events are wootiki, small fluctuations in a huge cosmic enfolding. And it was between these two points, complete and completing, that the Awb lived and sang.

Wootiki and wootika were more than inverses. The correct proportion of each could best be discovered through song. When the notes and counter notes of completing and complete intertwined harmoniously the rule-changing ceremony was declared wootika and disbanded for another four years.

It was said that when wootiki and wootika danced in a way that enriched them both, then all in the world was beautiful.

≈≈≈≈≈

At the mine in Australia, Noom found an abandoned passageway that led to a small chamber. On Mondays when the sound of the didjeridu was still fresh in his mind he would go there and, after extinguishing his mine lamp, sit in the darkness. If he remained quiet, in time he would begin to hear a faint rumbling. When he tried to listen to the deep sound directly it would fade away, but if he listened near the sound he thought he could just make out the words, "I am. Am I?" The two short phrases rotated, leapfrogging over one another like an endless metronome. Noom experienced profound comfort and calm when he imagined he was hearing the very sound of the earth turning easily on its long slender pivot. A perfectly frictionless bearing oiled only by its own whisper.

ΩΩΩΩ

In 1084 at a village near Edo, Japan an orphan was apprenticed to a master-maker of temple bells. The master, a man in his fifties, had earned his reputation after he cast four of the finest bells ever to be heard in Japan. They were called crawler bells because of the belief that the voice of these bells travelled more slowly than other forms of sound. The fourth of the bells, named the water-stone bell, was installed in a monastery near Kyoto.

From high on a ridge, housed in its own building on the temple grounds, this bell rested, comfortable in its harness. Struck three times

145

daily, twice in the morning and once in the evening, it was deeply cherished by all who heard it. In the mornings the sound would probe the valley mists, its deep sonorous tone sliding over the ground, cautiously working its way down the mountain side. The water-stone bell was unhurried, washing each bamboo leaf as it passed. At dusk when the air was dark and cool the bell would raise its pitch slightly, wandering far into the night bringing hope to the weary.

After hearing this bell the boy travelled all the way to Edo, its sound ringing in his ears, to learn the secrets of such a wonderous device. During the next twenty years he mastered metal casting, the knowledge of alloys and most important, the secret geometry upon which the bell shapes were based. Gifted in mathematics, he came to believe it was possible to construct the bell of his dreams, one which when struck would continue ringing forever. Continually regenerating in its own timely fashion, it would ring to the ends of the earth. A bell which, once set into motion with a single strike, would finally ring through all of space. A bell whose musical agility matched that of space itself.

On the master's seventy-fifth birthday the apprentice approached him with the idea. Thereupon the master went in seclusion. When he returned he summoned his student and said, "The tone of a once-struck bell would indeed be very special. If you can hear it in your mind I believe it can be made. However, I am too old and you must continue the journey alone."

Shortly thereafter the apprentice left the village bell-foundry and wandered into the mountains to be alone. There he stayed for fourteen years, living in a narrow crack in the rocks and meditating beside a small waterfall. Each day he painstakingly constructed a new bell in his mind and calculated the different harmonics, of which there were 233 variations generated by his secret formula. The apprentice visualized complex patterns created by imaginary nodal meridians which revealed the vibratory properties he was searching for. Testing all the variations of each mind bell was a laborious and time-consuming task. One evening just before dark he struck the right combination and heard in his mind the sound of rapidly spinning music that rolled on and on and on. Quickly before the light failed the apprentice scribbled the bell's signature in geometric code on the back of a dried bamboo leaf. At last he had heard the once-struck bell. He listened to it all through the night and by morning had heard all the major tonal variations and rhythms. The sound was not constant; it swelled and danced, moaned and shouted. Long melodic structures nimbly rotated through endless spirals. Enfolded within the bell's tone was the infinity of music.

In the morning he meticulously checked the tiny ideographs and diagrams drawn the night before. They were correct. With a happy heart he set out to return to the foundry and finally to construct the magical bell of his dreams. But on the way, while stopping to offer prayers at a mountain shrine, he suddenly realized that the fabrication of a physical bell was unnecessary. The ringing would be with him forever. So the leaf was left at the stone cairn where a warm summer rain washed it clean, and the apprentice was never heard of again.

However years later there appeared on the Yoneshiro River a very odd ferryman. If children were present and the river surface silent and smooth as glass, the old man would stand quietly, listening intently and then exclaim, "Wind chimes!" Watching the incredulous children closely, he would widen his eyes and add, "But no wind."

§§§§

When Jay awoke, he looked around for Noom and found him missing. It was only when he started building a fire that he noticed the note. Written in the calligraphy of a draftsman it said BACK, AFTERNOON. This was the second morning that Jay had risen to find the old man absent, and Jay wondered where he had gone.

The night before, after Noom finished his flute, they talked late into the night, and the conversation was still in his mind as Jay started a fire. He had been trying to describe to the old man how he sometimes went back over the decisions in his life trying to find a reason that would explain the current path he was on. For Jay, knowing how the past influenced him was very important.

"Sometimes I tell myself that I shouldn't have traveled right after I finished school. I tell myself that maybe I should have gone on and got a

Master's or something. Sometimes I really regret that I didn't get something started right then," he said.

"When was that?" Noom asked.

"Let's see, it was about six years ago," Jay remembered. "I left for Europe in July. I was glad to have school finished and just wanted to get away from it all, take a little time for myself. So I took off."

"And when you remember leaving how do you talk to yourself?"

"What do you mean talk to myself?"

"Just now you said that you tell yourself what you shouldn't have done. How do you say that to yourself?"

"Well, I just say 'you shouldn't have done' whatever it is I'm thinking about."

"And what kind of a voice do you talk to yourself with?"

"What do you mean, what kind of voice?"

"Is it, say, a soft gentle voice or a harsh voice?"

Jay stopped a moment trying to recall the tone of his internal monitor. "Well, I suppose it's kind of stern. It sure makes me pay attention," he laughed nervously, "I can tell you that for sure."

"It sounds like it would. Do you speak to your friends with that tone of voice?"

"You mean out loud?"

"Do you talk to them aloud with one voice and inside to yourself with another?"

"Well, now that you mention it I suppose I do."

"And which voice do you talk to them out loud with?"

"I've never thought about it, but I suppose it's the friendlier one."

"And why wouldn't you speak to yourself with that same voice?"

"I've never thought about it, I guess. What difference would it make anyway? I still regret that it's turned out the way it has."

"The way we talk to ourselves in our head makes a big difference in the way we feel toward ourselves. Self-esteem is our reputation with ourselves. The character of our internal dialogue has a lot to do with establishing that reputation. The character is formed by the tone and pitch of our inner voices. The words used and the inflections at the ends of sentences all have a big impact."

"Are you saying that the way I talk to myself, the tone of voice that I use has an impact on the way I feel?" Jay was curious, here was something he had never considered before.

"That's just what I'm saying. For instance, the pronouns which you use while talking to yourself direct your mind in different ways. Try saying these two sentences silently to yourself and notice the feeling that goes with each. 'You are stupid,' and then, 'I am stupid.'" Jay silently repeated each sentence to himself, first one and then the other, stopping between them to notice the particular feeling each evoked.

"And do you notice a difference?"

"Well, yes I do. It's funny, at first I didn't notice much but then the 'you are stupid' made me slightly depressed and the 'I am stupid' seemed funny."

"Isn't it interesting that by changing pronouns you can change the way you feel. I call them the you-voice and the I-voice and they turn out to be very different. You can notice that the character of your voice changes when you switch from I to you. You can discover the phenomenon of tonality when you switch from one voice to the other."

Jay repeated the sentences silently to himself again. "You're right, there is a tonal difference."

"Also there are usually specific words attached to each voice. With the you-voice often go the words should, can't, never, always. With the I-voice go the words want and am. I want or I am. An interesting part of internal voices are the unspoken sentence endings. With the you-voice, an unspoken sentence ending of 'and you always will be' is often added but left unspoken. So the full sentence would be 'You are stupid and you always will be'. The unspoken sentence endings seem to be embodied in the character of the voice. To the I-voice is added the word 'and'. So it sounds like this, 'I am stupid and ....' When you used the I-voice you found it was funny because of what came after the and. Maybe it was 'and I don't believe it' or 'and I want to change it' or perhaps something else. The sentence ending used with the I-voice is more generative, the ending used with the you-voice leaves you feeling stuck. When you think about it you will realize that the you-voice refers to the future and the I-voice refers to the present. I tend to think of the you-voice as the voice which shakes a stern finger at me. It is the voice of judgment. The I-voice is much more the voice of fact. If you tell yourself something in the I-voice which isn't factual, the sentence tends to be changed until all parts of you can agree on the statement."

"You said the I-voice refers to the present. What about the sentence 'I wonder what I will get for Christmas?'," Jay asked.

"Just say it in its full form. 'I am wondering what I will get for Christmas and'. This will orient you to the present and tend to gather more information in connection with your wondering. Try talking to yourself in the I-voice. Use the pleasant tonality, the pronoun I, the words 'am or want' and add the word 'and' at the end of each sentence."

ₒₑ ₒₑ ₒₑ ₒₑ

One afternoon Noom stormed into the stone house and sat sullenly by the fireplace. "What is it?" asked Derry looking up from her herb cleaning.

"I can't do anything right."

"What's gettin' at you, child?"

"I just can't do anything right."

He had been chopping wood and had broken the handle of the ax. Something in him also broke and he felt defeated.

"Come," she said setting her herbs aside. She led him from the house outside to sit under the green willow tree. He sat clutching his knees and looking at the ground. Derry took her time, letting the breeze blow some of the frustration off the boy's hunched shoulders.

"Child, there is something you ought to know," she began. "Each of us is in a way two different folks. One person is oh so wonderful and the other is just awful. Just plain rotten awful. You see, we've got this story about ourselves. And in this story we're real perfect, wonderful like. And when what we do doesn't live up to that story, then we split apart into those two people. Then the wonderful person tries to drive that awful person away. Calls him names and throws rocks at him. Every time those two folks fight they seem to hate each other just a little bit more. When you're feelin' down, like you do now, it's a sign that you just split yourself into those two people. You didn't live up to your own secret story and now you're gonna punish that other person, that bad one. And it makes the bad person real mad because he feels like he can never please that real good one. The bad one takes to feelin' sorry for hisself, 'cus he thinks he deserves a whole lot better. Now this story that we all got is kind of like a myth. Each of us has our own myth and it comes from the peculiar notion of what that good person thinks the bad one should be like."

"Well, what can I do?" whined Noom.

Derry reached up and picked one of the small green leaves from her tree. She pinched it between her thumb and forefinger, feeling the waxy surface. "Them myths must be crushed, just squashed flat. Sometimes it hurts a tad when we have to make up better stories for ourselves. That new story has got to be about who we are instead of who we think we should be. Each time we erase a myth and replace it with a better story, then we draw them two people in us closer together."

Holding her hands wide apart, she drew them steadily closer as she spoke. "As those two folks get closer they get to know each other and become friends. Then they begin to hold hands and get friendly like and then one day them folks may get to huggin' and in the wink of an eye just pop right into each other. When you give up the wantin' to be perfect you git the chance to become whole."

"So what is my myth?" asked Noom looking up from the ground for the first time.

"I don't know, it's your private affair."

"But how will I ever find out?"

Derry looked at the tiny leaves of her tree. She had planted it in front of the house when she moved to Missouri and it flourished under her caring hand. "The answer to the question, 'What should you be like?' is the key to your own myth. The answer will give you a peek inside. When you're feelin' all sad and hurt like you are now, just ask yourself that question 'cause the answer is your myth." Derry smiled at the boy and tilted her head to the side. "So, child, what should you really be like?" she gently patted his shoulder. "Fix your ax now and get back to chopping again."

The Structure of Delight

≈≈≈≈≈

As he climbed Noom remembered the last time he was on the mountain. His teacher played a flute and when he was finished placed it in the small stone crypt with the others.

"This is the last song," he told Noom, "and when it is time you will come here and play it again so the mountains won't forget."

"But how will I know what to play?"

The man looked at Noom and replied, "You will remember and you will help the mountains to remember."

"But I've only heard it once, just now."

The man looked at the mountains all around them. "Once is enough," he said quietly. "Once is plenty."

Over the years, Noom worried that he wouldn't be able to carry out the ritual. His teacher gave the training and instructions only once and Noom had observed, not participated.

"Of course you'll worry," his instructor chided him. "How do you prepare for something you'll only do once? However, you'll find that your worrying will have been wasted. When it's time, everything you need will be available."

Step by step now, Noom began to hear the song. He smiled, remembering that old fox, his Hawkeen teacher, who gave him what seemed at the time an impossible task. As he climbed higher the melody became clearer.

ΩΩΩΩ

The spatial arrangement of a lightning flash has perhaps a greater influence on the resulting thunder than its temporal organization. A pulse of thunder begins in a channel of hot gases, under high-pressure, created by a lightning stroke. Initially the high-pressure core expands as a shock wave but it soon relaxes and becomes the familiar acoustical wave.

The sound of thunder is determined by a number of things. The sequence and geometry of lightning strokes, atmospheric conditions and the location of the hearer all have a bearing on the nature of the sound. A lightning discharge has many components: Stepped leaders, advanced leaders, return strokes and dart leaders. These are names for the flash seen when lightning zig-zags and forks. Macro-, meso- and microtortous channels abound. A single lightning system may originate at an altitude of up to five miles and travel over a range of fifteen to twenty miles, having two to three dozen major channels. When lightning occurs on this scale even the gods listen, for it results in one of the loudest sounds in nature.

Between the lightning channel and the listener, a thunder signal is altered by the medium through which it travels. The atmosphere attenuates, scatters and refracts the sound. Low frequency sounds reflect from the ground, skipping across the land. Because sound travels faster in warm air that it does in cool, a temperature gradient tends to curve the sound upward.

Thunder from the same lightning flash sounds different at different locations since each location has a unique position and orientation with respect to the lightning channels. A few feet one way or the other is enough to hear a different thunder. A hundred yards to the side reveals an entirely different thunder symphony. Thunder storms will have as many facets as listeners and every one is unique.

Each protracted sequence of rumbles, claps, booms heard in the peals of thunder originates when energetic flashes crack the sky. Desert peoples have an extraordinary memory for different thunder signals and they report a rare but remembered thunder song. It is described as a ripping noise, one that can be imagined as the tearing of some cosmic cloth. When, Inya, the Big Thunder People, walk the earth it is best to stay indoors.

In the past every living thing was significant to the native people of Australia. At times as a source of food, at times as a symbol of the past or a portent of the future.

Around the campfire one evening Noom listened as the didjeridu sang the song of woiju. Human voices helped to tell the story, but it was deep within the spirit tube from which the real song originated. It was a song of an insect living in the desert land, woiju, the sand wasp. Woiju, the song

153

went, digs a hole in the ground where it sleeps, then it comes out and flies away. Woiju is not good to eat, but neither is it to be feared. Rather, it is revered as a close associate of the earth, from which all life comes and to which all life returns.

The small sand wasps are found primarily in the sandy ridges of desert dunes where they dig their burrows. In the sand around each entrance exist distinctive marks made and maintained by the wasps. These patterns are of great interest to the desert's human inhabitants, for woiju is very busy and knows many things. Unlike insects such as ants, bees and social wasps, the sand wasp is a solitary creature and this was the first characteristic which attracted Noom.

Later he learned the song of woiju very well. It kept him safe in the mine, his own burrow. If danger lay ahead, ominous woiju patterns would crowd his dreams, alerting him.

§§§§§

The night before, after Jay experimented with his I-voice, he urged Noom to elaborate. While trying the different voice combinations he felt a brief surge of excitement. Maybe the old man was right after all, maybe he did have some control over the events in his head. The glimmer of control filled him with a curious expectancy.

"You see, I think of it this way," Noom paused. "We have something in our heads called the mind police, and they police what and how we think. Now the mind police don't care what they enforce, but once they are instructed to enforce something particular they are pretty thorough in the task. When we were young, we were surrounded by the voices of different authorities. And slowly these voices became internalized in the form in which we originally heard them, the form of the you-voice, the voice which became the mind police. The mind police function for the benefit of others not for the benefit of yourself. I can't think of any case where the I-voice wouldn't serve you just as well."

"Let's go back to what you said about the I-voice. You said to use the forms 'I am' and 'I want.'"

"Yes, I did."

"If I think only about what I want, won't I become pretty self-centered?"

"I don't see how."

"Okay, let's say I'm with someone and I'm only thinking about what I want. In my head I'm only using the I-voice. Shouldn't I be thinking about them? I don't think it's going to work out very well between us."

"I don't understand why. You keep forgetting the 'and' part. For instance, if you're with someone and have a sack of cookies, you say to yourself, 'I want all the cookies and I also want this person to like me.' When both desires combine it leads to compromise and in this case sharing. Do you really think that you need the mind police to tell you to share or could sharing come naturally to help fulfill all your desires? It doesn't work too well having the mind police coerce you into sharing because then you tend to feel resentful. 'I have to share,' instead of 'I want to share.'"

"So you're saying that adding an 'and' to your internal voice leads to compromise?"

"That's right. If you don't, it puts you in a bind. If you satisfy just the mind police, then you feel resentful. Using the I-voice aligns your mind with all of your present needs and integrates them into a course of action which goes a long way toward satisfying all the parts of you." Noom paused and looked into the flames. This was the first time since he met the young man that he felt Jay might be catching on. For the first time this evening the young man had stopped his compulsive finger drumming for an extended period. He seemed to be able to sustain a small amount of contact with himself without the need to brush his hair back from his eyes or engage in other self-distracting behaviors.

"Spend some time practicing," Noom continued. "Have as much internal dialogue as you want, but start each sentence with 'I am' or 'I want' and use a gentle voice, the one you use with your friends. It will help to give you the feeling of being open and generative. It's an interesting feeling, peace with just a tinge of excitement. A feeling of relaxation."

"But I thought the goal was to stop all internal dialogue."

"Where did you get that idea?" Noom laughed.

155

"I don't know. Isn't that what all the mystic masters teach, that you shouldn't have any internal dialogue?"

"I don't know what the mystic masters teach. Sounds like the mind police to me. I don't know what you should or shouldn't do." Noom peered at him closely. "How do you really want to be? Using the I-voice stops the arguing in your head and you'll find that, with practice, problems will automatically be resolved before you finish your internal sentence. If you really don't think that you're capable of conducting your life in a enjoyable way then let the mind police run it, that's what police states are for."

Jay smarted from Noom's insinuation. He didn't like the idea that his life was being run by a police state in his head, but neither was he ready to give it up. "What about a sentence like 'I don't want to be hungry?'" he challenged.

Noom smiled and sat back. He had to admit the young man had spunk. "Negation is a property of language, not events," he said slowly. "We might say there is a state called hungry and a state called full, but the state of not hungry is only possible through language. Any state other than hunger is known directly for what it is. A particular state can be known without direct comparison to another state. Knowing something directly is more powerful than knowing it through negative comparison. Your I-voice helps to know the world directly because it uses present desires and feelings. The you-voice tends to employ negation by comparison. The I-voice helps you proceed directly to any desired state."

Noom had suddenly become uninterested in continuing their discussion. He yawned and stretched, saying, "It's late and my desired state is to get some sleep. We can talk more tomorrow."

ΩΩΩΩ

Once when Jay was between jobs a friend gave him a short-wave radio to keep him company. From his basement apartment he strung a wire out through a crack in the window sill and up to the top of a brick chimney. Most of the stations Jay received broadcast in languages he didn't understand, but he listened to them for the interesting cadences he found in foreign words. Jay invented countries and customs to go with each new language he heard.

Karmavania was one of his favorites. He imagined it to be located in a remote corner of the Himalayas. There the inhabitants had an all consuming interest in the manufacture and wearing of hats. All news or music broadcast on Karmavania National Radio concerned the price of hat futures or coming trends in millinery. Songs were written and sung of great moments of the Karmavanian hat wars and when Jay began quoting KNR to his friends they wondered if he was finally going a little too far.

However, the most unusual station Jay listened to was positioned at 5Mhz. It broadcast the time, Universal Coordinated Time. He listened to the ticking of the seconds leading up to a minute mark when a crisp male voice would say, 'At the tone the time will be twelve hours' and thirty-seven minutes, Universal Coordinated Time'. And then a tone would sound and the next minute began to be trimmed away, second by second, till the voice spoke again. Jay wondered where the used seconds went.

He imagined somewhere an electronic signal drew a line through each second and then pitched it on the slag heap of used time. Shiny new seconds crowded down a chute with fed them into a time guillotine where they had but a brief moment of existence. Then the beep would cleave them cleanly in half, and the parts would drop away on a heap of discarded time. Each split second with a different story to tell. Each with a different memory. Jay suspected at times that there must be a way to rebuild the seconds and use them again. Somewhere must exist a cosmic body shop that refurbishes seconds, where the halves are joined and repainted, where the dings are hammered out and they become as good as new. And Jay wondered whether his life was one that ran on this secondhand time.

For a period in his life, whenever he went camping he would take the portable short-wave radio and set it to the time station and listen to the seconds ticking away deep into the night as the fire died. Through the night, as he slept, the radio beside him would continue marking second by second the length of his life. 'At the tone the time will be ....' Throughout the night the tone precisely marked births and deaths, keeping count of the wait in between.

157

The station occasionally carried information on global weather or sun-spot activity, but it was the time that fascinated him. The constant everlasting beating of what he imagined to be the electronic representation of the heart of the cosmos, Universal Coordinated Time.

Jay learned the station was operated by the National Bureau of Standards in Boulder, Colorado and visited the Bureau to find the source from which the regular ticking emanated. In a large gray concrete building he was directed to a long hallway. Near the end he found what he was searching for, the Mother Clock. Through a large plate glass window he gazed into an empty control room. A single office chair sat in front of the banks of instruments and monitors. The red eyes of digital readouts blinked every time the Mother Clock's heart beat. At the end of the lonely hall, staring into the lifeless room where the clock lived, Jay read the pamphlet explaining the clock's operation and learned that the instruments in the control room monitored the heart beat of atoms. By the time he left he understood that the Mother Clock included everything that had a heart beat itself. Anything composed of atoms was in its own way a Mother Clock. Even the atoms within his own heart had a heartbeat. Jay never tuned to the station again for he knew time was being kept.

$\pi\pi\pi\pi\pi$

Frank Sherman had peculiar trains of thought. Noom could never quite understand how they fit together, and after the first year of school he quit trying.

"There are a couple people I want you to get to know," Frank said, eyeing his young student through thick glasses. "I think you've met one so you might as well know them both. The first is Pythagoras."

"Who?"

"Pythagoras. You know the guy with the triangles and the theorem?"

Noom expected to be introduced to someone just down the hall or in the next room. Often Professor Sherman's disregard for the organizing principles of historic time threw Noom into momentary confusion.

Frank waited for Noom to indicate at least a passing knowledge of the Pythagorean Theorem and then continued. "Pythagoras was the first to understand the scientific properties of harmonious music. He stretched a string and established that it produced a constant note. Then he found out that another string stretched to the same tension which was half as long or a third as long or a fourth as long, when played with the first, produced a harmonious sound. Seems he became an expert at fractions." Frank's eyes flicked over the bookshelf before him. "Anyway, using his system you could get two notes or two thousand notes to vibrate harmoniously. From that time forward music had a language. He devised a very simple system which equated pitch with length, the marriage of music and geometry. Before Pythagoras we couldn't have built a piano." Frank stopped and stared at Noom. "You know, they say that when Pythagoras discovered his right triangle theorem he sacrificed forty oxen to the gods in thanks. I think if it had been me, I'd have given the party after discovering that music business."

≈≈≈≈≈

At the crypt Noom finally stopped to regain his breath. The mountains were still as they waited in the midday sun. They had waited patiently and were in no hurry. Aging humans would come, climbing slowly, to play the last song and then place their flutes into the stone box with the others. They had waited for many men with old and tired knees, and they would wait for this one. The music would then slowly fade, year by year, as winter storms washed it away. The song would be eroded like the mountains themselves. Fainter and fainter it would became, until just before silence again reigned, another old man with wavering knees would climb to refresh and regenerate the music in the mountains. Each wooden flute was placed on top of the ones which came before and slowly worked its way to the bottom of the pile, turning to dust and vanishing completely.

At this altitude the grass left unharvested by alpine rodents was dry and lifeless and brown. Winter storms would come and deposit light dry crystalline water over the peaks to insulate them during the winter. Then the heat of spring would melt the snow and send it trickling back down the mountains. The water would find its way to the river where it would navigate a clear passage to the ocean, waiting again to be swept up by the winds and returned to the winter peaks.

Noom looked out over the valley and knew that winter was near. As he raised the wooden flute to his lips and began to play he remembered his teacher's words. Yes, once was plenty. From the morning he selected a branch, the ritual rule dictated just three full days to construct, play and deposit a flute. Noom found satisfaction carrying out the tradition. With this final action he would complete the last of his duties and obligations, his self-imposed discipline would be lifted.

Just as the sun shifted to the slant of afternoon, the small wooden flute voiced its song in rich, vibrant notes. Noom held the last note until he heard its echo, until the mountains again remembered the chorus and could sing on their own. Then he lifted the rock slab covering the crypt, allowing a full blast of mountain light to enter. After the new flute was deposited with its ancestors the chamber was plunged back into darkness to begin the long wait for the next offering. The ritual was complete.

$\pi\pi\pi\pi\pi$

"And the second person," Professor Sherman said continuing, "is Jean Baptiste Joseph Fourier. He was the son of a tailor and educated by monks. Along about 1822 he published some of his theoretical ideas on the subject of cooling."

"Cooling?" Noom asked.

"Yes. He was interested in what happened to molecules when a material cooled off. He showed that the flow of heat between two adjacent molecules is proportional to the infinitely small differences of their temperatures. He demonstrated that any function of a variable, whether continuous or discontinuous, can be expanded into a series of multiples of that variable. And, of course, the series now bears his name. He understood that when waves act independently of one another the displacement of any particle at a given time is simply the sum of the displacement that the individual waves alone would give it. It's what is now called 'superposition'." Noom's eyes were starting to glaze, but Frank continued. "The importance of the superposition principle physically is that it makes it possible to analyze a complicated wave motion as a combination of simple waves. And the simple waves that Fourier specified are sine waves. In short, Fourier said all music is made up of sine waves. In fact almost all sounds are made of sine waves. The character of a sound's particular tone is directly related to the sine waves compose it. Doesn't matter whether it's a tuba or a violin." Frank paused and then glanced at Noom. "What if Pythagoras had met Fourier at my beef barbecue? Wouldn't that be something?"

§§§§§

Jay spent most of the morning searching along the base of the cliff. He was searching for another Hawkeen carving but didn't locate a mark of any kind.

As he strolled along the cliff he found that the two voices Noom spoke of the night before argued in his head. His you-voice was loud and strong and then he found that he could translate into the I-voice and feel a small measure of relief in the process. After lunch he sunned himself beside the cave's entrance and was just dropping off to sleep when a slight tremor running through the ground startled him. Jay sat up and looked around. He wasn't sure if it was a small earthquake or if he had been dreaming. He waited for a new development but nothing happened, so he went back to his nap. Then he was awakened again by whistling. Long before he could see Noom he could hear the melody being whistled repeatedly. When Noom finally arrived his face was drawn with fatigue but he seemed cheerful.

"Where have you been? Your note didn't say anything about where you were going." Around noon Jay had panicked briefly that Noom was leaving him in the mountains alone. He was glad to see the old man.

Noom needed to sit a moment while he rested his legs. "You know those old ghosts I was telling you about? Well they're gone now. What a great afternoon. What have you been up to?" He smiled broadly and drew a deep breath.

Jay didn't have the faintest idea what Noom was talking about, but he was eager to report his experiences with internal dialogue. "It's weird how language can change the way you feel."

"Language does all kinds of things. It is a way that we keep time in our heads for instance." The color was coming back into Noom's face as he rested.

"Time?"

"Sure. When you switched from the you-voice to the I-voice today you may have noticed the sensation of having more time."

"How do you know that's what I felt?"

"I can tell by your behavior. You seem more relaxed, am I wrong?"

"No, the I-voice has been running through my head."

"It's fun to be able to stop and start time, make it run slower and faster. If you think you're out of time change your internal language and you'll have all the time you need."

"Show me how to do that."

"Let's wait till this evening, then I'll show you a way."

They sat enjoying the sun until Jay broke the silence.

"You said that pronouns make a difference and you've talked about first and second person pronouns. What about third person?"

"I think of the use of pronouns in internal dialogue in this way: When I'm using the first person I am myself, when I use the second person it's like I'm talking to myself, maybe up to ten feet away. With the third person or 'he', I'm beyond normal conversation range with myself, say ten feet to infinity. So in the way that you're asking, the third person pronoun is a more extreme case of the second. To test for distance, say the sentences 'You are stupid' and 'He is stupid', both referring to yourself. The use of pronouns defines the distance of one part of me from the other. It's difficult to make yourself feel bad with internal dialogue if all parts occupy the same location, as in the case of first person. Three things seem to be important here: The choice of pronoun, the quality of voice and the choice of modifying words. Using the pronoun 'I' in a nice tone of voice and the words 'am' or 'want' will make everyday life much more enjoyable. All parts of yourself integrate, become friendly and work in unison."

"But wouldn't I need to talk to myself using the other pronouns sometimes?"

"You can talk to yourself anyway you want, however you now have some knowledge of the consequences of your choice. Take care in choosing so you get the results you want."

"Tell me a little more about time," Jay asked.

"Well, for starters, we are formed by our futures instead of our pasts."

"That doesn't make any sense, the future hasn't happened yet. Our past is what we rest on."

"That's true, but I said formed. What we imagine can or will happen has a much greater effect on us than what has happened. Only if we imagine our future as a continuation of our past, will our past have much bearing on our lives. If something terrible happened to you in your past, it will only continue to effect you if you imagine that the event will recur at some point in your future. We can easily be free from our past if we exclude our past from our future. Also if something in your past was wonderful, then make sure that it is included in your future in order to get more of it. The I-voice roots us firmly in the present with our attention directed to a future which we desire. The you-voice tends to recreate our past and plant it firmly in our future, using the part of the sentence that's unspoken but understood, 'and you always will be.' If you don't want to 'always will be', you can simply drop it."

 ❧ ❧ ❧ ❧

Derry and Boondoggle kept a close watch on the boy's inner weather. If storms or long periods of fog loomed on the horizon, they would intervene. At these times Derry would question Noom about his internal dialogue. If he seemed troubled or distant she would ask, "Child, who's talkin' in there? You or someone else?"

Noom was mystified that the old woman could tell so easily about the voices in his head. In the beginning he was convinced she was some sort of witch who could read his mind.

"What do you mean me or someone else?"

Derry would smile and set him down. "Is someone tellin' you what you should or shouldn't do? Is someone tellin' you what you should or shouldn't be?" She would question gently. "Be careful lettin' other people talk in your head. They don't have to live your life and suffer the mistakes, you do."

"How can you always tell what I'm thinking?" he asked.

She would laugh. "I can't really, I can just tell how you're thinkin' it."

Slowly Noom came to notice that often his mood was dependent on who was talking in his head.

"Child, there is enough bickerin' in this world anyway. Just tell them to go away and leave you be."

ππππ

"So you see," said Frank, "chaos is the safest place for secrets. They won't be lost because they can't degrade anymore. If they do, then they start reappearing."

Noom had no idea what Frank was talking about and it was apparent because Professor Sherman suddenly stopped and looked searchingly at his student.

"The brain, son, I'm talking about the brain." White dots began appearing on the right side of Frank's head as he tapped his temple with the chalk. "Don't you see, music is just sine waves and lengths. A very simple code. The brain doesn't store information in an orderly way, it's stored in chaos. That way nothing every happens to it, it can't get scrambled because it already is scrambled."

"Then how do we ever remember anything?" Noom asked.

"Ahhh. That's the beauty of it. When you think anything your brain automatically organizes and aligns with that thought. We might go beyond that and say the reorganization and alignment is the thought. In any event, when you think apple your brain is automatically tuned to the apple mode and any information that was ever entered in the apple mode magically appears. It has to, that is the only way for it to exist. If you then think of a lump of coal, the apple information is scattered into chaos as your brain reorganizes into the lump of coal mode. What I have told you about Pythagoras and Fourier seems to have vanished. When I speak their names you reorganize again and the information returns. Most of the information we're not thinking about at the moment is scrambled.

However, I think it's probably scrambled in a way that's very easy to unscramble. It's probably as simple as Pythagoras and Fourier found music to be."

"Are you saying the brain is something like a combination lock? It's always set at some combination and if there were a door for every combination then wherever the lock was set, it would open some door?"

"That's about it."

"Well I don't quite see how you get the apple combination which opens the apple door."

"It's simple. Just think apple and presto, you have the right combination and the apple door swings open."

"I just have to think about apples and everything I know about them is available?"

"Not quite, but that's where things get interesting. First off, don't think about apples, just think apples. And second, apples, apple pie, rotten apple and George Appleton may have combinations which are very close together but not quite the same."

"Who's George Appleton?"

"An example. Now, the best apple pie you ever tasted may have been entered into your brain under the combination of apple or pie or the day of the week you ate it or the color of the plate you ate it from. Or finally it may have been entered under the combination of good tastes. So to find the memory of best apple pie you may have to use the combination of Monday afternoon."

"If I entered the experience of good pie under days of the week, wouldn't it be pretty hard to remember?"

"Of course." Frank sat still staring at his pupil who was momentarily stopped by the obvious. "Do you want the secret to being smart?" He finally asked in a whisper.

"Sure."

"Being smart has to do with cross combinations. Combinations that exist close to each other. If when you ate the pie, you filed it under Monday, rotten, George and hot steamy things, then when you think good apple pie all those doors open just a bit and let you look at it. If when you think a thought just one door opens, you're pretty dumb. But if a million doors open a crack then you have the opportunity for amazing thoughts."

Noom was puzzled. "So how do you do that?"

"By being broadly aware. By noticing all sensory perceptions in each situation. When you notice anything it's given a combination code and instantly retained in your brain."

"That sounds awfully hard."

"It sure seems that way in the beginning. Once you have learned something, then forget it. It won't be lost, just stored in chaos."

Noom wondered if Frank was finished with his thought. He had studying to do and had been at the office a long time. But then Frank's intensity began to rise. Noom knew there was more because he always felt a slight quiver when the professor spoke in that slow, quiet way.

"Son, chaos contains everything, even things you never did know. When it's constrained or aligned it will deliver anything which was placed in its midst. Chaos is not the same as confusion. It is the most fundamental arrangement possible. It is events crushed and ground into their tiniest bits. Chaos is what happens when events are unconstrained. Think of it this way; if your brain contained all possible notes of all possible instruments, you would still play just one song at a time. And while you're playing that one song all the rest of the notes would remain unused. If you kept them in a bushel basket somewhere, it would contain musical chaos. Once your song is sung let it break apart into separate notes and fall back into the basket and gather out new notes for another song."

Noom rose to leave and Frank stopped him at the office door. "By the way," he asked innocently, "do you know any good recipes for barbecue sauce?"

§§§§§

That night in the cave Noom's vitality seemed completely restored. "Okay, now I'll show you a little about time dilatation," he told Jay. "Get comfortable and take a couple of slow breaths. Imagine a still clear pool of water in front of you. When you inhale imagine the calm of the smooth surface. When you begin to exhale imagine a drop of water falling into the center of the pool creating a small splash and watch the ripples expanding outward. As you exhale say the word 'sssssssssssssssstop' quietly to yourself. Let the drop fall with the first of the 's' sound and let the pool be still again when you reach the 'p'. As you inhale listen and I think you'll hear a sound that you've heard before but have forgotten."

Jay closed his eyes and began to breathe long slow rhythmical breaths.

Very quietly Noom whispered, "Form your lips to make the sound but let the air move so slowly past the tip of your tongue that no sound is made." As he watched he could see Jay's lips close at the end of each exhalation when he silently pronounced the 'p'."

Jay had the odd sensation of time expanding slightly and he wondered what he was to listen for. So he continued imagining the pool of water, watching the small ripples that the falling drop made. With each breath he got the breathing, the speaking and the imagining to coincide more closely. Just after he quit worrying what he was to listen for the reverberation which existed between the beats of the Universal Time clock suddenly came back to him. Opening his eyes he asked, "How did you know?"

"I've listened also." Noom smiled. "It's a sound you need to remember. We have no concept of cause and effect without time. We have no concept of meaning without the concept of time. Meaning is a time-based activity. Sometimes we just need to stop and remember."

Jay was surprised by the experience. "Is that how the Hawkeen do it?"

"It's one of the ways. And while we're on the subject, you should know that the word Hawkeen comes from another language and in rough translation means something like 'person of excellence.' To be Hawkeen is to be in a state of excellence, so it's really also a verb. And for that matter so is the word 'mind'. Mind is what the brain does. Mind is a verb. Often you can learn more by hearing in your mind than with your ears," Noom said, tapping his temple with his finger. "Pronouns are one of the ways the mind discusses itself."

"Then you're saying that it's something like a code."

"I suppose you could say that." Noom paused looking out of the cave's entrance into the night. "Your comment reminds me of the Code Talkers."

167

he said, warming to another story.

"Code Talkers?"

"During the Second World War the Marines recruited Navahos to serve as radiomen in the Pacific. The idea was that they could speak freely in their native tongue which would serve as a code. The only way to break the code was with a native speaker, something the Japanese didn't have. Actually it was a code within a code because the Navahos used the names of different birds to describe different types of aircraft and so on. Birds that were known to them on their home reservation. The Marine units could communicate over open radio without the trouble of encoding and decoding messages.

"And were the messages ever intercepted?"

"Of course, all the time, but that didn't do the Japanese any good. All they could do was listen and wonder."

ΩΩΩΩ

Jim Yazzie was recruited into the Marines in 1942 and went to a camp in California to become a Code Talker. For a Navaho boy this was a bit frightening. By the time he had completed his training Jim's excitement had grown and he was eager to be assigned to a fighting unit in the Pacific.

Ado Takayama was a university student at the start of the war and quickly enlisted in an intelligence unit. 1942 found him stationed on the slope of a lonely volcano far out in the Pacific ocean. The island was picked because it was well situated to intercept the radio traffic of the American forces. Ado was good at his job. He spent long nights huddled over the charcoal heater in a shack perched high on the mountain. Each night he would bring a small pot of tea and some rice balls for nourishment during his vigil. Listening for radio signals, Ado meditatively touched the sensitive tips of each index finger to the head phones straining to expand his acoustical universe. Constant storms throughout the Pacific basin generated static which his keen ears penetrated to pick up garbled Yankee messages. Ado was used to the waiting, for he believed that he might be the one to copy down a message which could finally break the American code. He would deliver it to his commander, written in meticulous script, and soon the imperialists would be driven from the Pacific islands.

Jim Yazzie was to be the first Code Talker on the air. The Marines felt they could now communicate in full secrecy and were eager to find out the range and clarity of transmission. The night picked for this test turned out to be calm and clear, ideal for radio traffic. The aerial was extended as high as possible and the generator revved to full capacity. Other Code Talkers throughout the Pacific were poised to receive these first Navaho words. Jim had never before worked with such a powerful transmitter and he was excited. They'd be hearing Navaho all the way to China tonight. Shortly after midnight Jim Yazzie switched on the microphone and waited for the antenna to build full power.

Ado, in his radio shack snapped straight up in his chair, bumping rice balls off the table. His receiver hummed as the static cleared. The weak background to which he was listening was suddenly clear and sharp. The ether was taut anticipating this important message, it was the strongest signal Ado had ever heard. And he instantly knew that his interception of this upcoming transmission would win the war for Japan. His vigilance had paid off, he would return to his homeland a victorious hero. Ado's fingers pressed the headset ever tighter as he waited.

Jim smiled at those surrounding him and leaned forward. Speaking clearly articulated Navaho, he said into the microphone, "This is Jim Yazzie and I'm on the air."

A thousand miles away Ado's brain was instantly filled with an ear-splitting blast of rich guttural sounds and it slowly ground to a stop as if congealed by mutton fat. In the morning they found him sitting frozen in the straight backed chair with his fingers still pressed to the headset. Rice paper and bamboo pen, carefully laid out on the table, were untouched. Gently Ado was pried loose from his equipment and his extremities massaged to restore circulation.

During his convalescence at the infirmary strange and troubling dreams plagued him, so he was reassigned to Tokyo to calculate naval fuel allotments while he recovered. After the war Ado finished his schooling and joined a small company that manufactured electronic equipment. Postwar prosperity and the transistor propelled the company into global

169

competition and Ado into a vice president's position. Having forgotten the war, he would stand at the end of the assembly line, watching boxes bearing his company's proud logo being stacked into huge creates to be sold throughout the world. The war far behind him, the economic future looked bright.

Jim's life was different. The code talking experience heightened his sense of pride in being Navaho, and he returned to the barren reservation never to speak English again. The first summer as his anvil sang under the cottonwood tree he knew he was finally home. He pounded out silver ingots, fashioning fine turquoise jewelry and stared at a horizon peopled only by the spirits of his ancestors. Accompanied by his dog, Jim Yazzie herded sheep on a lonely mesa and listened to the mysteries of the wind, far from a world which watched the electronic flicker of toys and tools. He worked quietly with his hands in a sagebrush emptiness.

One afternoon thirty-five years after being discharged from the Marines, Jim was standing outside a discount store in Winslow, Arizona. His eyes kept returning to a box in the window, the bright logo was intriguing. Then he noticed the box contained a 40 channel CB radio. Back at his hogan, Jim soon had the radio installed in his pickup and the next day drove to the top of a nearby butte and shut the engine off. Youthful excitement returned as he keyed the hand-held mike and waited, letting the antenna load. Leaning slightly forward, he spoke in proud and meticulous Navaho, "This is Jim Yazzie and I'm on the air again."

Half a world away Ado Takayama lurched upright from his futon. The dreams had returned.

Chapter Seven

§§§§§

In the morning the two men sat in the sun by the cave's entrance. "How you see things in your mind makes a tremendous difference," Noom began. "There are those who say life exists only in the mind. I don't know if that's true, but I do know how you view your life is how you will find your life to be. If you carry two versions of the world in your head, how you think your life should be and how you think it actually is, you will be unhappy. If you imagine a perfect world or a world that is unattainable, your own experience of reality will never compare to your ideal. And you'll be continually unhappy. If your version of the world is incomplete, there is room for you to finish it, to make it more the way you want it to be. The trouble arises when you confuse what is complete with what is not.

"Most people consider their circumstances in the world to be fixed and immutable. We have an odd belief that we are born with abilities and that our natures remain fixed. For people who hold such beliefs education makes very little difference. However, the underlying idea of education is that our natures aren't fixed. There is a certain factual component to the world, events which do seem unchangeable; these are the events we can depend on. Factual things in the world seem to be fixed; however, what the facts mean is not fixed and this works to our advantage."

"What do you mean, factual things?"

"The melting temperature of ice seems to be fixed, and it's just as well because otherwise it can't be counted on. If you say that you've had a fight with someone, then the meaning has already been fixed in your head. If you say that you had a disagreement, then the meaning is changed and if you say that you had a discussion then the meaning is changed still further. When someone views a discussion as a fight it becomes reality for them, the nature of the world automatically changes. When something is named, this tends to fix reality in a specific way. When something is unnamed, or renamed in a more fluid or open way, then the world can have multiple meanings. And with multiple meanings you have choice. With choice the world becomes varied and rich. People have extremely strong views of the nature of the world. To them the world's nature is self-evident because every discussion is a fight and every question an attack.

"The most joyous fact that I have ever run across is that minds are changeable. We can change our minds. What a wonderful discovery. When each of us really makes that discovery for himself the world becomes new and fresh and original. If you can change your mind then you can change the world. It's as simple as that. If you can change the meaning of one small seemingly insignificant thing then you can know it is possible to change the meaning of everything."

"If that's true, then the temperature of melting ice would also be changeable."

"As a matter of fact it is. The temperature of melting is dependent on pressure, increase or decrease the pressure and the temperature changes."

"But two and two still equals four."

"Two what plus two what equals four what? Integers, rabbits, drops of water? Over what time period? Under what conditions? When you generalize, you lose the richness and possibility of the world. Generalizations are fun and on occasion useful, but the details, the specific is where the action lies."

"Then you're saying that it depends?"

"Of course, and I could answer that depends also depends."

ΩΩΩΩ

Some insects possess eyes designed to use polarized light as an aid to maintaining direction during their travels. This explains the remarkable navigational skill of many ants and moths and, of course, honey bees. A large hunting ant, the bulldog ant of Australia, has multi-faceted eyes of which each sub-unit contains its own lens. This desert ant is a solitary hunter; it never forages along a scout's scent trail. And because the desert is devoid of most landmarks the ant must rely on sky light to guide it. The atmosphere polarizes sunlight, in particular ultraviolet light to which the ant's eyes are sensitive. It is interesting that the ultraviolet part of the spectrum is the least affected by atmospheric disturbances.

The sun is the one body in the sky which lends itself to direct navigation. It lacks polarized light and is also the most brilliant celestial object. To an ant this disc becomes particularly meaningful. But for the ant the importance of the sun as a guide is its lack of polarization rather than brightness. Bulldog ants can distinguish the differences between thousands of points in the sky. However, they lack a nervous system complex enough to retain signals from so many sources. An insect's primary task in navigation is the retention of consecutive dead-reckoning summaries. A bulldog ant is very good at adding and subtracting. It keeps a running total. The rest of the information is lost as soon as it has been calculated. To say that an ant has no memory is not quite right, because it can remember the location of home. So these ants know two things, their present location and the location of home; memories of other locations are discarded after they have been processed. If a bulldog ant traveled through Portugal, for instance, the trip would be remembered only as it figured into the ant's current location.

Humans have the opposite problem. We remember everything and can't add. We remain blind to the ultraviolet which ants see so well. However, some of the Viking explorers made up for this defect. To sail with confidence for Greenland and Newfoundland they used sunstones, dichroic crystals, which can serve as polarization analyzers. These crystals are found today as pebbles on the coast of Norway.

When the sky was overcast and gray the Vikings could peer through the crystals and see much as an insect does. The sun stones figured prominently in some of the old sagas, as well they should, because their magic allowed a human eye to be transformed to that of a honey bee. There exist no polarizing crystals in the eyes of insects; the ability of their visual cells to respond to polarized light is the result of a molecular oddity.

The eyes of some creatures use mirrors in addition to lenses. Certain crustaceans, shrimp and crayfish, for example, have mirrors in their eyes, the operation of their eyes depending on reflected light. These mirrors are multi-layered, constructed of alternating bands of different materials and have properties not possessed by ordinary metallic mirrors. In some creatures each eye contains a single mirror in the shape of a half hemisphere. In others, the eye is multi-faceted, each facet with its own mirror system. And the mirrors of compound eyes operate on different optical principles from those of single eyes. The compound eyes of nocturnal animals differ in still other ways.

Perhaps that's part of the reason the Vikings explored, searching for new places to see with transformed eyes. Driven forward on a long journey finally to behold with mirrored, multi-faceted, crystalline eyes.

ᔕ ᔕ ᔕ ᔕ

On summer evenings in Birch Tree, while Derry prepared her herbs, she would set the oil lamp close to the window. Moths were drawn to the light and walked across on the outer side of the window pane. She enjoyed watching them and always waited for a certain type of moth. It was white with just a tinge of old ivory spreading out across the under-wings. It would alight on the window without a sound and delicately pulse its wings while the larger, crazier moths flew in circles, banging against the glass.

When one of the special moths came, delicate and shy, Derry watched closely because the light reflected from its' eyes had a bright pink glow. It gazed at her through the glass with small unblinking crystalline eyes set close together, high on its head. The intensity of the light from its eyes was a sharp contrast to the delicate complexion of the whitish wings and body. When she put her face close to the window she could just make out the tiny movements of silent breathing. After she extinguished her lamp and went to bed, Derry would imagine these moths, gliding through the blackness, the butterflies of night.

Eldest Son was a painter. Any surface became his canvas; fiber, sand, wood, stone or skin. He decorated everything around him, his house, his didjeridu, dancing boards, carrying dishes and even himself.

On flat sheets of bark he painted the dreamtime stories. With infinite patience he would place tens of thousands of tiny colored dots, each adding to and giving significance to an overall pattern. Using the tips of dry grass stems, Eldest Son meticulously painted his world with colored ochres.

"This is Wandjina," he told Noom, pointing to the broad beaded outlines he was now filling in. "This is Wandjina, he made 'em people to go about in the right ways."

Noom noticed a curious thing. Whenever he studied one of the paintings he would experience an odd state. Any knowledge of his current physical status simply evaporated. He couldn't tell if he was hungry or had just eaten; he didn't know if he was hot or cold, aches or pains just vanished. At times it was difficult to tear himself away and return to the ordinary world. He suspected that Eldest Son painted, in part, to enter the state where concentration was so easily maintained it became extremely pleasurable.

"When you paint, what happens?" Noom asked pointing to a half-finished painting.

Eldest Son sat back on his heels and scratched his beard. His brow wrinkled as he struggled to find an answer Noom could understand. Finally he shrugged and said simply, "No time."

Noom began to notice that concentrating on visual patterns, particularly those of a tiny scale altered his perception of time. And when time was altered so, too, were many ordinary sensations of the world. When time stopped physical sensation dropped away, and he remained suspended with no separation between himself and the colored dots. Art, Noom came to understand, was the destruction of time.

He found that while working on engineering problems that frustrated him, he would start making tiny dot patterns at the corner of the paper with his drafting pencil. His frustration would quickly wash away and be replaced by an insight that would allow him to solve the particular problem. Noom's supervisor began saving the dot doodles and displayed them on the main bulletin board. The patterns were circled in red pencil and underneath was written, 'YES, YOU TOO CAN BECOME A COLLEGE EDUCATED ENGINEER.' Noom took the ribbing with a smile, because as simple as the dots seemed, they were a powerful tool for him.

ππππ

The beginning of his senior year found Noom sitting again in Professor Sherman's office. During the summer Frank added a painting to the room and sat admiring it. It was an oil painting of a man contemplating blue-prints spread out before him. Turning to Noom he asked, "When you think of a problem how does it appear to you?"

Noom was never able to predict what Frank would come up with next. "Well, I suppose it's always huge. Isn't that what a problem is?"

"Good point!" Frank was feeling particularly energetic at the beginning of the new school year. "Is it bigger than you or smaller?"

"Well, it certainly isn't smaller."

Frank sat back in his chair and began gazing at the ceiling. "Son, I know you know about scale and I know you know about points of view. But what you may not know is that your brain uses those very same conventions during its operation."

Noom settled in for the professor's discourse. "The first thing you have to do when you're solving a problem," Frank continued, "is to get the whole thing into a single picture. No matter how big the problem is. You may even have to move back a little until you can see it all. But you must make sure all of the problem is within a single picture in your mind. That's the first step. There is no point in starting to solve any problem until you've got it into a single focused picture." Frank held his chalk poised in the air ready for his next point.

"How tall are you anyway, about six feet?"

"Yeah. I guess," Noom stammered, caught off guard again. "Almost."

"Now the second step, and this is where the trick really lies, is to keep moving things around in your mind until you're larger than the picture."

Frank stopped with the chalk still in the air. "You may have to expand yourself or squeeze the picture down a little to make it work. Either way, get it small enough that you can rise above it in your mind. You have to change the scale and make it smaller than yourself. When you've made it smaller, move the picture down just a little, so that in your mind, your point of view is from above the problem picture." He glanced at Noom. "Now think of a problem."

"What kind of problem?"

"Any kind of problem. A mining problem or a problem from your past that's always plagued you or any problem that you can imagine that you might want to solve someday in the future. This is a problem-solving algorithm. Remember that word?"

Noom nodded.

"When your problem picture is larger than you are, your brain identifies it in a certain way. When you get it into a single clear picture that's smaller than yourself, then your brain isn't afraid of it anymore and can really begin to work clearly. Single, clear, smaller, lower. Simple." Frank tapped the side of his head once with the white chalk to make his point.

ΩΩΩΩ

In Australia a dust storm is an awesome meteorological event. Wind lifts dust particles and small pebbles from the ground and moves them into the air as in a terrestrial hurricane. These storms are sometimes called haboob, a term derived from the Arabic word for violent wind. At ground level they can be life threatening.

The cloud masses often form almost explosively just before noon when the air temperature drops in the wake of a developing cloudburst. Downdrafts may reach velocities which are roughly proportional to the height of the cloud top. Tornadic vortices form not only inside dust storms but also along their leading edge. When warm air is pushed up over the edge of the advancing front of cold air it gives rise to small whirlwinds

Although visibility can drop to zero in such a storm, victims caught in the giant whirlwind tend to try to keep their eyes open as the world spins and rages around them. There is excitement in observing such power. The track of a dust storm can be read from the pattern it leaves on the sand. And many of the world's people seek out these sand seas as a place for meditation and introspection.

Traveling across a vast dune field one can inspect the last storm's signature. Out of chaos come regular and definite sand shapes. Wandering among them in a wordless desert allows one to inspect the beauty created by a ravaging storm. Mountain tops are sought out for insight, but deserts remain the perfect ground for reflection.

∾∾∾

The single entry of the fisherman's diary reads:
Eighth moon, 1243.

A dry dawn echo
The boundary scrambles under my shadow
Morning morning, twice.

No other notation seems to have been made that day.

ΩΩΩΩ

Fireflies belong to the beetle family. Throughout the world nighttime is occasionally lit and decorated by the bioluminescence of roving fire beetles.

In New Guinea fireflies gather in trees in dense swarms, flashing on and off with a definite rhythm, each beetle blinking in perfect unison with the others. Where forest meets river, trees with fireflies on every leaf flash in the night.

Humans have the capacity to dance or march in unison but synchronous activity is rare in nature. The ability which allows a group of organisms to repeat an action simultaneously and at regular intervals seems to be confined to man, a few kinds of crickets and certain fireflies of the Pacific. The light producing organ of the firefly is activated by signals originating in its brain, but how the fire beetle keeps time is unknown. The nervous system of the small beetle meters time in flashes which range in intervals from every half-second or so up to three seconds. These neural delays march steadily forward hour after hour, night after night, keeping steady time. Fire beetles are truly the insect clocks of darkness.

Firefly constellations have been known for centuries. Their nightly displays of bioluminescence radiate cool light from millions of members in single sharply defined pulses. Long before the electric light fireflies on the rivers of New Guinea were patiently drumming out their nightly photic messages. Along stretches of a dark river an individual tree may silently pulse, providing a beacon for the night rivermen who use the firefly trees as navigational markers while gliding over silent waters. And it could be that the specific frequencies of the night beetle's light coupled with its rhythmic pulsing is of more interest to the eyes of distant stars than all the racket humans create.

When enough small and insignificant actions become coordinated and entrained, beauty and power are created. Order arising from chaos is the most powerful of all. Random neural discharges of the brain must first be linked and combined before the magic of thought and understanding appears. But the nightly messages of the fire beetle of New Guinea, continually spreading throughout the galaxy, may be beyond our comprehension.

§§§§

By the cave's entrance Noom was relaxing in the sun now that his Hawkeen duties were finished. During his tenure as Region Master he had made changes in the rituals for his region. He would be the last to visit the crypt. Noom considered himself the last of the generation of Hawkeen who had seen the group enter the modern era. It was with a sense of completion that he conducted the flute ceremony. He had fulfilled the duties and obligation to the old ways. The old man took delight in being the pivot around which one chapter closed and another opened. Few others had the opportunity to experience the distance from the Stone Age all the way to the Space Age.

179

The primary task of his trip into the mountains was completed. Now he could turn his full attention to the young man before him. "It is possible to see without seeing meaning," Noom continued, his brown eyes sparkling.

"I don't understand what you mean." Jay was unsure where the morning's discussion was leading.

"Most people see what the world means to them instead of what it looks like. Now there is a deep paradox in the middle of this. Values become the lens through which meanings are formed. Values and beliefs become the lens through which we look. There are those who believe that it is impossible to see at all without seeing with meaning, but it is possible. The naming part of your brain is where a lot of meaning is created, so the path to seeing without meaning begins with the shutting down of the naming department. Can you see a color without knowing its name?"

"I've never really thought about it."

Noom chuckled. "Probably not," he said. "The process of perception is ongoing and naming stops this procession. While the movement of meaning continues the world is incomplete and possible. When meaning is specified the world is complete and stops, set in concrete. A name turns the infinite into the finite."

"So how do you keep meaning fluid?"

"One of the ways is to practice finding several unique meanings for each situation. Realize the meaning you give any event and try using the opposite meaning. Try giving every event at least three different meanings and see how this changes your world."

"Why can't I just give an event the right meaning off the bat and be done with it."

"Because I've told you, an event doesn't have a true meaning. Reality is an abstraction because meanings remain arbitrary." The old man paused and looked far into the distance. "Everything is at the same time; nothing is vice versa. There is that and this."

πππππ

"And once you've gotten the problem picture in order," Frank proceeded, "add the minimum that is necessary when you're working on it. Anything more than what is necessary is extra. And extra detracts. Try to keep from adding surplus information, because then the problem starts to grow and get away from you. A very fine line exists called the optimal. It is the most favorable, a place where any more or any less detracts. A large part of life is searching for and attempting to ride the optimal line. I don't know if the point is to be on the line exactly, because that results in perfectionism. The point is to remain near the line as much as you can. I call it my optimal lion and try to keep it around most of the time."

"You don't really have a lion, do you?" Noom laughed.

But Frank was serious. "Of course. What would you expect me to have, an optimal rabbit?" He looked long and hard at Noom. "Son, nothing is completed in this world unless it is completed first in your mind. When something is completed in the mind then it can be completed in the world. Know what you can do and don't know what you can't do. Many people talk and think about what they can't do. They define themselves by what they can't do. What you can't do is of absolutely no use to you, unless you're trading it for sympathy or pity. Sometimes in those cases it can be worth a lot. But if you have to display a lack of power repeatedly to get someone to loan you some of his, then it is difficult to develop your own. Spend most of your time accumulating power instead of avoiding it. Beware of relationships in which you're encouraged to disperse your personal power." Frank thought for a moment, "I can't think of any time when self-reliance wouldn't be an asset."

"But don't some people fight to be the most powerful?" Noom asked.

"Of course. They are people to avoid. Seek people whose power you can compliment. In those cases the total becomes greater than the sum. Some marriages are like that."

"Is there a Mrs. Sherman?" Noom asked tentatively.

Frank's face lit up. "Yes, there is. And she's a lot smarter than I am. She's an artist."

"What do you mean smarter?" Noom couldn't imagine Mrs. Sherman doing calculus any more rapidly than Frank.

"Well, I don't know if it's smarter exactly. Let's just say that she amazes me at times. I think what I do is easy and what she does is hard because it's foreign to me. Her mind works in ways that remain an absolute marvel to me." Frank's memories were far from the office and his voice became very soft as he spoke. "Yes, Mrs. Sherman and I got hitched forty-two years ago and we've made a good team. Plowed a lot of ground together, smartest thing I ever did. We're stronger together than apart. So I guess that's what I'm saying: Avoid those people you're weaker with and seek those you're stronger with."

≈≈≈

In the muddy waters of the Yoneshiro River lived a mighty carp. This carp was a divining fish, it told fortunes. The fish dwelled under a large black boulder at the edge of the river. There it had been born and there it had lived for over four hundred years. Over time its golden color aged into a dark russet brown with a single black spot across the hump in its back. The carp was particularly fond of honey covered rice balls.

A supplicant would walk along the river until he reached the black rock where he pounded on a special stone left just for that purpose. The fish would swim to the surface and with an unblinking eye examine the seeker thoroughly. For simple questions the carp required a single rice ball and for very difficult and profound questions the number could increase to four. It was only after the fish passed its three hundredth year that it would even consider a five-rice-ball question. The old carp would eat the balls one at a time from the fingertips of the questioner and then dive deep into the water to retreat under its rock, digest the rice and think over the question.

It is said the carp told fortunes because a fisherman once befriended it. One afternoon when the fisherman drew in his net, it contained a single young carp. Just as he reached to pluck the young plump fish from his net it turned so quickly that head and tail became one. The fisherman was surprised and withdrew his hand. The image of a circular carp firmly implanted in his mind, he asked aloud, "What have I caught here?"

The fish answered,

"My root retreats around the beginning,
a hushed firefly on the path
touching thunder."

The fisherman immediately prostrated himself in the bottom of his boat and pleaded forgiveness for disturbing such a fish. He released the young carp quickly. Thereafter, on the first day of the new moon, the fisherman would row to the quiet spot by the rock, share delicacies with the fish and listen to its words, recording them in a small diary.

This diary, the only record of the carp's words, has been protected at a Shinto shrine since the death of the fisherman in 1261. It contains 503 entries with notations and comments, all written in the fisherman's spidery script.

∾ ∾ ∾ ∾

"When I was younger I could remember anything whether it happened or not," Derry said one day. The dogwoods were in bloom and the bees were busy.

"How can you remember something that didn't happened? It's either real or it isn't."

"Then what's that?" Derry pointed just above the horizon.

Noom turned and looked. "There's nothing there. I can't see a thing."

"I know you can't, child. Pretend. If you pretend that you can see it well enough, then maybe, just maybe you can catch a glimpse."

The boy stared hard. "What am I supposed to see?"

"There." Derry suddenly pointed again. "No, now it's gone. Oh, well maybe later. When I was a little girl my grandmother would tell me 'bout her grandmother. 'Sometimes if you look at somethin' real hard it'll just go away. When you can do that,' she told me, 'then you can go and visit my grandmother.' I tried and tried. I looked at different things every which way, till I was 'bout cross-eyed. But then one day after I came to this country, I was walkin' along the stream in the bottom of the holler where we lived watchin' out for the places where a special lily grows. And this dragonfly he starts to followin' me. Flappin' 'round and 'round in a circle. He was a shiny blue all over and he just kept goin' in smaller and smaller circles, flappin' faster and faster. Well, I got to watchin' as he was a-flappin' faster and faster until he was a-goin' in such a tiny circle that he was just standin' still flappin' real furious. He was a-buzzin' real loud and then that critter just completely went away and all of a sudden there was my grandmother's grandmother sweepin' the dirt path to her house. Just like that, no warnin' or nothing. So," Derry said, "keep your eye all sharp, because your grandmother could pop up just like that."

"But my grandmother is dead."

"Sure she is, and can you remember her? Can you remember her when you were little? Do you remember what she looked like and how she talked?"

"Well kind of."

Derry moved around behind the boy and took his head in her hands. "Then just put her there in the distance," Derry whispered behind his right ear. "Just down under that big dogwood tree. Can you see which side she's on?"

"Well I can see her, kind of."

"And I'll put my grandmother's grandmother there in the same place."

"We can do that?"

"Sure we can, child," she whispered. "As surely as the sun's goin' to rise."

"And what about Boondoggle's grandmother? Can he see her there too?" the boy asked.

"Boondoggle doesn't have no grandmother. He was found as an infant mule under a rock by some root diggers passin' through." She directed his attention back to the tree with her hands. "Can you see your granny now?"

"Yes. I'm just starting to." He could feel the gentle pressure of Derry's hands and just make out the faint image of his grandmother rocking back and forth in her rocking chair.

"Now make her come closer and closer until you can just about touch her."

"I can see the rocking chair."

"And now hear it squeakin'." Derry directed the boy's attention. "Now make her go farther away. Farther and larger as she goes. Back down to the tree."

Noom's head moved very slightly backward as he imagined his grandmother moving farther and farther away as she got bigger and bigger.

"Now, hold her there and I'll move my picture until they are at the same place and the same size. You keep watchin' and maybe our grannies will get to talkin'."

The skin behind Noom's ear began to prickle as he saw an image which seemed to slide back and forth through his picture. Suddenly he could see an old woman leaning on a broom talking to his grandmother. Under the dogwood tree they spoke in a language he couldn't understand. The other woman admired his grandmother's knitting. Then the image began to fade and Noom was left listening to the squeak as the old chair rocked slowly back and forth.

"How did you do that?" he wanted to know.

"I didn't, we did."

"What were they saying? I couldn't understand any of it.

"It sounded just like the old country."

"Could you understand what they were saying?"

"Oh, child," Derry told him, "they was just talkin' about their grandbabies."

"When I was in Australia I met people who use their eyes in amazing ways," Noom said. "Some aborigines could focus one eye independently of the other. When they were out hunting or just out, for that matter, they would begin scanning the landscape. Sometimes it was possible to see for fifty miles or more, so there was a great expanse of land to watch. They would quit talking and all you could hear were the whispers of their feet roving across the desert. Their eyes would slowly scan from side to side. They had a funny trance look to them. If someone spotted something in the distance which was of interest to him, one eye would focus on that object and the other eye continue scanning. If the object was of great interest then both eyes would focus on it and the rest of the landscape would be forgotten. If not, both eyes would continue scanning. It seemed a very efficient way to hunt or search for resources in a meager land."

Jay tried to imagine what it would be like to be dependent on a barren landscape for one's dinner. But all he could see was miles and miles of empty sand.

"There were many objects which might be an animal," Noom continued, "so one eye would linger and watch while the other eye continued searching. It was an eerie feeling walking silently with half-a-dozen aborigines, mile after mile. They would walk all afternoon without saying a thing. Silently gliding over the hot ground, each with each eye moving independently. An old woman's son tried to teach me how to do it. He would take me out to sit on the side of a hill so we could see far into the distance. 'You must not talk,' he would say. 'You must not speak aloud or talk in your head. Especially not talk here.' He would tap his temple. Then he would have me move my vision slowly from side to side. 'See all, see everything. All, sky, ground. Distant, close, everything. Let all come to you, no hurry, let it come to your eye. Some things take long time to get to your eye, wait for them. Then when something finds you, go to it with one eye. You go there in your head. One eye wait and other eye go. One eye here and other eye there,' he told me. It was a very odd sensation, for the few brief instants that I could do it, of being in two places at the same time. Then my eyes would begin to water from the strain and I'd lose my focus. 'Too much talk,' he'd say. 'Too much talk.' I never did get the hang of it. Those people thought that the ability was very important. They said you could go to something they call dreamtime with your eyes."

"Dreamtime?" Jay asked.

"Yes. Dreamtime, long ago time. It wasn't so much the past as a timeless time. Perhaps all time. 'Ride your eyes,' they would say, 'and go to dreamtime.'"

ΩΩΩΩ

At the north pole the sun moves in an orbit that loosely follows the horizon. But at the equator it cuts across the horizon twice daily, once in the morning and again in the evening. As a consequence of these motions there is little seasonal change at or near the equator and dramatic differences at the poles. At the north pole the sun will orbit above the horizon for half a year and below for the other half. During the time of the equinox, twice yearly, the sun will follow just along the horizon. It appears to be continually setting or rising, depending on one's particular inclination.

Ancient peoples who lived at the equator and the Arctic were both influenced by the sun and its passage but in different ways. Equatorial people perceived the sun as going up and down and Arctic people perceived it as going around. As a very subtle consequence, these perceptions organized their mental worlds differently. For equatorial people, things have tops and bottoms and for Arctic people things have sides.

When missionaries began teaching Arctic children the English language they were dismayed to find that the children rotated letters, top to bottom, at will. These children couldn't seem to understand that a 'T' or an 'A' had a strict and unvarying orientation top to bottom, so 'p's' were often confused with 'b's'. What the teachers didn't notice for a long while was that the children didn't rotate letters from side to side. So 'b's' were never confused with 'd's' because this would involve a rotation of sides. Also 'p's' weren't confused with 'd's' because this would involve a double rotation, top to bottom and side to side.

Equatorial children have the opposite problem. Much more often they rotated letters side to side. Arctic children were more sensitive to symmetries around a vertical axis and equatorial children more sensitive to symmetries around a horizontal axis.

People who live in trackless areas of the world, the Arctic and deserts, and depend on the land for a livelihood develop tremendous mental map-making abilities. Eskimos of old could draw from memory extremely detailed maps, covering hundreds of miles, that were more accurate than those compiled by the first European explorers. Furthermore, they could read a map however it was handed to them. Orientation made no difference.

For Europeans north has a definite meaning and they create and read their maps with this alignment in mind. For them the North Star lies in an unchanging and dependable direction. But for Eskimos the North Star lies in the general direction of up and so is of very little use in orienting maps or anything else for that matter.

Cultures that have depended on the ocean for food learn to visualize a medium through which they can look. They have the usual perspectives plus one which might be called an x-ray view. They often represent creatures or events as if they could see all the way through them.

Thus sea-hunting Eskimos of the far north are skilled in several novel ways of viewing the world. They can rotate mental images and become proficient at aerial and x-ray perspectives. Since they are most sensitive along the vertical axis they have great skills at imagining mirror images, because mirrors rotate only on one axis and not the other, rotating left and right but not up and down. Eskimos were unimpressed when they first encountered European mirrors. Amazement was left to equatorial people.

Of the capital letters in the English alphabet, nine letters are symmetrical on their horizontal axis and eleven letters are symmetrical on a vertical axis. Four letters remain symmetrical on both and the remaining ten are symmetrical on neither. This would seem to indicate a latitudinal average of all the origins of the English alphabet at nine-twentieths of the distance from the equator to the north pole, or 40.5 degrees. This places it on a line that passes just south of Homeworth, Nebraska, just north of the birthplace of Euclid and through the center of Wofosi, the temple of the sleeping Buddha on the outskirts of Peking. In Japan the line stretches across the headwaters of the Yoneshiro River and in the Southern Hemisphere a similar latitude cuts off the southern tips of Australia and the Andes. Hawkeen knowledge runs worldwide along these two hemispheric meridians.

When Jay was in high school he took a drafting class from a German cabinet maker, Heinrich Toller. The teacher was massive and gruff, mumbling and growling most of his sentences. He came from the tradition in which learning was achieved through repetition and concentration. When discipline was a problem in one of his classes he would take the offender next door into the wood shop and place his hand in a vise. He then begin his particular way of teaching. "You're not paying attention are you?" Heinrich would state. If the boy tried using excuses the vise tightened an eighth-turn. "Now, are you listening?" And Heinrich would continue, an eighth-turn at a time, because he knew that at some point the pain would clearly focus the boy's mind on his present situation: His hand firmly stuck in a vise that was controlled by a direct and powerful man. "You come to this class to learn. Yes? Not to throw spitballs. Yes?" The vise would tighten fraction by fraction until Heinrich received an affirmative answer. Through the doorway Jay watched boy's faces go white with fear. "Now that I have your attention," Heinrich would say, folding his arms across his chest, "I want you to listen very closely. Drafting is like a family. The big kids can take care of themselves, it's the little kids you have to worry about. Yes? And when you go back in class take care of all the little kids in your drawings. Yes? No more goof-off. Yes?" If Heinrich received affirmative answers he would leave the boy to extricate himself from the vise and re-enter the drafting class. It was Heinrich's way of demanding that his students pay attention to the details. He felt that mastery was in the details.

That year Jay learned to draw objects from different views. He learned to visualize in cross-section or three-dimensionally. He learned isometric and orthographic projection and other perspectives. Jay was a good student and always wondered where the time went when he sat down to draw. He would hurry into the class and get his drafting tools out, begin working and soon the bell would ring signaling the end of the hour.

Each drawing had to be completed to Heinrich's satisfaction before he let a student begin the next. Some students were still working on the second or third drawing at the end of the school year; Jay completed forty-one. Drafting was the first time he enjoyed precision and he was fascinated that Heinrich's thick hand could draw fine details with microscopic precision. When Jay was ready to have his drawing graded, Heinrich would hold the board with the drawing attached and examine and measure all the dimensions with a drafting ruler. Jay waited for any faint flicker of praise or recognition. But Heinrich would just make an arcane mark in his grade book and tell Jay to start the next drawing. Before the year was out Jay began to understand that the reward he sought was one that he could give himself and from then on his confidence grew. "You have to take care of the little kids," Heinrich told him, "the big kids can take care of themselves." Jay began to see the need for praise as his own little kid and started heeding his own judgment of his accomplishments.

The last week of school Heinrich took Jay into the wood-working shop and closed the door. "You know all I can teach you about is drafting. From now on it's up to you to figure out that drafting isn't really about making drawings of objects." Jay was puzzled.

"Yes?" Heinrich questioned.

Jay glanced at the vise and quickly nodded his head.

In the years that followed Jay never made another formal drawing. But something had changed in the way he thought about things, he had been able to see events and situations clearly. Perhaps he would again.

§§§§

That night in the cave Noom continued to expound on dreamtime. His memory of Australia and its people were an important part of his life. The richness of the experience always returned when he talked about it.

"Did you know that when you enter dreamtime you can relive your memories any way you want?" Noom asked.

"I can't enter dreamtime, I'm not an aborigine."

"Don't worry about that, from a certain point of view neither are they. Let me give you a brief idea of what I mean." Noom searched for an example to demonstrate his point. "Let's see. Can you remember learning to ride a bicycle?"

Jay nodded.

"Remember it now." He paused waiting for Jay to recall the memory, "Are you riding your bike or do you see yourself riding the bike?"

"What do you mean?"

"In your memory, do you remember being on the bike, feeling the handle bars in your hands, seeing through your own eyes? Or do you see little Jay in the distance riding his bike?"

"I remember it the first way, as it happened to me. I'm coasting down a long driveway."

"Okay. Now start again and float up out of yourself and watch the boy Jay as he coasts down the long driveway on his bike.

Noom waited as Jay stared across the cave remembering. "Could you see him?"

"Yes. I've never seen it that way before. It's very different." Jay paused, fascinated with the novelty of what he had just done. "I watched myself coast down the driveway and then crash."

"How far were you from yourself as you watched?"

"Oh, maybe ten feet. I was a little behind and kind of up in the air," Jay explained.

"Now, I want you to try it from a hundred feet away. Just watch Jay as he coasts down the long drive and crashes."

"Okay. I can see myself bumping along on my bike and then it goes into a rut and falls over."

"I want you to remember the event the first way, ride your bike and crash at the end."

Jay flinched. "It hurts. I remember the feeling of skinning the whole side of my leg."

"That's right. Two distinct ways of remembering exist. The first is remembering an event as it happened to you and the second is remembering it as you would watch it happening to you. Using the first way, you can feel what happens and with the second way you just see what happens to yourself, so let me call them attached remembering and detached remembering. Do you understand the difference?"

"With attached one feels and detached one looks from a distance."

"That's right. Now you have a choice as to how you would like to remember riding your bike down that long driveway and then crashing. Try both ways and see which you like the best."

Jay looked up toward the cave's ceiling and remembered the event first one way and then the other. Noom could tell which way he was remembering by Jay's slight shudder when he relived the pain of crashing.

"That's weird. Remembering it the attached way I get hurt and the detached way I don't."

"That's right," nodded Noom. "Let's see which way your brain likes remembering best. Do you remember learning to ride your bicycle?"

"Sure."

"Which way?"

"That's really weird." Jay stopped and his mouth hung open. "I just automatically saw myself riding down the driveway, detached."

"Your brain now knows that it has a choice and it picks the one it likes best. If remembering any event causes you pain or embarrassment or discomfort you can try detached remembering and see if you like it better. There are many little pains in our lives, and the normal operation of our brains accesses these memories. Each time we do, we feel the shadow of the original pain and don't know where the hurt comes from. If you practice the detached way of remembering your brain will begin automatically to change your memories so the information is still retained but not the pain. In one sense, there isn't a lot of difference between remembering and imagining. You can attach or detach while remembering or imagining."

"If it works for small pains, what about big ones?"

"Is this an imagined big hurt or a remembered big hurt?"

"It's something that happened to me and when I remember it I hurt a lot."

When Jay was sixteen there was a person whom he respected and admired very much. One Friday afternoon in August his mentor casually and unexpectedly unleashed a scathing criticism of his personal worth. At that moment something within him had broken and for fourteen years he had been unable to affect a repair. Every time he recalled the event he felt the pain again.

"Using detached remembering works for little hurts," Noom said, "but big hurts or fears require something extra. There are two steps, the first you already know, it's detached remembering. For a big fear or hurt you first remember the event in the detached way. Then, and this is the second part, you remember the event backward very rapidly in the attached way.

"How can you remember something backward?" Jay laughed.

"Easily. Have you ever seen a film being rewound or run backward?"

"Sure."

"It's a poor memory that only works forward. You can remember things backward as well as forward. You just start at the end of the memory and go back to the beginning. Now, this second part needs to be done very quickly. Say in a couple of seconds."

"Okay, let me see if I've got it. First, I remember the event as it happened but in a detached way; next, I feel the event backward rapidly in the attached way. Then what happens?"

"You said you have an event which caused a major pain or fear, so complete step one and then step two and find out what happens. The important part is to feel the event backward a few times until you can get it to run backward really fast, to where it goes zzzzzzzzzip backward."

While Jay restructured his painful memory Noom got up and took a short walk outside. He kept glancing at the night sky as if he expected the weather to change but the stars twinkled and the air was still. The completion of the ritual observance often set into motion certain natural events which Noom would need to monitor. So he kept a sharp eye on the weather to be forewarned of the wakening of powerful forces. When he returned he asked, "Well, how did it work?"

"It's strange. I can't say exactly."

"Do you still remember the event?"

"Yes, but I don't feel the same way about it."

"Does it scare you or cause you pain when you remember it now?"

"That's what's odd. It isn't traumatic any more." Jay slowly looked around as if he were searching for something lost.

"Do you like the way in which you respond to the memory now?"

193

"When I remember the event now ...." he paused. "That's very strange. It's all right. I've remembered it hundreds of times before and always the same bad feeling came, but now those feelings have vanished. I wouldn't have believed this could happen. I never thought I would get past that memory. It seemed like a large black canyon right in front of me. Too long to go around and too wide to cross. And now it's behind me," Jay brightened. "It really is."

"I want you to notice that the remembering is still there, all that has changed is the way you feel."

"What would happen if, when I remembered something else that is really bad, I did this same thing to it?"

"I don't know what would happen. You have the knowledge now, how you use it is up to you. My guess is your past would become far less painful. But some people need painful pasts to justify the way they act. Self-pity seems to require a painful past. The question is whether you can live without painful memories. Some people think that's all they have of value and are frightened of living without the pain. They think it gives them the grounds to be self-righteous and feel noble so they can express their bitterness. They have proof that the universe cheated them and they demand an accounting. The sad part is that the universe doesn't care, doesn't care at all. If you do decide to start changing some of your memories remember to make the nice ones even better."

"How do you do that?"

"Simple. Always remember your pleasant memories in a very attached way so you get the full benefit of the good feelings. For instance, remember when you were a kid eating a particularly delicious ice cream cone. Then flip back and forth between remembering actually eating it and watching yourself eat it. Which do you like better?"

"Eating, of course."

"Of course," Noom smiled. "Remember your triumphs and victories and the good times of sharing something special with someone, remember them all in an attached way. It makes your life richer."

"I've been thinking about all of this and I begin to wonder. What else can I do with my mind? Maybe a better question would be what can't I do with my mind? What are the limits?"

Noom stirred the fire. "Let me rephrase your question a little. What you can do in your mind and with your mind may be somewhat different. That's something the Hawkeen are very interested in, how your mind affects your body, how your mind affects the world around you. The answers to those questions can only be known by experimenting. However, what you can do in your mind follows a general and straightforward rule. You can do anything in your mind that you can imagine doing. If you can imagine it, you can do it, so in that sense you're limited only by your imagination. How a particular activity of mind affects your body or your world will need to be tested. I suppose I'm speaking of the difference between imagination and experience. In some ways they are quite similar and can be exchanged one for the other. In other ways they differ, which can lead to disaster when one is exchanged for the other." Noom was silent for some time as he watched the flames. Finally rousing himself from his thoughts he smiled. "It's a paradox."

"So if I can really imagine having a greater imagination, then are you saying what I can do in my mind is unlimited?" asked Jay.

"That's about it."

"Wait till I get back and tell some people about this."

Noom stirred the fire more and then started speaking in an old and quiet voice. "Son," he said looking at Jay, "you must remember what I just told you about testing in the world. You may think what you just heard is great news but many people don't. Knowing that you have unlimited freedom of mind may be very exciting to you, but to many it is the most terrifying news they could hear. To institutions and religions and governments, an unlimited mind is a dangerous thing. A lot of folks have much invested in their limits. Take a very hard look at education of any type and notice whether it is directed toward freeing your mind or installing some new set of limits. If you speak too loudly of freedom in an area of limits, the boundary police will soon come, and what they will do is not pretty. People fight and kill over limits not freedom. To be unlimited is to be peaceful. But tonight," the old man said suddenly, looking up, "you can think every crazy thought you can imagine because I won't tell, and if

195

it's crazy enough I may even join you. Dreamtime is a wonderful place to explore."

ππππ

"What this is really all about," said Frank, "is space. Space of mind. The shape of your mind-space determines what your world will be like. Try to bend your mind and shape it different ways. Use anything you can imagine, and find out how it works. Nothing exists out of mind, there is no inside or outside of mind. If you get really good at it, you may become wise enough to imagine a stick with only one end. What a sight that would be, a one-ended stick," Frank marvelled.

"I don't see how I could ever do that."

"Good point!" Frank said, brushing the chalk from his hair. "Practice!"

≈≈≈

Sixth moon, 1247.

Garden on my moon;
blind raven near the bramble
the summer echo has latched.

Chaos in my venom ....
Water flutters near the knot
an empty perfect wave.

Dust scrambles on hushed rivers
the orchard has fallen,
extinction over a myth.

The carp was talkative that day.

"Some folks get all messed up. It's like they got a big ball of snakes in their heads," Derry said. "Heaven sakes, child, a big ol' ball of black snakes or racers or somethin' all stuffed in there. And I go to see 'em and shoo those snakes off. I just tell 'em to git and point the way. And then them folks settle down and we can talk some. I find out about their funny notions, notions that stick in the minds like leeches. Then I pick 'em all off. Folks got these funny notions about always wantin' to be right. That's what them leeches stick to, notions. Causes folks to get all flustered and confused." She turned and gave Noom a stern look. "If you want to be right, you can be. That's no particular trick, but you'll miss the whole rest of the parade. Them notions will blind you so you can't see at all."

"What parade do you mean?"

"Oh, child," she laughed, clapping her hands together, "it's the longest parade there ever was. I'm in it and you're in it and even old Boondoggle's in it. Why, it'll take a lifetime to see just a part of it. Yessiree, a full lifetime isn't near enough, but it'll have to do. Now let's get on to thinkin' of some pie. What color do you think would be best?"

ᷳᷳᷳᷳᷳ
They came from a round hole in the sky (the Awb sang)
glowing like dark fire.
This, the Raven said, was a star.
Badly it came upon them, the downward thinking.
Then the Two Rock People spoke to them,
be impervious as we are
be solid in your trouble.
For today it did not happen that way.
It will point away, out from under your skin.
Today, now, all the dark fire will burn away.
In days to come you will carry unseen possessions in your hands.
All is well again, taste the sun.

The Structure of Delight

ΩΩΩΩ

It is said that long ago in the Himalayas there lived a master sculptor. She retired from the world to work on her creations alone in a cave that looked out on mountain peaks.

At first, the woman used stone and small pieces of firewood. But she was restless, searching for the perfect material. In her search she carved on a single strand of her own hair for over three years. The woman was seeking to shape pure essence, and in time her work made use of fewer and fewer tangible materials until finally they were dispensed with all together.

Then, tiny and cautious, she began whittling the empty air with the sharpened edges of butterfly wings which she kept in a small wooden rack beside the tea pot. These new creations pleased her. She polished them with the tip of her finger until they were beyond reflection. Until light passed unnoticed.

When finished, a sculpture would fit comfortably in her hand and had the strength to crush bone. Each was carried to a special location and left there to grow within its own light. Perhaps just below the sharp turn in the rocky path over the gorge or beside the red lichen boulder washed bright and clean by a sudden afternoon shower. Perhaps left at the center of a meadow where a cloud pattern lingered one day. Each a perfect thought.

Chapter Eight

§§§§§

When the sun rose on the seventh day, gray clouds threatened in the east. Overcast skies pressed heavily on the land as a gathering storm grew. The wind was restless, prowling and turbulent, rushing under the trees in short sprints and then rising high into the atmosphere. As the two men readied their gear outside the cave, Noom sniffed the air and eyed the horizon. Like the wind he was restless, the forces were beginning to stir. The turbulence had started during the night, and now they would have to hurry to reach his destination by mid-afternoon. When his sack was filled and buckled tightly, the old man pointed east, directly to the darkest part of the morning. "There's where we're going."

Jay squinted and looked far into the distance where dark clouds obscured the morning sun. "What's there?" Jay didn't like the thought of traveling when there was a storm brewing.

"We're on a plateau and out there," Noom pointed, "is the eastern edge. About ten miles from here we will reach a rim. That's where we're going."

"And what's there?" asked Jay still squinting to the east.

"At the rim the geology and plant life change abruptly. What lies beyond is a new and entirely different world." Noom examined the sky as wisps of dingy clouds passed over them, like geese fleeing before a storm. A much higher storm ceiling was forming and it concerned the old man. As he elbowed his way into his jacket Noom glanced at Jay, staring into his eyes. "Yes, entirely different. We need to move quickly now."

ΩΩΩΩ

When Jay was sixteen he spent the summer hoeing corn. The rows
were a quarter mile long and he hoed them two at a time, walking in the
furrow between them, hot in the sun. He and a cousin walked the long rows
side by side, hoeing in silence. A quarter-mile down and a quarter-mile
back, one half-mile for a complete circuit through the corn. Row by row
they worked across the field, only to begin at the beginning again with new
weeds to hoe. It took a week for them to hoe the entire field, just enough
time for new weeds to get a good foothold.

Young sunflowers, burdock and mullein greeted them every foot of the
way. Russian thistles, bull thistles and sow thistles defiantly sprouted in
their path. Lamb's quarter, milkweed, dandelion and last year's alfalfa were
all cut away so the corn could grow. Amaranthus retroflexus, the common
pigweed, died with the flick of the wrist.

Jay learned to hoe first with one arm and then with the other,
switching every ten minutes or so, letting the alternate shoulder rest. An
irrigation ditch ran along the head of the field and with each circuit the
boys drank ditch water and cooled their hands and feet. They sharpened
their hoes with a flat file, preparing for another half-mile of weeds. Jay's
hands would redden and swell under his leather gloves. Their tennis shoes
slowly filled with dust from the clods of red dirt while they labored through
the corn.

The field was forty acres, a quarter-mile square with 528 rows. Every
day they would make eleven circuits through the field. Five in the morning,
then a lunch of scrambled egg sandwiches and Kool-Aid beside the ditch
and then six more in the afternoon, finishing just at sundown. Five-and-a-
half miles of hoeing each day and thirty three miles for the six-day week.
Every Monday morning each boy was faced with thirty three miles of corn
to hoe and the next Monday it would be repeated and the Monday after that.
They started hoeing the first week of June and quit the first of August when
the corn plants reached the tops of their heads. Jay kept his mind occupied
during the long hours by calculating distances and amounts. He estimated
the number of weeds they hoed and learned to recite the alphabet
backwards. But what kept his mind engaged, when he ran out of things to

calculate or memorize, was imagining what lay under the ground.

Throughout the field the boys found the pot shards and artifacts of a civilization which lived on the land long before. They found worked and polished bone fragments and flint chips. These they stuffed in their pockets to save and examine at their leisure in the evening. The most exciting find was a stone axe that was displayed prominently in the center of their collection. Chipped and abraded from a slab of dark green basalt, it was their prize.

Jay became fascinated with the idea that the surface of the ground divided two distinct realities. One included his hot sweating labor and the other embraced what lay below the ground in the cool darkness of the long ago past. He imagined that his hoe continually cut into the surface of that other world. The metal hoe blade reached just below the ground where a magical people now resided. Once they had lived on the surface and probably hoed corn just as he did. But they were transformed by time and now inhabited the deeper region, below the ground. For a time Jay entertained a notion that in the cosmic scheme of things one must walk the ground and labor at the end of a hoe before one could be admitted into the magical realm.

And he began to think about the root systems of the corn plants, how half of each plant existed beyond his eyes, deep in the ground. One half grew into the sun and sky and the other half into the dark and damp. He began to visualize plants as two pyramids with their tips meeting at the ground surface. The upper pyramid inverted and resting on the lower one. He began to know that each plant needed both domains to grow and flourish. And indeed that is what their hoes were for, to separate the upper weed pyramid from the lower. When the weeds were cut just at the point where both worlds meet, both parts would die. Jay began to understand that the stem which connected the upper and lower was the critical point of life and growth, and if it was damaged both worlds would perish. And it was his job that summer to sever the stalks of a million weeds right where they were most vulnerable, right at the interface where root and leaf meet.

He imagined each corn plant growing as deep into the ground as it grew above. And as the corn stalks grew taller Jay imagined a whole field of

201

corn roots growing ever deeper, drawing nourishment from the lower world. For each broad green leaf shining in the sun there existed a powerful hidden root structure. It was the first time that he began to suspect that something lay beyond his immediate vision, a power which could only be seen with inner vision.

During the long summer Jay searched for a tie to that power. It seemed to him that no matter how hard he tried, the connection was kept small and slender, eaten away by an invisible cutworm.

That fall when he returned to school Jay had hoed 264 miles of corn and seen the field cut away at harvest. The corn plants had gone to the silo for fodder and the roots left slumbering through the winter to nourish the underground inhabitants.

ππππ

"You ever do much fishing?" Frank asked his student.

"No, I grew up in Nebraska."

"They don't have fish in Nebraska?"

"Not a whole lot."

Professor Sherman leaned back in his chair, relaxing. "Well, in my experience there seem to be two types of fishermen. Those who fish lakes and those who fish streams. I don't know why that is." He stopped for a moment to puzzle over the thought. "And there also seems to be a difference between those who like to fish with bait and those who fish with lures. And those who like to catch big fish and those who just like fishing. Or those who wade in the stream and those who fish from the bank. Come to think of it, fishing seems to be a varied endeavor." Frank's wandering eyes lingered, showing interest in the lower corner of his office as if a huge volume of water might suddenly come gushing into the small room creating a trout stream as it ran over the desk and out the door.

Noom glanced over his shoulder at the spot to make sure it was just his instructor's imagination. "I don't quite get your point," he said turning back.

"Well, I've always wondered why it is that you can go to the center of a lake but not a stream."

"You can go the the middle of a stream, you just wade or row out to the middle."

"Maybe," mused Frank, losing interest in his imaginary stream. "I know how to find the center of, say, Lake Michigan but how do you find the center of the Mississippi River. I've always wondered about that. I've had a theory for a long time that at the center of every river lives a whale of a fish and that fish personifies the entire river. I know that at the center of lakes no such fish exists because I've checked it out. But I've never been able to figure out how to find the center of a river. If my theory is true think what lives at the centers of the Amazon or the Nile." Frank glanced back at the corner. "Monster fishes."

Noom was momentarily distracted by the thought of drowning in a second story office in South Dakota, just one week before Christmas. "Well, couldn't you calculate the water flow along the river and find the average point?" he finally managed to say.

Frank waved his hand. "Nope. Calculus or any other math skill isn't of much use in this case. No, what I'm really hunting for isn't the geographical center or the hydrological center or any of those, but the center of what the river means."

"But a river doesn't mean anything."

"Oh, but it does. But only at its center," Frank's voice softened as he looked directly at his most promising student. "Engineering is of no help in finding the center of a river, but it's there just the same, right in the middle." He moved his hand close to his chest, gently tapping his shirt pocket with the chalk. "Right where that fish lives."

Second Moon, 1237

The living thunder expressed
one hushed moment
dust murmuring over his verse.

The Structure of Delight

Bone from your birthright
twilight touching.
A sparkling echo, the loud glimpse.

Under the twilight tide
our shape has stopped.
Willow rises through her stone.

This page of the diary is one of the few containing a drawing. It is believed to have been made by the fisherman. Short heavy pen strokes fill the entire page and partially cover one of the verses, line crowding word.

The drawing shows a turtle emerging from reeds along the bank of a river. The hexagons of its shell are clearly depicted, and the center of each hexagon is marked with a faint symbol. Monk scholars have referred to this page as the Mud Tortoise entry and doubt that the drawing depicts an actual event, since the Second Moon would have found all turtles hibernating in the river's mud. It has been suggested that the drawing is an unconscious rendering of the fisherman's service to the carp, as scribe and younger brother. The drawing remains a mystery, its purpose unknown.

However, closer examination reveals a distinct ink mark where the turtle's tail drags through the mud. The line cleverly depicts the hexagonal tiles of its back and then recedes far into the distance beyond the Mud Tortoise. This line marks the path the ancient reptile has taken, creates the tortoise itself and then continues to indicate its future path. Past, present and future all represented by a single line. As the turtle slowly makes its way from the river's sticky black mud and through the slender reeds its shell appears as an intricate geometrical knot constructed entirely from a single thread. The turtle is given flesh and substance through the weaving and intertwining of its own time-line. Spinning and knotting, the line achieves a luxurious cat's-cradle of depth and understanding. Given its great age and long experience, the turtle has attained a rich brocade of pattern. A pattern which will grow until the day when its time-line is pulled taut from each end, unravelling all the knots in micro-seconds. The tortoise pattern will vanish as in a magician's trick, leaving only the flash of a single lightning stroke where it once had been. Then the line spirit will begin again, spinning a new topology, anticipating with tiny nimble fingers, brilliant pattern and endless possibility. The purity of the straight tortoise time-line, weaver of its own destiny, will knit its substance once again.

So in the fisherman's drawing the princely Mud Tortoise remains, rugmaker of the universe, patiently threading the strands of its own experience into a profound tapestry of personal meaning.

§§§§§

After they had walked a little over a mile Noom stepped off the trail and parted some low bushes to expose a small spring. During the past few days Jay had learned not to be surprised at the old man's actions. He was beginning to grasp the fact that Noom seemed to have an intimate knowledge of the area and its resources. Without a word he unhitched his pack and removed his canteen. He cautiously set it to catch the small trickle and like Noom rested while it filled.

"I talked a lot of noticing differences because navigating through life is greatly aided by noticing differences. But you should understand there are two ways to do it. They differ greatly." Noom bent down and picked up a rock, handing it to Jay. "Now, let me explain it this way. Tell me how heavy the rock is."

"Well it's about medium heavy."

"What I'm speaking of is gauging differences. One way of gauging is to compare and the other way is to contrast. Now, you could compare it to this rock," Noom quickly picked up a slightly larger rock and handed it to Jay, "but when I use the word compare I mean to contrast. If you gauge the differences in weight of these two rocks by contrast you will notice that one is heavier and one is lighter. If you are really perceptive you might even come close to the percentage of difference. To contrast is to gauge the difference between it," Noom pointed to one of the rocks, "and it," pointing to the other. "In contrasting things are considered as parts and judgments are made without meanings. To compare is to gauge the difference between me and it, things are considered as wholes and a judgment is made about

205

meaning. Gauging by contrast can be duplicated by instruments. We use scales or rulers or voltmeters or any other instrument that we can devise to duplicate our own native abilities of contrasting. What I mean by comparison is the gauging of differences by feelings. Comparing involves value judgments and contrasting doesn't. So when someone says compare this and that you have to find out whether they want you to compare or to contrast. Comparison is a type of perception that depends on memory and imagination while contrasting doesn't. This point is subtle, but important. At some very basic level we can do both. I think that brain cells probably have two modes of operation, that each cell can engage in two distinct and quite different processes. Compare and contrast. Gauging differences by contrast is the basis of science and gauging differences by comparison is the basis of religion. In science the central question is the difference between it and it. In religion the question is the difference between it and me.

"Which is better?"

Noom glanced to see how the canteen was filling. "That depends on what you have in mind. Comparing and contrasting are both necessary in any activity; however, their ratios may vary. Comparing and contrasting combined in the optimal proportion creates enjoyment in everything you do. We might even say that delight is the indicator which lets you know when compare and contrast become properly balanced for any particular activity."

"So how do you tell when you're comparing and when you're contrasting?"

"It takes some practice, but here is a general guideline. If you have much emotional involvement you're comparing and if not, you're contrasting." Noom took one of the rocks from Jay's hand. "For instance, consider the questions: How heavy is this rock? and Is this rock too heavy? These two questions will separate the two types of gauging. In the first question we must ask contrasted with what? And with the second, we ask compared to what? Contrasting finds natural differences and comparison finds differences which ascribe meanings. Generally we use the words compare and contrast interchangeably, but be aware, they are very different." Noom tossed the stone up into the air and let it fall back into the palm of his hand. "Another general rule is, if a device, real or imaginary, can find the difference you're searching for, then you're contrasting; if a machine can't accomplish the task, then you're comparing. In ordinary thought we alternate very rapidly between the two." He handed the rock back to Jay. "For instance, if we were to place these two rocks on a balance-beam scale it would rapidly contrast the difference in weight. Then we might compare that difference to something else and give it meaning."

Jay sat with a stone in each outstretched hand waiting for Noom to continue, but the old man just stared at him. The silence continued until Jay's arms began to tire and he finally asked, "What do you want me to do with these rocks."

The old man slowly leaned closer. "I want you to find out the difference in between them."

~~~

Fifth Moon, 1221

My feeling this morning
Is from my root
What next?

The fisherman pondered long on these particular words of the mighty Yoneshiro Carp and found himself profoundly moved. Rowing against the current in his small wooden boat or patching nets, the verse would wander into his mind bringing any activity to a halt. He intended to write a long commentary on the verse and for over a year struggled to form the words correctly.

Finally one evening he sat down to begin. Spreading the diary out before him on the thin straw mat he lit a candle. Placing the reed pen beside his diary he vowed not to move until he knew why the verse affected him so and had written down the reason. But it was not to be. Throughout the night he strained to exhaustion and beyond until he was kept awake only by the continuing battle. Repeatedly he began anew struggling with the words as beads of sweat dripped from his face, each illuminated by the silent flickering of the single soft candle. Just when dawn reached his hut beside the river the fisherman read the lone haunting verse again. He suddenly knew he had nothing to add and seizing the pen in a quick hand wrote, 'Just so!' Leaving the diary open so the ink could dry, the weary fisherman was asleep before the sun rose and shone through his window.

§§§§§

Jay felt uneasy standing with a rock in each hand. "I don't understand what you mean by in between. There isn't anything in between these rocks but thin air."

Noom gently lifted the stones from Jay's outstretched hands. "Relax, son. There is something I want you to understand. It is at the same time both very simple and very difficult." He stared far into the distance watching the dark clouds as he organized his thoughts. "Meaning," he began slowly, "is what connects mind and body. The meaning which you or I or anyone else gives to an object or event is how we represent that object or event in our minds. Emotions are a response to what happens in our heads and they register themselves in our the bodies. The particular emotion or emotions which are registered are determined by meaning. I'm saying that meaning connects mind and body. When we believe the world is meaningless, then the connection between mind and body is weakened. And when the connection is weakened we begin to feel afraid. Humans have a great fear of feeling nothing. Change the meanings which you ascribe and it will change how you feel." Noom stopped watching the coming storm and turned to Jay. "The shamans and healers of this world attend to this connection, and one becomes a shaman only after mastering meaning. The first and only rule is to understand completely that meaning is arbitrary. After that the rest is just training. To change another person's meaning is to change his reality; this is the task of a shaman. To be able to change one's own meaning is the task of a Hawkeen. When the difficult becomes simple, all is obvious, and the Hawkeen operate only within the obvious."

"What do you mean the obvious? What may be obvious for you may not be to me."

"Of course. What I'm trying to tell you is that the Hawkeen will not attempt the difficult. They will first reduce the difficult to the obvious, and when that has been achieved the rest is automatic."

"You make it sound so simple. It might take a long time to really figure something out. To change it from being hard to being obvious. That might not be easy."

"Obviously," Noom said with a straight face. "Let's go." He pointed to the overflowing canteen. "You're full now."

The second year Noom was in Australia he fell while climbing down a shaft and broke his arm. The mine's dust and water coated the ladder rungs with a slick slimy mud and the young engineer in an unmindful moment fell far into the darkness.

At the infirmary Asha came to see him "Well," she said, "who are you?"

Noom could see that she didn't understand English very well. "No, you mean how are you," he corrected.

"No. I mean who are you? Not the same fellow I knew. Different fellow now." Asha smiled. "Who are you? Man with broken arm, man with good arm?"

When she left the infirmary Noom was annoyed, but that night he thought over what she had said. He thought about what was him and what wasn't him, what was part of him and what wasn't. During the dark of that night he decided something very important, and in the following days his arm mended quickly.

When he next saw her, Noom gave a big wave using his healing arm. Asha clapped her hands together, "So now you strong fellow man!" she said, her eyes brimming with delight. "I been worried that when you fall Chindi Man come quick into your mouth and eat all around inside."

"Chindi Man?" Noom asked, still holding his arm high in the air.

"He been like a ghost, that Chindi Man," she explained. "So I didn't know who you been, Chindi Man or that crazy American fellow who don't watch when he's been goin' down into the mine." The small deeply wrinkled woman stepped forward quickly and snatched the sleeve of Noom's upraised arm, pulling him close. She looked up into his face and with a serious whisper said, "Now you know. If ever Chindi Man been comin' around, you just tell 'em, 'shoo, shoo'."

And she made him promise, carefully repeating the words in her own tongue, "Tsa, tsa."

§§§§§

They walked most of the morning in silence, Noom ahead and Jay struggling to keep up. For the first two hours the old man followed the landscape, then he turned and began to cut across gully and ridge, one after the other. Each time they were walking up a slope Jay's pack seemed to get heavier, but the old man never varied his pace. He kept his eye on the sky and moved quickly, racing the weather. The unsettled air created a sense of urgency within him, and the old man pressed on mile after mile. Just when the faint disc of the sun could be seen in an opening through the clouds directly overhead they stopped suddenly and ate lunch.

As they rested, Jay asked, "You said something about mastering the obvious. I've been thinking about that, and it's starting to make sense to me. For the past few years I've been attempting to understand something that's seemed hopelessly scrambled. But when I stand back from it like I did last night, what's wrong with my life seems a little more obvious"

Noom reached into his sack, "Let me show you something." He rummaged around in the mysterious pockets and finally withdrew a ball made of canvas. It was very worn and the seams had been restitched many times. He handed it to Jay. As Jay moved it from hand to hand he found it was surprisingly soft and seemed to be filled with tiny pellets.

"What's inside?"

"They're seeds from a kind of pod tree in New Guinea." Noom smiled.

"And this is what you wanted to show me, an old ball filled with seeds from a pod tree?"

"Patience. That's only the surface," Noom explained, taking the ball back. "What I'm going to show you is how to use it. Stand up now."

The two men rose and Noom instructed Jay to stand with his feet spread the width of his shoulders.

"Hold your hands out flat in front of you as if you were supporting a tray." Noom corrected Jay's arms until his elbows were close to his sides and his forearms extended out in front of him parallel to the ground.

"Hold your palms up and just imagine supporting a tray in front of you. Noom placed the ball in Jay's right palm. "Now look at the horizon."

Jay stood looking straight out in front of him.

"Can you throw the ball to the other hand?"

Jay easily tossed the ball to his other hand. "That's not so hard, what's the point."

Noom chuckled at the young man's impatience. "Can you throw the ball back?"

"Sure," and he tossed the ball back to the hand it started from.

"Now slowly throw the ball from hand to hand about once a second or a little less. From hand to hand." Noom watched and then corrected the throwing. "You don't need to throw it so high, six inches to a foot is high enough, just up to the level of your chin. Settle down into a steady rhythm and you'll find that each throw takes a little more than a second."

When Jay was throwing the ball from hand to hand smoothly and steadily Noom said, "Now look up about thirty degrees." Noom waited until Jay completed a few tosses in the new position. "Now look up at a sixty degree angle." Again he waited until he was sure Jay was proceeding smoothly. "Now close your eyes." Noom watched, pleased with the young man's easy rhythm. "That's right," he whispered, "a nice steady rhythm, hand to hand."

On one of the tosses Jay missed the ball and began grabbing wildly for it. He finally got it back under control and stood a step or two away from where he started.

"Better to drop than to fumble. If you miss, just let it drop to the ground and then pick it up and start over. Dropping is part of what you're doing. Now begin again."

211

"It's like my right hand doesn't know what the left is doing." Jay laughed and started tossing the ball again. When the rhythm was established he began moving his eyes up from the horizon until they were finally closed. After a couple of dozen tosses he rocked very slightly backwards onto his heels and then corrected forward till he was standing straight again.

"That's right." Noom said quietly.

The movement was very slight, his head moved only an inch or so, but the old man was watching sharply. Just as Jay regained his balance he missed the ball and let it drop to the ground.

"You quit watching the ball in your mind just before it fell didn't you?"

Startled, Jay opened his eyes. "Well, yes, but how did you know?"

"You were watching the ball in your mind up to that point and then your mind wandered off to something else, didn't it?"

"Yes, as a matter of fact it did. Am I supposed to keep the ball in mind as I juggle?"

"On the contrary. You can let your mind think anything it wants, anywhere or anyway it wants. Or you can think nothing at all. Just juggle the ball evenly from hand to hand with your eyes closed. Try again now."

Jay started and when the rhythm was established, his body tilted slightly backward and recovered again as the ball moved smoothly from hand to hand. His facial muscles began to relax and his breathing deepened. After a while he missed the ball and let it drop to the ground.

"That's enough for now," Noom said as he picked the ball up and dusted it off. "You can practice more later. What was it like just at the end?"

"It was strangely relaxing."

Noom sat down and rolled the ball with his fingers feeling the seeds inside as he spoke. "Were you surprised?"

"As a matter of fact I was," Jay exclaimed. "I was surprised that I could do it at all and surprised that it seemed so comfortable, like I already knew how to do it somehow."

"This is probably the most beneficial technique I know for starting on the path as a Hawkeen." Noom smiled. "Very simple and very deep. I'm still finding things out forty years after I first learned it. If you want, make a ball like this and juggle it daily."

"How many times?"

"Work up to around a thousand."

"A thousand? Isn't that a lot?"

"You figure it out. A thousand tosses is fewer than you think. I've known people that go to ten or twenty thousand at a time, but a thousand seems about the right number."

"I don't think I'll ever get to a thousand. How do you get the hang of it?"

"Practice! For the Hawkeen, this type of juggling is participating in something they call hycation, the seeking of order in chaos. They use it for other things also. For instance, it is impossible to continue experiencing panic while juggling this way. So it's comforting to know that you have a way to end extreme anxiety immediately at any time you want. Returning chaos to order. When the voluntary becomes automatic you will begin to understand hycation. This practice connects one part of you with the other. In order to complete the exercise those two must be joined and function as a single unit. And when they do, both flourish. The cord which connects is strengthened and the two parts begin to support and enjoy each other."

Noom returned the ball to his sack and began telling a story. "There was a period in my life when I was a river pilot for a shipping company. It was my job to guide the boat safely down the river, making sure that the passengers and cargo arrived safely. It was an interesting job and I learned a lot from it. One thing I noticed was that there were different kinds of passengers, those who thought about the currents and rapids which we had already passed through and others that worried about the river downstream. They wanted to know what would be around the next bend. Their questions were very distracting at first. They diverted my attention from the task at hand. Unlike my passengers, my attention was on the river immediately ahead, the water and rocks that were approaching and how the boat was responding to the helm. It was important to feel the rhythm of the river and pick a short path ahead that would use the currents and ride the rapids. Choosing which side to pass an obstruction would have consequences farther down stream." Noom stopped to reflect. "It was one of

213

the most important summers that I ever spent."

"Why did you quit?"

"In a sense I didn't." Noom pondered. "I just became a river pilot on a much larger river, the Yukon of the soul you might say." He stopped and looked at Jay. "You know, there is a legend of a people who came to this continent long ago in small boats. And the legend has it that their boats were navigated by the blind."

"Blind navigators?"

"Exactly. There came a time in the history of these people that required them to make dramatic changes. And so a vision came to these people, a communal vision, a vision of a land far from their own. They were already something of a sea-faring people, but they rarely left the sight of land. They plied the warm coastal waters in small open boats. This migration to a new land would require them to be at sea for many months. So the problem arose as to who would lead them through unknown waters. They thought and prayed to find a solution until one night a blind woman among them spoke up. 'I have given it much thought,' she said, 'and now know that I am the one to lead you.' 'How can that be?' the sighted asked. 'There are two reasons,' the woman answered. 'One, I can see our destination as well as any of you, perhaps better.' The people thought this over and they had to agree. 'And second,' she said, 'this journey is larger than any we have attempted before. The others have involved using landmarks that can be seen with the eye. This journey is without landmarks that can be seen. It will use landmarks that can only be observed with mind, and for that I am best suited. The loss of my sight has allowed me to concentrate on the eddies and currents of a much larger world, and that knowledge will be needed for this journey. When I first lost my sight I also lost what was familiar around me, but in time I found new landmarks, landmarks in a world where I can never become lost. Each of you, when you leave the safety of the shoreline, will become disoriented because you will lose what is familiar. And the fog will obscure your vision. But my vision has seen through the fog. I know exactly where I am at all times.' The people discussed this at great length, but they knew that she was right, and in time they set out in confidence with the Blind Navigator leading them. The woman rode in the lead boat blindfolded with cloth to protect her pale eyes from the salt spray. From time to time the tiller-man would call out for directions and she would answer, setting a steady course. True to her prediction the woman led them unerringly to their destination."

"So how did she do it?" Jay asked.

"After she lost her sight the woman learned of a compass which was unswerving in its accuracy. A compass which can't be drawn off course here or there, but one that remains steady and true. She could see space itself and so was never lost."

"Space itself? I can't imagine what that would look like. Are you really serious?"

Noom let his eyes defocus while he peered straight at Jay. "It is said to be as clear as you can possibly imagine."

"But you look through space, you can't see space."

"Well, that's one way of looking at it. If you think of space as having certain properties, you can begin to experience them, and one of the ways is with an inner vision. If you can think of space as being thicker or thinner then it can bend and flow. Objects are the things which determine the density of space. So when you look, look between objects and begin to sense how space is modified by them. Around large objects space becomes thinner and more uneven. Smooth, fat space is empty space. Most people look at the objects in space, but try sensing the space around and between objects.

"How do you tell the difference?"

Noom returned his focus to Jay's face. "You look. You look and see."

"Well, what I mean is how exactly do the objects change space?"

Noom scratched his whiskers. "Space is modified by rules so subtle that they cannot be expressed, only experienced. Space can change the color of light and the color of light can change the character of space. In a certain light space becomes very clear and sparkles."

The Structure of Delight

Third Moon, 1253

A shadow hidden under her skin
touched moments repeat.
Intricate illusion.

A wandering river;
expanding under dry willows
The shade escaped.

ΔΔΔΔΔ

On occasion we have an idea that is so clear and simple and elegant that we become astonished, as if a rare and precious meteor fragment just landed at our feet. We pick it up and examine it closely. And we ask ourselves, where could this have come from. Looking back to the blue sky we marvel. But we can never figure out what to do with the idea. Some meteors become doorstops or paperweights. The same is true for these special thoughts. We marvel at their novelty for a while and then tend to forget them. But ideas, like a seed crystal, need to be nurtured so they can grow and influence us. An idea with beautiful symmetry must be planted deep in the mind with long and considerate reflection. Then it can be the seed crystal of thought that will grow, reflecting it internal beauty and geometry.

§§§§§

"Did you ever see space clearly?" Jay asked

"Yes, I did as a matter of fact," Noom laughed. "Right after I left Homeworth I awoke one morning from a dream in which I'd come to the startling discovery that I could wear socks of different colors."

"What do you mean different colors?"

"I understood with a frightening clarity that I could wear socks which didn't match."

"And that was what you saw?" laughed Jay, "that you could wear mismatched socks?"

"Don't laugh. I'm still discovering the difference that idea made in my life. Later I found out that I could go without socks altogether."

ππππ

"Son, lines can locate position or define space," Frank said, pointing to the upper corner of his office. "A grid may be a collection of points or a collection of cells depending on whether the lines are used for intersections or boundaries. Defining intersections is very different from defining boundaries, as a river is different from a lake. Intersection is the birthplace of surprise and is necessary before bounding begins. Some people seek the essence of a river at its headwaters and others at its mouth. But the center lies somewhere in between, in the body of the river. Somewhere between the head and the toes. They remain difficult to find, these centers, but I've always thought that if you could find one you could live there forever. Live on that river forever, always knowing where you were in relation to its center." Frank brushed the chalk dust from the front of his shirt. "You're a good student and will make a good engineer. This school has taught you engineering and mining engineering in particular. But there is a whole section of knowledge that isn't taught here and isn't taught anywhere that I know of. It is something that you'll have to learn on your own, or all of the teaching and training that you have received at this institution will be of little or no use. Don't even try to use it. You will try to use your clever engineering mind to try to solve certain problems in your life, problems that by their very nature aren't amenable to engineering solutions. All things have centers and these centers have knowable meanings which are recognized by your own center. You can know the meaning of anything by checking your own center. Rivers are a natural place to hunt for surprises, as they journey far to drink of flowing water. Some surprises are large and slow moving. When at the river they drink deeply. Others are swift, traveling with the speed of mind. They travel along rivers seeking their own centers."

217

"A surprise has a center?"

"Sure it does. At the center of a surprise is the source of delight." Frank stared unblinking through his wire frame glasses. "Now what's this about no fish in Nebraska?"

§§§§§

During the time they had spent together Jay noticed that Noom's moods were even and stable. This was the longest time he had been alone with just one other human companion and he noticed that contrasted to the old man's his moods were wild and erratic. So he asked, "Noom, how come you never get angry?"

"Who says I don't?"

"Well, since I met you, you haven't."

Noom waited before answering Jay's question until he had the young man's full attention. "Jay, moods can be managed."

"But my moods just seem to come and go," Jay complained.

"You make them sound like the weather."

"Well, sort of, I suppose."

"You're not going to start claiming that your brain is a robot again, are you? Remember when we spoke of primary and secondary feelings?"

"Yes."

"Well your moods are secondary feelings, they're a response to the way you think."

"How can that be?"

"When you remember something as attached or detached does that change your mood?"

Jay tried it for a moment. "Well, yes. I suppose it does."

"That's an example of changing the way you think. You thought the same thing but in two different ways, and so the result is two different moods. We can have primary and secondary feelings because we have two different nervous systems, voluntary and involuntary. What we think seems to run the voluntary system, and how we think seems to run the involuntary. When you consider the entire process it becomes an interesting problem of how to combine two messages in such a way that they don't interfere with each other. Contained in each of our thoughts is coded information that lets our bodies know which mood to feel when we think that particular thought. This gives the thought meaning."

"I'm not sure I understand. Explain some more."

"To make it simple: Imagine the single word 'elephants' printed on a page. Now it could be printed in many different type faces or colors of ink. And none of that would change the content of the printed word 'elephants'. The letters remain in the same order in relation to each other, but we can print it at different places on the page or upside down. So we might say that the letters themselves make up the content code and the way in which the letters are printed make up the mood code. Printing the word elephant must involve some type face and some color, for without them we have no word. Thoughts are the same way. Every thought is the combination of a content code and a mood code. The mood code can be changed just as easily as specifying another type face and color of ink for the word 'elephant'. Whether you remember something in an attached or detached way radically alters your mood code. As a result the mood associated with the memory is changed. Pleasant memories are coded one way and unpleasant memories another. Mood coding can be changed and therefore meaning can be changed. That's why I keep telling you that the world itself has no meaning, it all depends on your coding. There exist general coding systems that are pretty much the same from person to person. That's one of the reasons that we can understand each other, but each person tends to have his own variations. A black mood may mean different things to different people. Your moods seem to come and go because you never knew there was a mood code, and the one you learned as a child has become automatic. So the source of a feeling or mood is not from the outside world but from the inner. When a hungry lion jumps out in front of us we don't react to the lion, but to the code in which the lion was perceived when we first recognized it. Granted all this happens so very quickly that we naturally assume we're responding to the lion. But a lion hunter will respond to the sight of a lion in a much different way than you or I might. The lion hunter will code the perceived lion in another way and may feel lucky that he now has a lion in his gun sights. Every thought includes both a mood and content code. People who respond to their content code more than their mood code have simply developed a fairly consistent mood code. Everything affects them about the same because every mood is coded about the same. You can change your own mood code for any thought you think. So you see that's why I speak of changing how you think in order to change how you feel. Our opinions and judgments of ourselves and the world are all included in the mood code. They remain a part of meaning."

"What about the times that I don't have much feeling about something, one way or the other? Does that have a mood code?"

"Sure, every thought is coded for mood. The case you're speaking of is coded fairly neutrally so your response is fairly neutral. Do you know the difference between excitement and anxiety?"

Jay needed to pause for a moment to understand Noom's sudden turn of thought. He remembered times when he felt excited and then times when he was afraid. "I'm not sure, they seem pretty close to together."

"They are very similar. One way to think of them is to think of the two halves of the water in your canteen. Thinking of the half that isn't here brings a feeling of anxiety and thinking of the half that is here creates a sense of excitement. Anticipating loss creates anxiety and anticipating gain creates excitement. The feelings are similar in that they both involve anticipation. They both include the future. If you wish to influence your body, your feelings or your health you need to pay attention to how you mood code your thoughts. This is what determines how your body responds. If you feel down, imagine what kind of coding would make you feel up. If you can't imagine it, then remember a time when you were up and notice the mood coding of your thoughts. It's no accident that people speak of feeling gloomy. If you could see the pictures in their heads the thoughts would actually look bleak. When people speak of a rosy future you can have some idea what their mental pictures actually look like."

"I'm not sure I believe all this."

"It's not important whether you believe it or not. What's important is that you now know it. You can keep the mood coding that you have now if you want. But it makes it more difficult to complain of your moods once you know how they are coded."

"You're making it sound like the world's just made up in our heads."

"It is. But that's a big jump. I won't argue over reality because I think such an argument is pointless. However, the one thing I am pretty insistent on is what we might call the flavor of reality. It's my contention that what we're calling the flavor of reality, its character, so to speak, is entirely arbitrary. It is something of a paradox that to comprehend reality it must have some flavor. Your life can be sour or it can be sweet, it's up to you. What I'm really saying is your experience of life can be sour or sweet, that your taste of life can change from moment to moment. So when I speak of not complaining I mean that a person who has stopped complaining is one who has discovered ways to change the flavor of his or her experience. The idea that all reality is arbitrary is pretty advanced. An intermediate stepping stone is the idea that reality is flavorful and you can choose the flavor which suits your taste. Beyond that, I think we actually do choose the one that suits our taste. Complaining is an indication that we really do prefer sour. From what point of view would your life appear sweet?"

"Well, I suppose I could come up with one."

"When you do, compare it with your sour point of view."

"But changing my point of view doesn't really change anything."

"It doesn't?"

"No, it doesn't. Picking a different point of view doesn't really change how the world is."

"And how is it really?"

Jay was at a loss for words. So Noom continued. "The world takes on the flavor of the point of view we use. If you want a sour world, look at it one way, if you want a sweet world look at it another way. You want a vanilla world, look at in a vanilla way. People and institutions have set themselves up in the business of discovering the way the world really is. Once they think they know, they'll tell you and expect you to agree. But the whole business is pointless because the character of the world is created during perception, so there never is a right answer. The idea that getting the right answer entitles you to go to heaven is nonsense. You get to live in any world which you think is right, and that makes the option of being wrong

221

immensely valuable. Complaining centers on the idea that the world doesn't provide the things I need, that it is somehow deficient. It doesn't make me feel the way I want to. It's a shabby world which doesn't give me what I want, and I'm going to complain about it loudly to everyone around me and let them know that I understand just how shoddy this world is. It has failed me and I deserve better." Noom paused to give Jay time to weigh his words. "Son, to complain is to demonstrate your inflexibility."

Throughout the morning's march Jay had been drinking from his canteen. At the end of lunch he held it up. "I can't believe it, it's half gone."

"And what of the half you still have?"

Jay blinked. "It's still here."

"That's right, it is here."

"Which half are you going to drink from?"

Jay was puzzled.

"Are you going to drink from the half that's gone or the half that's here?"

"The half that's here. How can I drink from the part that's gone?" Jay asked.

"That's what I was wondering. When you think of the half that's gone how do you feel?"

"I don't know, maybe a sense of loss. It certainly doesn't make me very happy."

"And how do you feel when you think of the half that's here?"

"I guess I'm glad I still have it."

"Were you going to think of the half that's gone while you drank from your canteen?"

"I don't know."

"Well, have a swig and find out."

Jay raised the canteen to his lips and then stopped.

"Makes it hard to enjoy either half doesn't it." Noom smiled. "You can measure the amount of water by thinking of how much is gone or by thinking of how much you have. Or you can measure your life the same way. Measure in a way that creates pain or in a way that creates delight."

"So you're going to tell me that it's my choice?" Jay's fingers began to drum silently.

"No, I wasn't, because you tend to measure by what's missing."

"Why do you say that?" Jay stammered.

"Remember back at the river you told me that you were hunting for something, something that was missing. If you imagine the missing part as wonderful, then every time you compare it with your own life you feel empty. Others might have a choice but I doubt that you do. Two automatic strikes every time you swing, doesn't make you want to go to bat much."

"So what do you want me to do?"

Noom grinned. "Well, you could pour the rest of the water out on the ground, then both halves would be gone and you could really feel miserable. It's going to be a long afternoon."

"I don't have to, I've got plenty of water right here," Jay said, angrily shaking the canteen. "I have it right here."

"You're right, have a drink and let's get going."

Noom rose, shouldered his sack and began walking.

Jay felt awkward holding the canteen in his outstretched hand. Drawing it close to him he listened to the water inside as he slowly shook the container from side to side. He took a long drink and tasted the warm slightly metallic water. His water.

"Why are you so hardnosed about everything?" Jay complained when he caught up with Noom.

Noom stopped and stared at the young man for several long moments. "Do you find softnosed people more attractive?"

ΔΔΔΔΔ

During the afternoon Jay lagged behind as the old man determinedly pushed ahead. Noom's slightly bowed legs steadily propelled him as if the ground itself pulled him forward. At one point Noom stepped to Jay's side and offered some advice. "Something that helps me walk is to breathe in for a certain number of steps and breathe out for a certain number of steps. Each number may be adjusted for the terrain or how tired you are or any other reason. The important factor is that one number must be odd and the other even. One odd, one even. For instance, three steps to inhale and four steps to exhale. I seem to like the greater number for exhaling but you can try it and see what you like. Two-three or three-two or three-six or any number combination that seems smooth for you, just as long as one's odd and one's even. One for inhaling and one for exhaling."

Jay began walking with a silent count. At first he had trouble keeping the count in his mind, but very quickly he noticed his pack was feeling lighter and his gait smoother. It was a strange sensation, being part of a rhythm that repeated itself in an unexpected way. A way that he couldn't quite put his finger on. Even though Jay found it odd, part of his mind relaxed and he continued the journey almost as a passenger.

ΩΩΩΩ

Raymond Begay was had been a graduate of the Rough Rock Community College for less than a year when the letter arrived. He had majored in range management and was currently unemployed. A good student, he had written an outstanding paper on the infestation of snakeweed throughout the reservation. But range management jobs were scarce so Ray lived with his grandfather, helping with the sheep. He hadn't wanted to work at any of the coal mines or the lumber mill. He was happier out alone with the sheep and his plant friends. Then one day the letter came in a fancy envelope.

It invited him to participate in a two-week event which was to take place in September on the edge of the Mojave Desert. Ray had trouble understanding what the letter was getting at. It seemed to be aimed at something called 'Experiments in the Radical Synthesis of Earth Forms and Processes', a subject the Cea Foundation seemed very interested in. Ray read through the release forms and material requisitions. And the forms for the film rights. He ran his finger over the heavily embossed stationary and decided to go. Grandfather would be able to handle the sheep for a couple of weeks in the fall, and Ray was bored anyway. He wrote 'Yes' across all the forms and sent them back. He didn't quite see how range management fit into a radical synthesis, but Ray had learned that there was a lot he didn't understand and so put it out of his mind.

What the Cea Foundation didn't know is that they had the wrong Begay. The communications between the Rough Rock Community College art department and New York weren't very good. The Foundation wanted an unknown Native American artist to give the whole affair some validity, and besides it would look good in the film.

Three months later Raymond patched the spare tire on his old pickup and set out for Needles, California with a shovel and a gunny sack full of snake weed.

When he arrived he found a small settlement of silver trailers housing the crew and participants. He was assigned his and told to proceed as he wished, so he slept in the front seat of his truck.

During the day Raymond hung out and listened. He wandered from project site to project site and watched. In the evenings when everyone joined in a circle around a large fire Ray paid attention and learned very fast. He picked up two words that he used whenever any one asked him a question. Valid and synthesis.

"So, Begay, when are you going to get started on your piece?" they would ask.

"Well, I've been wondering whether this synthesis is valid," Ray said looking into the distance. This seemed to satisfy everyone and they would become quiet for a moment, not wanting to interrupt an Indian's thoughts. But Ray was still puzzled. He didn't have the faintest idea what these people were doing here. So he continued to listen and look inscrutable.

He heard endless talk about art. Art this and art that. What art was and what art wasn't. One timid member of the group finally said something about beauty one evening and was quickly laughed down. The word caught Raymond's ear. Finally here was something he knew of and in his excitement he asked a foolish question.

"Does art have anything to do with beauty?" he asked. He really wanted to know, but the group thought he was asking a philosophical question and fell silent. They were somewhat intimidated by the question and wondered if finally the quiet and smoky eyed Native American had spoken from the wisdom of his ancestors. Ray just wanted to know what in

225

the hell was going on.

While other members of the group were setting up lasers and acrylic reflectors, digging pits for solar furnaces and mounting interferometers on thirty-foot towers, Ray examined the plant life in the valley. He pitched in, helped on one of the projects that seemed to have as its goal reflecting early morning sun light onto a certain rock. Its creator, a big fat man with a beard and a torn tee shirt, ran around the site bellowing. When Ray asked about the purpose of the installation the man answered, "Hey, Begay, I thought you redskins knew about earth magic."

Now Ray had two words he understood, beauty and magic. These two would be enough. In Ray's mind the two concepts joined into a single Navaho word, 'hozro'. It meant being in harmony with one's environment, at peace with one's circumstances, content with the day, devoid of anger and free from anxieties. That night he dreamed what his art project would be.

On the morning of the last day Raymond Begay selected his site, one that gave him a clear view of the western horizon. With his shovel he meticulously cleared and leveled a six-foot circle, transplanting any plants that needed to be moved outside the circle. When the ground was smooth and covered with clean packed sand he retrieved the sack from his truck and placed the dried snakeweed around the perimeter to form a boundary. By noon he was ready to begin. Facing north, he placed himself at the very center of the cleared circle and began to chant in a barely audible voice. Occasionally Ray would lean forward and with the tip of his finger make marks in the sand, marks which grew into a design as he chanted. First north, then east and south he prayed and drew until finally just before sundown he was facing west surrounded by a sand design whose only opening pointed directly to the spot where the late afternoon sun would touch the horizon. In that opening lay a single white bone. Ray now sat and waited cross-legged with his eyes closed, deep within himself.

The filming crew was busy this last day recording the construction and operation of the different projects. They decided to wait until Ray was finished and then have him explain what he was doing before the cameras.

Just as the sun touched the western rim of the world Ray slowly raised his head and in a quick exhalation shouted a single word which echoed throughout the small canyon. The entire Cea Foundation project stopped in its tracks and watched as the sun began to darken. Slowly at first and then more quickly it began to glow a emerald green. Streamers shot out, coloring the sunset and the clouds danced. By the time the green disc dropped over the edge of the world Ray's work of art was finished. Only then did the camera crew leap into action, but by then it was too late. The moment passed.

A dry autumn moon running behind broken clouds guided him safely homeward. By midnight Raymond Begay was safely back across the Colorado River, gassing up his truck in Kingman, Arizona.

《《《《《

From another time
beyond the great bitter river, they travelled.
Wrapped in a holy mist, The Searching People
followed an outstretched finger
watching with quiet hearts
until the first glimmer of tomorrow came upon them
just before they arrived.
Such a place!
Stone Man Mountain blinked his eye,
and Fire Rock awoke.

Chapter Nine

~~~

Eleventh moon, 1257

Over one mountain
a thunder repeats,
single cloud far from the rain.

Near my spidery evening,
and before the moment.
This old path meets a stranger.

While dry water sleeps, gate beyond the gate.
This spring young stranger,
his summer long stone around our lingering dust
when splendid echoes descend.

§§§§

In the middle of the afternoon the two men arrived at their destination, a sandstone ledge several hundred feet above the desert floor. The mesa across which they had traveled ended suddenly and from its edge they could see far to the north.

"This is the place," Noom said, "where the world changes."

Beyond the ledge the land fell away down the steep hillside to a plain engraved with a series of small arroyos. The land was empty except for one small cone-shaped hill about a quarter of a mile beyond them. The cone was a bleached yellowish color, bare except for few stunted piñon trees.

The old man placed his sack against a tree and sat down using it as a backrest. He watched the darkening sky and rubbed his knees. The storm that had been brewing since morning was slowly gathering its full strength. On the plain small dust devils sprang up and ran across the ground for a few moments before they unwound and scattered.

Sitting beside the old man, Jay watched them whirl and run their course. But his mind was elsewhere. "I've been wondering, what does one need to do to join the Hawkeen?" he asked.

Noom took his time before beginning to speak. "The original concern which gave rise to the Hawkeen was the desire to understand how fear operated. A long time ago unknown individuals sought to find the origin of fear in order to free themselves of it. At the time it was thought that fear was an external event, that it came from the outside, that it was something which happened outside of one's being. They discovered that fear was closely related to perception, so they became interested in the mechanics of perception. During their investigations they found that fear was an internal event and was therefore arbitrary, and this notion became the basis for the Hawkeen. Investigations by the Hawkeen, then and now, are intensely personal. They asked of themselves, 'What can I control?' and found they couldn't control or change the past. The Hawkeen aren't much interested in the past because it can't be changed."

"Then should I forget my past?" asked Jay.

"No, keep your past. Besides forgetting a past requires a lot of effort, as a matter of fact forgetting anything takes effort."

"What do you mean forgetting takes effort?"

"Well, sometime you might give it a try. What would you have to do to guarantee that there is no possibility of ever remembering again some specific bit of information? Once you know something, basically it's yours for life. Knowledge is easy to gain, hard to get rid of." Noom paused, returning to the thread of his discourse. "The original Hawkeen did discover, however, that they had direct control over how their pasts affected them. And to implement this control they developed astonishing body awareness. Some of them became so aware that they could monitor their own metabolism. They found that even though they might have little control over an original experience they possessed a great deal of control over the structure of its memory. And this is where they applied their energy, changing the emotional structure of any fear-causing memory. From that first interest in fear the Hawkeen spread that concern to all facets of the operation of mind. It's something which still continues today and I suppose will continue. The Hawkeen believe in self-determination, and they enjoy creating their own fates. They value competency, not falling prey to every passing trend. They value integrity. They are peaceful and appear magical without being magical. They know that the one thing which is absolutely controllable is the inner life, the very inner core, the foundation of self. They continue to study and experiment. They're teachers, they give freely of themselves." Noom paused, turning to Jay. "Now, let me go back to your original question. I don't know if you'll understand this, but the only requirement to joining the Hawkeen is to become proficient at minding your own business."

Jay was silent as he studied his shoes. "When can somebody do that?"

"Whenever that person is prepared to supervise his own instruction."

ππππ

Professor Sherman removed his glasses. Holding them toward the light, he tried to determine whether the glasses needed cleaning or whether his mind was a little cloudy.

Noom gazed out the office window admiring the campus in its late spring foliage, knowing he would miss these talks with Dr. Sherman after graduation. The past four years had had a profound impact on his life, and he felt a sudden pang of sadness, knowing that the weekly visits with his teacher were about to end.

Frank lowered his hands into his lap, holding his glasses delicately with the thumb and forefinger of each hand. "Son, the whole trick is to handle one's environment skillfully." His roaming eyes stopped and focused clearly on Noom. Noom knew better than to ask what Frank was talking about so he waited.

"I'm talking about reality. We can handle any situation or let the world do it. On a large scale it doesn't really matter very much. Either way everything gets resolved. Whether it takes just a second or an entire ice age,

231

everything will be resolved in time. Every hope and dream, every illness or difficulty. They all will be resolved."

Noom was feeling cocky. "If what you say is true then why do anything?"

"Good point," said Frank glancing down at his glasses. "The only reason that I know of to get involved with the world is that you might want to pick the time and type of resolution. If you let the universe decide your life, it will pick a time and circumstance that fits its needs, not yours. Keep in mind that everything gets resolved sooner or later. Maturity is when you stop complaining over the way things get resolved. You either accept a situation or change it. Control yourself or control your environment, accept or change. These are the only two options. The universe in all of its complexity fits between the verbs 'to be' and 'to do'." Frank held his hands out, palms facing one another. "These are the constraints, and life as we know it takes place between those two verbs," he said nodding toward the space between his hands. He glanced at his student. "Hold your hands out."

Noom positioned his hands like his teacher's.

"Now, look carefully at the space between them, because that is where your life will be formed. The proportion of being to doing that you choose will determine your life's character."

Noom sat staring at the space between his hands. It seemed insignificant but then he let his eyes relax and his focus drift far into the distance. For a brief instant he had the direct impression that he was seeing micro-worlds spinning into formation and then dissolving again.

"That's right," said Frank very quietly. He waited as his student watched the dance of possibility between his own hands, then speaking very slowly and meticulously he continued. "The intersection of imagination and reality is the source of all personal power. An idea or wish only becomes powerful when it intersects with reality." Frank's index fingers began to turn toward one another. Gently they probed the gap between his hands until they met just at their tips. "People are impoverished no because they lack imagination, they remain impoverished because the lack intersection."

Noom stormed into the house one afternoon after a confrontation with Boondoggle. When the screen door slammed, Derry looked up from her needlepoint to see what the ruckus was.

"That mule is just plain rebellious."

"Oh, no, child. Boondoggle is a different kind of a mule entirely."

Noom found a slice of pie in the pie safe and brought it to the table to eat. He began to eat and the old woman folded up her needlework, putting it away in her work basket. "You see there are rebellin' types of mules and then there are revoltin' kinds of mules."

"Well, he's ornery."

"Oh, no. That's where you're wrong 'bout Boondoggle. Now most of your mules are rebellin' types, but that's where ol' Boondoggle is different. Rebellin' is not doin' something that somebody wants you to do. That's when you're just an ornery cuss, not doin' what somebody wants just to spite 'em."

"Well, that's what he's doing," Noom complained between bites of pie.

"No, I think you've got it wrong. You see, when you don't do what somebody wants you to do, that's rebellin'. But if you do what you want to do then that's revoltin', and Boondoggle is a revoltin' kind of mule. He don't care so much what you think is right as he does about what he thinks is right. Rebellin' is when you want to hurt somebody and revoltin' is when you want to help yourself. So in a funny way rebellin' is when you say 'no' and revoltin' is when you say 'yes'. Rebellin' is when you fail at revoltin'. Mules are famous critters for rebellin', but Boondoggle is famous because he's a choice-makin' mule."

"Well, I don't like him very much."

"Oh, child. He always gets the upper hand because you're always rebellin' with him. Start revoltin' just like him and you'll get alone fine."

Long after Noom left Missouri he remembered the choice-makin' mule with considerable fondness. For it was Boondoggle who taught him the subtle but life shaping difference between rebellion and revolution. Taught him that rebellion kept one bound in conflict and revolution freed one of it.

ΔΔΔΔΔ

Navigation is the art of finding one's position or course. It is the province of the Rainbow People and whoever practices it walks among them.

The skill of navigation is only necessary for those who intend to travel into charted regions or to return from uncharted ones. If one wishes to explore uncharted territories and has no desire to return, navigation is of no use. Those who have no interest in where they have been or where they're going may wander and explore free from the burden of constant navigational observation. There may be some who choose such a path; however, those who have taken it are seldom heard from again. It is unknown what lies in uncharted directions. Those who don't intend to return keep no maps.

Navigators have a definite sense of the future. The uppermost thought in their minds is how to proceed. Their awareness of themselves and their world is exceptional because they have mastered their own attention. Above all a navigator relies on courage, relies on a clear mind. If confusion or fear creeps in, all is lost. Self-confidence is the ability to imagine any future and remain fearless.

Navigation, generally, is one of three types: Auto-pilot, point-to-point and overview. Auto-pilot is the navigational method of the infant. With this method the self is the world; therefore, the person resides at the very center. It is navigation by a single point, me. Who I am is all that matters.

Point-to-point navigation is the method of the child. This method recognizes more than one center or point. With multiple points the world can be known and navigated by following lines which connect these remembered points and experiences. Navigation by line is to live on a specific street and attend a specific school, to know the direction to the park and to know the way home.

Overview is the method of the adult. This view is adopted when the interconnecting lines become numerous enough to form a surface. It is the beginning of map making, the first glimmer of the 'big picture'. Suddenly the earth becomes unified through continuity of surface. One begins to live on the earth instead of at a specific location.

The three major types of navigation: Point-making, line-making and surface-making each proceed by adding a dimension to the previous method. But there exists a fourth and rarer type of navigational skill, the method of the mature. It is adopted by one who is certain and allows him to live in the cosmos. Using the fourth method, location within space becomes less important than the properties of space itself. In a galaxy with a billion billion suns specific location lacks significance. To the mature, location makes little difference; they know at all times where they are because they know their own minds. These navigators, who truly know who they are and of what they're capable, have little need to know where they are because they're never lost. They know they have never been lost, are not lost now and will never be lost because all centers remain connected. Connected not by line or surface, but connected by pattern. The pattern of chaos.

When the inner stone turns on silent bearings all places and times become home. When the mind becomes as certain as stone then any personal address will do. When the private self ceases to wobble and rotates with stability and equilibrium it grinds all doubt into a fine powder. Then higher and lower dissolve, closer or farther connect and before and beyond become now. The navigation methods of the infant and the mature are separated only by the accumulation of skills and experience. In the beginning identity of location is necessary, later the location of identity is unimportant.

§§§§§

"Until you really know what you want to become, you're waiting." Noom rearranged his sack to make himself more comfortable. "I'm speaking of what you want to become in the next minute or in the next ten years. It doesn't really matter. Once you know what you want to be, what you want to be like, then you have a path to follow. We're constantly beginning and only realize it when we have finished."

"But when we're finished then we're dead," Jay countered.

Noom turned his gaze toward the young man and smiled. "If you think of it that way, you wouldn't want to do much would you?"

"I don't suppose so."

"I'm speaking of small configurations which build into larger ones. Becoming and being, doing and done, happening and happened, ripening and ripe, feeding and fed. Satisfaction comes only when we can say 'It is done.' Many people exist who are fascinated with beginnings. Historians are like that. Proper beginnings remain important; however, it is proper endings which create satisfaction. It is very important to know the difference between completing and complete. When is a breath complete and another begun? When is a day complete and another begun? When is a storm complete and another begun? Satisfaction is the feeling which exists between boredom and anxiety. Boredom is moving too slowly, anxiety too fast."

"So, how do you tell?" asked Jay.

"Tell what?"

"How do you tell how fast you're going?"

Noom chuckled. "Delight. Delight is the speed indicator. You know of the Three Bears don't you? There's too fast and too slow and then 'just right'. But your 'just right' may not be someone else's, everyone has different speeds. And everyone can change speeds. We learn more slowly in the beginning than later on because completions are made as we go along."

"But when I anticipate something that seems to drive it away."

"I'm talking about expecting rather than anticipating. Expecting is different from anticipating. Expecting is the determination that something will be done and then enjoying the process of seeing it through. Expecting is concerned with getting and anticipation is concerned with having. They are very, very different," Noom warned.

"But when I think about working things out it's seems impossibly hard."

"When you experience delight, work is without effort."

ΩΩΩΩ

1. My mind restores for me
2. I wish it to be
3. It is becoming
4. It has become so.

𝕮𝕮𝕮𝕮𝕮

"We come again, Inya," The Dance Master spoke.
    And the chorus sang, "Aligned, aligned,
    being accurately aligned,
    at the White Spot place.
    Slim Water leading the way ...."

The Dance Master carried power in his hand. His rattle, backed by the steady beat of the drums, cut through the heavens magically like a spirit blade. So now, Inya, awaken.

The Awb lived in an arid region without flowing waters. They had no lakes or streams. Their daily water came from small seeps hidden at the heads of secret canyons or under lonely sandstone overhangs. These precious seeps, where water was painstakingly collected, were honored and cared for by the villagers. The Awb remained confident even though they lacked plentiful water. They were confident because they maintained one of the most dependable of water supplies; they had a vast well in the sky. They were masters of the sky which they watched and studied. Cloud patterns and the movements of air fronts were noticed and discussed. Crops were planted, corn and beans, with the knowledge that the sky would protect them once again, keeping the Stomach Stalker from the door.

"Intending again, Inya."
    "Roundbill Crane at the Water-bottom,
    waiting at the moist place.
    Under greasewood, Toad Man watches.
    This is how it starts and is reckoned ...."

The Structure of Delight

The night before the Sky Dancing a full moon would ride low over the eastern horizon. The night sky watchers called out, "Tsik, tsik. Go, go," urging the North Star to commence its wanderings. "Follow the pale brother, for tomorrow we dance."

This dance was unlike a slow harvest dance. It was meant to quicken, to excite. Eagles screamed from the roof tops, ruffling their feathers, preparing to fly before the storm. They listened to the singing, tensing their wingtips. The dry buzz of the rattle directed the liquid power of the drum as nerve directs muscle. When lightning crackles, dancing through the sky, dark moody clouds swarm and cry. A communal forging of the village life force was pounded out by solid feet on a hot dry afternoon. So now Inya, listen.

"Come here, my Grandchild, Mud Turtle Man speaks!"

"From the Bitter River we came.

Follow, follow

The mountain tops joined, giving strength.

The Black Stone People in the home of the Center Bead

condensing their beauty.

Its inner form, whose feet are changing ....

Going about ...."

When wootiki became wootika, when the completing became complete, then Inya, the Big Thunder People, would walk once again. The sky would open and become bond to the land. The seeps would continue dripping, corn would grow to the sun and all would be right when the Sky Well was blessed again. Air transformed into water, an annual celebration of ordinary affairs.

"Returning once again, Inya."

"This earth was soft, and there my good desire ended.

Then you may depart.

The way before us is pleasant.

Pleasant it has become again, as you will see ...."

Once each year was enough for the Awb. The rest? Just practice.

Snap, contact.

△△△△△
The future is a representation of what will be, of what will happen. The future is static, it is the imagined consequence of present circumstances. Fundamentally, we can only have two concepts of time, ongoing and finished. Any finer distinctions of time, of which there are may be a dozen, always relate back to ongoing or finished. These two, leapfrogging forever, precede us and direct all of our actions and activities.

An incredible discovery was made long ago that futures are imaginary, and because they remain imaginary they can be shaped and molded. After we reshape our future our behaviors change automatically because the future is the province of resolution.

Actually we may have many futures, all of varying time lengths. Next, tomorrow, Christmas, this lifetime. They extend before us beckoning like golden promises. And the strongest among them at any moment is the most operational, the one that has the greatest effect. How we see ourselves in our futures mobilizes all our resources toward becoming the person we picture. Now is dynamic, then is static. Now is ongoing, then is finished. Time leapfrogs, that is its nature.

What is ongoing? What is finished? "You must decide," said Old Man Toad, "it's all in the mind."

△△△△△
Ssssssssssssssssstop
Thhhhhhhhhhhhrough
Rrrrrrrrrrrrrrrrrrit
Freeeeeeeeeeeeeeee

ΩΩΩΩ
"One time I worked at a gold mine in Wyoming. And there was a man there named Riley," said Noom, beginning a story. "Old Riley was a blaster, he loved dynamite. Early on he figured out that dynamite packed a punch and didn't see why he should put himself out doing a job when explosives

could do it just as well. So one day he was trying to empty a mine car, but the ore was sticky and wet and it stuck in the car. The boss told him to get a pick and shovel and clean out the mess. But Riley thought it over for a while and then rounded up a stick of his beloved dynamite, plastered some of it on the bottom of the car, lit the fuse and ducked back around the corner. When the smoke cleared, there was the ore car just as empty as you please and Riley hadn't shoveled one shovel full. There was only one problem, the bottom had a big dent in it. So Riley, the ever ingenious blaster, took the rest of the stick of dynamite and plastered it on the inside of the car, right on top of the big dent. He lit the fuse, ducked around the corner again and when the smoke cleared Riley found he had used too much. The bottom was blown out of the car. The shift boss came along about this time and Riley got fired. So he gathered up his lunch bucket and went home.

"That evening when the night shift was arriving, the change room was filled with the news about Riley. Didya hear about Riley?' they all asked, and the story of his firing was told and retold. Then the door opened and in walked Riley, set his full lunch bucket down and started changing his clothes to go to work. Somebody finally worked up the nerve to ask him if he had indeed been fired for blowing out the bottom of an ore car. 'Yup,' said Riley, 'it's a fact.' And he went right on changing. The questioner asked him what he thought he was doing getting ready to go to work on the night shift if he was fired. Riley tipped back his hard hat and looked the questioner square in the eye. 'Pard,' he said, 'if a person listens to them bosses, he'd never have a job.'"

"So what happened to him?" asked Jay.

"That was the end of it. Nobody ever said another word to Riley about it, and when I left two years later he was still going strong on the night shift."

❝❝❝❝❝

Many, many lives ago, there lived among the Awb a boy who was very poor. From his mother he inherited one small corn field. This patch of ground was all that stood between the boy and starvation.

The field lay one day's travel from the village. And in the spring at planting time the boy would go to the field, say his prayers and begin to plant, singing his planting songs. After the corn sprouted he would go every few days to tend to his corn. Coming and going, he would pass other fields that were bigger and greener than his but he didn't lose heart. His field was a great distance from the village, it was also a poor field. It wasn't in the bottom land where the moisture accumulated from winter snows. It was higher up, on a windy rocky point.

The first year the grub worms ate most of his corn, but he tended it anyway. The second year there was no summer rain. Although the corn started well, by late summer it withered and there was little to harvest. The third year sand storms lashed the field, splitting the corn's broad leaves until they hung in tatters. In spring of the fourth year his corn looked promising. But again the wind began to blow. It blew down the wind breaks he so painstakingly constructed, burying the young corn with sand. The boy stayed by his field and fought against the sand trying to save the sickly corn plants. But the wind continued and would not let him rest, not even at night. That year he wouldn't grow enough corn to eat during the winter.

Despondent, the boy sat in the middle of his field on a rock and sobbed. Then he heard a small voice. "What is this? What is this?"

The boy stopped his crying and looked all around his ruined field.

"What is this? What is all this crying?" A blue spider beside him spoke louder.

"Who are you?" asked the boy wiping the tears from his cheeks.

"I am Blue Spider and this is my home. You are sitting on top of my home."

"You live here?"

"Yes, under this rock. What is all this crying? Are you trying to water your field?"

"Four years I have come and planted and four years the corn has failed.

What am I to do? I'm afraid that I will starve this coming winter."

"Perhaps you will," replied the spider.

"But what am I to do?"

"Grandson," said the spider, "this is a poor field. Four years you have come and planted as I have watched. And four times your corn has failed. This is a rocky place with little moisture. The wind blows here, it is a poor place to grow corn."

"But I have no other fields, this is all that was left to me."

"Yes, yes I can see."

"If I can't grow corn here then I will surely starve."

The spider scratched its belly with one of it's legs. "Perhaps this ground has other uses. Perhaps you will have a harvest yet."

"What other uses?" the boy asked.

"Give me your hand and we will go into my house where we can talk."

The boy held his hand down so the spider could step into his palm. He began to shrink and shrink until he and the Blue Spider were the same size. Then the spider led the way under the rock to its home.

Inside were baskets which the spider had spun full of hard red flint and white beads made from shells. Colored feathers hung in nets from the ceiling beams and in the corners pungent herbs were neatly stacked on jeweled rocks.

"This field of yours is no good to grow corn, but perhaps you could use it to learn to make sacred ground," the spider said.

"Sacred ground? What is sacred ground?"

"Sacred ground is a place where truly magical and mysterious things can happen, like my home here."

"Then will I have a place that could grow corn?"

"No, no, grandson," the spider frowned. "Then you would still have a poor field and the ability to make sacred ground. Sacred ground is for people. In the beginning you will still be poor but with an ability."

"How can this be? This ability?"

"You must listen and train very hard to complete this ability."

The boy thought and thought. "So it is," he said finally. "At least I will starve with an ability."

"So it was," replied the Blue Spider. "Now listen!" and the spider began its instruction. "You have two and only two tools at your disposal: time and pattern. Time will be regulated by your song and pattern will be directed by your sight. Before and later remain the province of song. Below and beyond, you will mark, drawing with colored powders. When your voice and sight are fully united, the ground around you will tremble. A boundary must be created, first opened and then closed. When line, color and song finally become correct, all around you will resonate. Sacred space is created by a special web of thought, gathered from the midden heap of your past and directed forward. When the lines of your thought combine with your singing words, a tiny rainbow point is created. You then expand that spot until it becomes a place where others can stand. This is the way," the Blue Spider said. "To know one thing, know a thousand. If not today then tomorrow. Begin expecting your place in this world with your coming ability," the spider told the boy. "Your field is poor, but you may learn to create sacred ground within the only world you have."

Throughout the following fall and winter the boy went to his field and practiced and practiced while the Blue Spider watched and instructed. The boy's feet became sore from dancing and his throat dry from singing. His mind became confused and tired, but he kept on.

"Ah yes!" the spider said.

The old spider encouraged the boy to continue practicing in spite of the cold winter wind and snow. Encouraged him to go far beyond anything the boy imagined he was capable of. As each part of the learning was completed the Blue Spider responded, "Ah, the ability grows. Just so!"

That winter the young man became a singer with the skill to create sacred ground at any place, at any time. And when spring came the Blue Spider led the young man into its house under the rock once again. "It is done," the old spider told him. "Now you have a name."

So among the Awb there arose a great enchanter, eating of the corn which winter grew.

243

§§§§§

"When we first met on the river you asked if there was a question that quietly guided my life. And I've been thinking about that question and I think I have it," Jay said.

"Have what?"

"You asked me if there was a question that guided my life, what would it be? And I think I know what it is, the question I mean."

Noom turned toward Jay. His attention was intensely focused on the young man. "Can your question be answered with a 'yes' or 'no'?"

Jay thought a moment, "Yes, I suppose it can."

"Then try rephrasing your question so that the answer will always be other than 'yes' or 'no'."

"How would I do that?"

"If your question starts with 'am' or 'will' then it can be answered 'yes' or 'no'. But if it starts with 'how' or 'what' or 'where' then the answer always depends on the context. And skip all questions that begin with 'why' because they have no answer."

Jay thought for a moment and rephrased his question in his mind. "Okay, it can't be answered 'yes' or 'no'."

"Now, if your question had an opposite what would it be?"

Jay started to tell the old man his new life question but an upraised hand stopped him.

"But don't you want to know what my question is?"

"It's not necessary. I'm more interested in the form that the question takes. Your question's pattern has more power than its particular content."

"That doesn't make any sense."

"Let me give you an example. Suppose your question was 'Will this last?' and you ask yourself that question quietly during every activity or experience. What would be your answer be?"

"My answer would always have to be no, because nothing lasts forever."

"That's right and so you would be perpetually disappointed."

"I didn't think of my question that way, but I suppose you're right. Are there really people who use that kind of question to guide their lives?

"A better question might be 'Are there people who remain perpetually disappointed?'"

"I suppose there are," Jay conceded.

"That's why I think the structure of a life question is important, you have to live with the consequences. If you change your question, you change its consequences. Life questions go a long way toward determining the quality of the life of the questioner."

"So what would be a better question than 'Will this last?'"

"It's not so much an idea of a better question as it is knowing the results of its structure. A life question's structure determines its power. If you want to be disappointed, then 'Will this last?' is a great question."

"Okay. If my question was 'Will this last?' and I wanted to feel different how might I change it?"

"First, you need to change it so it can't be answered 'yes' or 'no'."

"Like what?"

"Well, you could ask yourself 'What about this moment will I cherish?'"

"Okay, I can understand how that makes a difference."

"That's right. Ask your own life question in such a way that you can act on the answer, so the answer will direct your activity. If the answer defines who you are or your state of being then you're sunk. If instead it gives you some useful information about how to proceed then it becomes a valuable question and enriches your life. Here are some rules of thumb for altering your life question." Noom began ticking the points off on his fingers. "The first we've already discussed, eliminate 'yes' or 'no' answers. Second, try changing the verb tenses. For instance, if your question is 'How will I get what I want?' you might change it to 'How did I get what I wanted?' Third, if your question refers to yourself and others then reverse them. In this case, if your question is something like 'When will they like me?' change it to 'When will I like them?.'"

"So you just reverse the direction?"

"Yes. Now putting it all together, if you started with the question of 'Will others like me?' Change it to something like 'How will others like

245

me?' or "What will others like about me?' Then try changing it to 'How have others liked me?' Then finally change it to 'How have I liked others?' or 'What about others have I liked?' Each question gives you a different feeling and view of the world. Finally, leave out all negation and comparison and try asking your question without reference to any person, yourself or others. So in this case we might ask something like 'How will there be liking?' or in a smoother form 'What in this situation is loving?' You see, all of these are very different structures from 'Will they like me?' You can fiddle with your life question in any way you want. You can change it completely or modify it or reverse it. Go ahead, give it a whirl."

Noom waited while Jay tried different forms and versions of his question.

"Okay, I've got a new one now. Let me tell you!"

Noom held up his hand again. "It's not necessary."

"Why? I want to tell you."

"Because I already know."

"You already know what I changed my question to?"

"I don't know the particular wording of your question, but I do know that it works very well for you."

"So tell me, how do you know?"

Noom was watching as Jay's enthusiasm grew. "Because it fills you with delight. Because it directs your activities in a direction that you find pleasurable and exciting. It will direct you toward 'the something' which you're looking for. A well designed life question becomes a self-correcting life map, a valuable something to possess. Then work is done without effort." Noom smiled.

~~~
Ninth Moon, 1239

Withered bitter sky
the foreign moon flutters,
winter one beginning.
A massive blind path.

Near the loud stranger
her echo shuddered
illusion rides all around.
A thousand thoughts
after this night will be ... always dawn.

This entry has always worried the monks at the Shinto shrine and its meaning has been debated endlessly. But in the end it comes down to this: the mighty mud carp had something altogether different in mind.

§§§§§

"You keep talking about work without effort, what do you mean?" Jay asked.

"There exist specific patterns for everything the mind does. One is the pattern of joy. Work done in that pattern is without effort."

"How can that pattern be created?"

"One of the simplest and most effective ways is to recall a time of delight. When you have fully recalled an intrinsically delightful experience the pattern is automatically created. While the mind maintains that particular pattern all experiences remain delightful. That is the structure of delight."

Jay stopped for several moments, and while he thought Noom gazed out across the desert. In the distance the old man spotted a lone eagle riding the turbulent air currents, and for a few seconds he gave the bird his undivided attention, almost as he were flying himself.

"Then what you're saying is that events don't necessarily create states of mind, but rather they're experienced through different states of mind." Jay paused while Noom continued waiting and watching the bird. "And events by themselves don't have meaning, meaning is created by the particular states of mind in which they're perceived."

Noom suddenly bounded to his feet and began applauding. "Yes!" he shouted. "Yes! I couldn't have said it better myself. Meaning is invented. That is the structure of delight. The ideas of cause and effect give rise to meaning. The need for the concept of causation is the root of meaning. A world without linear causal relationships is for most a world without direct meaning. Have you got it?"

Jay was startled by the old man's sudden exuberance and could only nod affirmatively.

Noom suddenly turned and pointed out over the desert floor. "Then keeping your present state of mind, look out there."

Jay rose to stand beside the old man and followed the line of Noom's finger. Far in the distance he could see a bird gliding high above the desert, fighting the air currents. "What's that, an eagle?"

"Yes," said Noom glancing at the clouds overhead. "An eagle flies before the storm. What does this mean? Does it mean the eagle is bringing the storm? Does it mean the eagle is escaping the storm? In short, I'm asking what is the relationship between the eagle and the storm?"

"I'm not sure there is one."

"Then the event, storm and eagle, has no meaning for you."

"I don't know about a meaning," Jay laughed, "but it sure does makes me happy watching."

"Of course," Noom grinned. "However, if you choose a meaning which is uncommon then you might be accused of magic. Magical meanings are resorted to when there is uncertainty about one's future. The Hawkeen have predicted that uncertain times are coming. They watch and keep an account of such things.

"How do they know? You said they weren't very interested in the past."

"Oh, you are getting clever, aren't you." Noom smiled broadly. "We have our ways. There are those among the Hawkeen who keep records, time records stretching far back in antiquity. These records aren't kept for the purposes of history, they're kept for the study of time patterns. A terrible period may soon be upon us. Magical thinking abounds during uncertain times, and I don't want you to be one of the ones who is paralyzed by fear. Keep your wits about you. Don't indulge in fantasies, indulge in futures. If you replace omens with choices then you will remain safe and all storms, like this one," Noom said, eyeing the steadily darkening sky, "will pass."

"When will it happen?"

"What happen?"

"The troubled times you're talking about."

"Soon enough," Noom laughed, "soon enough. But for now I want you to look directly at that small hill." He pointed to the yellow cone. "That is the last remnant of a very old mineral deposit. It's been eroding over untold centuries and what you see now is all that remains. It is connected to an enormous wheel on the plains north of here."

Jay squinted in an attempt to see farther into the distance.

"No, no," laughed Noom. "It's an imaginary wheel. One which stretches from Utah to South Dakota, from southern Colorado to northern Wyoming. All together it covers parts of six states. The outer rim is marked by seven geological features each equidistant from a central mountain peak which is called the collection point. And through a long series of mountain lakes and ridges, the entire drama of the western heartland can focus on the single small cone you now see before you."

"That?" asked Jay pointing at the mound.

"That." Noom nodded. "It's called the discharge point. The wheel, collection peak and all the rest, all the way to this knoll is one half of a mammoth geological formation. The other half is integral to the functioning of the whole. This half I've told you about and the other you'll have to discover on your own."

"How did you find out about all this?"

"I know something of the earth," Noom stated simply. "I've mined its veins and listened to its heart. Its geology is more than the mere distribution of minerals. Huge organizations exist on a scale that can only be seen from very high," Noom craned his neck upward, eyeing the dark clouds overhead, "very high beyond the atmosphere. It is said that when the wheel turns lightning dances on this insignificant cone of dirt. It is also said that if you keep your eye on the strike point and go there you'll find crystallized lightning."

"Come on, I've swallowed a lot these past few days but this is too much. You're putting me on. There is no such thing as crystallized lightning."

"In a way I suppose I am," Noom smiled. "Anyway that's what the ancients thought. What really happens, I suppose, is that the

249

mineralization of the dirt at the discharge point is of a type which the heat and force of a bolt of lightning will crystallize. A very uncommon occurrence, I might add."

ΩΩΩΩ

After the Blind Navigator guided her people to their new homeland, she spent the last of her days teaching. She felt it was her duty, for she knew that one more great migration would occur. This last migration would happen long after her death and the death of her children's children. It would occur long after her people had forgotten her name, had forgotten their sea voyage and had forgotten the language she now spoke.

So the Blind Navigator had a wrist band made which would serve as a map when the time of the last migration came. Many attended her classes because the skills of navigation that she taught were useful for various kinds of journeys, personal and internal ones as well as the massive migrations of whole peoples.

Toward the end of her days the Blind Navigator summoned the most promising of her students. Out of an old wooden trunk she withdrew a small bundle. Carefully unwinding the soft leather wrapping she freed the bracelet. While caressing the incised inner surface with the delicate tips of her old fingers she whispered, "You are the one. Your training is not compete. Your training will never be complete. There is much to be learned by you and by those who follow you. In truth, all I have given you is the map to learning because that is all I can give. Every time and every life is different so I have no maps that mark destinations, only beginnings. However difficult it may seem at times, always remember that every boundary contains the instructions for its crossing." The Blind Navigator smiled and then continued. "Wisdom is what you accumulate along the way. Wisdom is the accumulation of the obvious, the bones of life. Go now and learn and teach, for in time these skills will be needed once again. The student slipped on the perfectly fitting bracelet and became known as the Endwearer.

§§§§§

"Sit down," Noom told Jay, "we haven't much time." The old man focused on a spot at the top of Jay's nose and very slowly widened his own eyes. Jay looked directly into those deep soft eyes knowing as they slowly blinked that he would relax and feel very comfortable. Jay's pupils dilated rapidly and Noom began speaking quietly.

"I know that certain things in your past weren't what you wanted, and I also know you have been wondering what you have learned, how it all fits together. You really don't have to pay attention because you will remember. You may not know it now, but you have formed certain images that will stay with you for the rest of your life. No need to remember them now and while you're sitting just as you are, your breathing has changed and you may feel the urge to move slightly. You may soon notice a mysterious sensation which will let you know the satisfaction of having learned so much. You can enjoy the comfort of knowing and I want you to delight in every moment of wondering what amazing experience might happen soon. It makes you curious when you can feel such delight in watching things unfold.

"When we're finished you can remember the spring where you touched the bubbles," Noom continued, "or fondly remember any other part you want. At the beginning there will be difficult times when certain thoughts float on the surface of your mind. Some may simply float away and others will sink deeply, it's not even important that you pay attention. It's not necessary to be aware of every odd thought that may come or go. You may throw an interesting question out on the smooth surface of your mind and watch an old truth swim up and nibble at it. Or you may wish to watch and wait. You've had a certain type of experience, this time we've spent together, and it's not even important or necessary for you to tell everyone what has happened. As your closest friends may be wondering when you return just what about you has changed, you must tell them carefully. Fortunately, you will be of some help in suggesting where they might explore. The structure of delight is a wonderful place to begin. When you're uncertain or have difficulty remember my words and all that I have told you, you will remember even what you don't now understand. The remembering will be easy and surprise you at the oddest times, as my voice will always be with you. It has been a particular joy to me spending this time with you. You have done me a favor, being who you are and allowing me to pass something along. Someday you may stand at a place much like this with someone much like the person you are now. Then you can know the full satisfaction of what I now feel."

The breeze along the rim began to rise and Jay knew what flourished beyond his shadow of doubt. Just as he was beginning to examine it the wind suddenly increased, buffeting the branches of the trees around the two men and kicking up dust.

Noom quickly rose and pulled Jay to his feet. "Now watch and listen!" the old man commanded.

ππππ

Professor Sherman sat, his hands in his lap, fingers intertwined. "Even more than we are doers, we become deciders." He continued, "Once the mind is aligned and clear, the doing is automatic, for then the universe can participate in our action."

Noom watched the rolling hills that spread beyond the campus. "How do I know where to start?"

"Son, all actions begin with the obvious. When you prepare to walk, which foot will go first? Left or right? The mysterious is knowable only through the obvious." Frank held his glasses up to the light again. "Yes," he smiled, "it is my glasses." And he proceeded to clean them thoroughly.

§§§§§

The two men stood far out on the ledge waiting.

"Most people don't like surprises and so they're never surprised," Noom shouted above the wind. "But you can learn to welcome surprise."

As if the skies were waiting for that very moment, a single brilliant shaft of blue lightning split the sky with an electric flash, striking the small hill. Before Jay could recover from his initial gasp the shock of thunder crashed over them.

"Jesus Christ, you weren't kidding."

"I never do," the old man beamed. "See where the lightning struck and mark the spot in your mind." He took Jay's hands in his and squeezed them long and firmly. "Now go, quickly."

ΩΩΩΩ

It is said that in the beginning when Thunder Boy awoke, he was hungry and alone. He searched for something to eat but found nothing. He cried and cried, but no one came. Starving and alone, he ate his own thunder and it gave him a bellyache.

Thunder Boy waited and waited for someone to come, and while he waited he searched in the sand. He crawled around and around until he created a small depression in the dust and there he lay, eating his own thunder, living with the bellyache.

In time, the others began to worry and gathered to discuss the troubled boy.

"Thunder Boy is sick," said Skunk. "Without thunder nothing grows."

"Dreadful," said Hummingbird. "Something must be done."

So Raven was sent and he asked Thunder Boy, "Why don't you come and fly as I do, high in the clouds?"

"Because I am sick and weak and no one will lift me up."

So Raven flew away. Then Gopher was sent and he asked, "Why don't you dig down deep as I do?"

"Because I am sick and weak and no one will dig for me."

So Gopher returned and everyone was silent, thinking hard. Finally Coyote spoke. "Let me try." The assembly nodded its approval and Coyote set out.

When he arrived he asked, "What is this small depression in the ground?"

"It is my home, the place where I stay while I wait," answered Thunder Boy.

Coyote sat down at the edge of the depression, crossed his legs and looked thoughtful. "You don't seem well."

"I hurt. I'm alone and hungry."

253

"Yes, I can see that," Coyote agreed. "You are sick because you eat your own thunder."

"But I have nothing else to eat."

Coyote scratched one of his ears and looked over his shoulder. "When I am hungry and there is nothing to eat, I pluck a hair from the end of my tail and eat that."

"But I have no tail."

Coyote examined Thunder Boy thoroughly. "True, I thought you had a long and wonderful tail, but you must have eaten it. However," he said gazing at the boy, "I will give one hair from the end of my tail, but you must eat it while you stand."

"Why must I stand while I eat it?"

"That's the way it is."

So Thunder Boy slowly stood up for the first time and Coyote waited until he gained his balance. Plucking a single hair from the tip of his tail, Coyote handed it to the boy.

Thunder Boy swallowed the hair and the swelling in his belly went away. "That was good. Give me another."

"What?" asked Coyote cocking his ear. "You must have mumbled. I didn't hear you."

"I want another hair from your tail," the boy spoke louder, taking a shaky step forward.

But Coyote still couldn't hear. "What? I can't hear you. Speak up."

This angered Thunder Boy and he roared, "I will have another hair from your tail!"

The blast knocked Coyote over backward. "Not unless you can catch me," and he began running fast to the East.

Thunder Boy thundered after him roaring and bellowing until the hair erupted from his mouth in a single bolt of lightning. Coyote leaped high into the air to catch the lightning which he fastened to his tail right where the hair had been.

Thunder Boy laughed and laughed when he saw how Coyote had tricked him. He quit the chase and started for home, but he couldn't find the small depression. It felt good to walk with his head in the clouds and feet on the ground. And it felt good to spread his thunder. So he practiced rolling it across the ground and up against the cliffs. "This is good," he said rubbing his belly. He leaped high into the air and yelled until the sound echoed among the grass and soaked into the ground. "Yes, this is very good." Thunder Boy began bounding across the earth doing his work, speaking freely for all to hear. In the mountains he found delicious hard crystals, in the canyons he ate tender sumac, saving sagebrush for lunch.

Spider collected thunder from the low places and spun it into snug warm blankets with multicolored designs. Corn Beetle gathered it by the mouthful to make smooth pollen balls to store inside a yellow gourd. And everyone was glad.

Thunder Man had finally come into the world rolling his own power, giving birth to the Rainbow People. Another swift slice of the waterknife.

¥¥¥¥¥

Jay had grabbed his pack and scrambled down the slope. He made his way quickly, stumbling over rocks and sagebrush. In the distance the dust from the lightning strike still swirled around the point of impact. By the time Jay reached the desert floor he realized he had never seen a bolt of lightning strike the ground, let alone dry powdery soil. Running smoothly across the empty plain he searched the sky for the eagle but it had vanished.

When Jay arrived at the cone he was momentarily confused. From the ledge he had marked the spot of impact in his mind as just below a small scrub piñon, but now that he was closer he realized that there were several small trees growing on the mound. He stopped to take his bearings. The yellow dust had drifted away and for a moment he feared he had lost the spot, but then he recognized the tree he was searching for and began climbing toward it.

Thunder rumbled again and he felt a cold drop of rain on the back of his neck. Then another as he scrambled up the side of the mound toward the impact point. At the foot of the tree he found what he was searching for, a small crater about a foot across. Extending into the air from its center was something that looked like a root. Jay sat beside the crater and caught his

255

breath. At first he was afraid to touch the glassy root because he thought it still might be hot. Then tugging gently upward with one hand and digging with the other he extracted the fragment from the ground. It was nearly a foot long, dark and slender, terminating at the end in a black crystal slightly larger than his thumb. Rain started to drum on his shoulders as lightning flashed in the distance.

He held the stem with one hand, the crystal with the other and began applying pressure. The root was tougher than he expected, so he applied even more force. Suddenly it snapped and the crystal broke clean. Rivulets of water ran down the hillside making the footing slick. As he scooped muddy dirt back into the crater the sky rumbled again and a steady rain lashed at him. Jay hunched down at the base of the tree trying to keep out of the rain as best he could. The pounding increased to a heavy downpour as he prepared to wait out the storm. Then he spotted a small patch of white bone just beyond his knee. Digging into the brown piñon needles Jay uncovered the perfect skull of a badger. His hands instantly remembered the special grip. Standing erect Jay held the skull aloft, pointing it toward the sky so the rain would wash it clean. The fear wolves silently took up their guard stations around him, for now they had something to protect.

∽∽∽

The last recorded words of the mighty river carp were written on the date of the First Moon, 1261.

The aimless path consumes,
Fluent rain falling
Delight becomes delight.

On that day the fisherman's script was strong and sure. The rest of the diary is filled with blank golden pages. Some have imagined their contents.

A native of the Southwest, Nelson Zink is a psychotherapist who lives and works in Embudo, NM. In addition to his regular practice, Zink co-founded The Embudo Center, an organization dedicated to the exploration of delight. TEC develops and conducts outdoor experiences designed to heighten sensory awareness and implement the ideas and ideals of this book.

For other delights
write:
Mind Matters
Drawer SS Dept. A
Taos, NM
87571